A Jack Wesley Novel

Shoving Back the Shadows

W. B Martin

Also by W. B. Martin

The Jack Wesley Series

>Trouble Leaves Too Slow
>Only Pretty Lies
>Chasing the Blackbird
>Shaking Off Futility
>Pleasure Smiles

Alternative History

>German Golfers Who Changed the World
>Sweetness in the Dark

Science Fiction

>Endangered Species

Young Adult Novels

>Cubo Zoan
>Vincent van Gogh Likes Cats

A Puhaka Books Selection

puhakabooks.com

In Memory of:
Stu 'Andy' Gillett

Notice

This is a work of fiction and as such all people, businesses and events depicted in this novel are either fictitious or are used fictitiously. Any similarities to real people or places are strictly coincidental.

Printed by permission of
Puhaka Publishing

Printed in the United States of America

Edited by T. Johns

Cover Layout by Morwenna Rakestraw

Version 1.2

Print ISBN 978-1-940554-12-9
eBook ISBN 978-1-940554-13-6

First Edition December 2017

Chapter 1

Chicago, Illinois

Jack Wesley lay awake in his bunk, the night air heavy. With no breeze, below deck was stifling.

The Newport 36 sailboat had two openings for air, not counting the small scooped vents in the deck. On the forward hatch he had erected his wind tube that was supposed to catch the wind and create a chimney effect. Tonight the lack of wind left the large nylon tube useless. The other opening consisted of the main companionway. Located near the boat's galley, it led out to the cockpit.

Next to the short steps to the deck was a pilot berth that Jack normally slept in. But it was too confined in this hot weather with its tight location under the cockpit. Moving to the forward V-berth had gained some measure of air from the forward hatch.

Normally on a hot night like this he would be sleeping on deck, as sailboats generally lacked air conditioning, at least medium-sized ones. Sleeping on deck was the typical solution most sailors resorted to in overcoming the stuffy confines below. But being close to downtown Chicago, deck sleeping arrangements were not an option.

Not exactly sure of the surroundings outside the marine shipyard where he was moored, Jack had waited out the repairs. The owner had been generous when the Newport's engine started acting funny and needed a place for immediate repair. Bad fuel had been the culprit. Now, after two days of cleaning fuel tanks and replacing fuel filters, the boat was ready to continue its journey.

Jack was attempting to become a 'looper', or a boater who circumnavigated the eastern United States. Using the Mississippi River, the Inter-Coastal Waterway, Hudson River, Erie Canal, Great Lakes and the Chicago Ship Canal/Illinois River, a 2400 mile trip would take him in a circuit. He had started in Washington D.C. the previous fall.

The Newport 36 belonged to his brother and the two had sailed for two weeks south as Jack learned the finer points of sailing. Then his brother headed back to work as the Chief-of-Staff for Wyoming's lone congressman.

The plan was that the brother would join Jack whenever he could get away. So far, Jack had only seen his brother once. They had enjoyed the Inter-Coastal Waterway along the Gulf Coast during the Christmas break.

Now that the boat had traveled up the Mississippi River and the Illinois River just before the spring floods, Jack was ready to hit the Great Lakes. Jack hoped his brother could join him for some serious sailing now that he knew more what he was doing.

But the early hot weather combined with bad diesel had forced him to endure one more night too close to the murder capital of America. Chicago was infamous for its strict gun laws and just as famous for its killing sprees. *It seemed that the bad guys didn't follow the law*, Jack thought. *Go figure.*

Growing up in the west, Jack had a more open view of the need to carry a weapon for self-defense. Lately he had been living in Wyoming and had come to appreciate the gun culture even more. After many years in law enforcement in Oregon, Jack had quickly learned that Wyoming was a very different place from the Beaver State.

"Too hot to sleep, eh pup," Jack said to his companion. Laying on the deck below him, his Airedale dog perked up at his master's attention. Coventry, or Tree for short, was Jack's constant companion, and although not a water dog, he had adapted to life on the water.

"Well, we have to be up early anyway to catch the bridges through Chicago. They don't raise the lift bridges during rush hour. Same as Miami on the Inter-Coastal. Pleasure boats take second place over the money earners."

Jack scratched behind Tree's ear as the dog rolled onto his side. The motion rocked the boat slightly. Lacking neighbors, Jack's berth in the middle of the shipyard was quiet. Although not a huge shipyard, the ways were clogged with workboats of various types being repaired.

Large, two-storied sheds ashore held small steel craft being built or refurbished. During the day, the place was a cacophony of hammers, grinders and welders. He was ready to shove off and head north on Lake Michigan for some solitude.

"Hey, maybe we'll catch up to that Dufour 44. I bet you'd like to see your friend again." Jack referred to a woman and her dog they had met on the Illinois River. Working their way through one of the locks, the lock master had requested that Jack raft up with the Dufour.

Rafting up inside locks meant boats would go through the immense locks together. Designed for large river barges, each lock could hold numerous small craft. By the small boats moving together, the lock operator would save water and time.

Jack and Tree had found themselves tied up alongside a very expensive sailboat. Her skipper was a very good-looking woman with a Jack Russell dog as a mate. The dog had appeared to be the only other hand on board as the boats were lashed together.

"You terriers all want to hang together. What's with that?" he teased his dog. An Airedale was the largest of the terrier group while the Jack Russell was probably the smartest of the breed. Both dogs were noted for their fierce disposition.

Tree didn't answer Jack's question, instead sitting up. Jack could see the dog's ears moving to a sound outside on the dock. Jack strained to hear what noise his dog was picking up but only heard the water lapping at the pier. Then he felt it. The Newport shifted slightly as someone stepped onto the side gunwale.

Tree responded with a low growl. Jack patted his dog to get him settled down but noticed the hair on the dog's back was standing stiff.

The boat shifted again as whoever was on deck stepped into the cockpit. With the shipyard vapor lights outside, there was enough residual light reaching the dock to make out a figure just outside the companionway. Jack reached for his security and shifted his position. With an open companionway due to the hot weather, the intruder took advantage of the easy access.

A large body in dark clothing stepped over the sill and placed one foot on the top of the steps. A second foot arrived as the person's lower body moved into the cabin. Jack waited.

The person lowered themselves down under the cabin roof and stepped onto the lower deck. With full headroom on the sailboat, the intruder stood up straight.

A beam from a flashlight hit him where he stood. Holding the flashlight in his extended left hand, Jack leveled his revolver onto the man's chest. The man froze.

Dressed in black with a hoodie pulled up over his head, Jack knew the type from thirty years on the police force. Tree's growl grew louder.

"Hey man, get that light out of my eyes," the man demanded.

Jack watched the man's hands to see if he carried a weapon. So far, Jack could see both hands and they were empty. He kept his revolver aimed on center mass.

"Buddy, you stepped onto the wrong boat tonight."

"What's you saying?" the man said. "I'm looking for my main man. Said he'd be sacked out here tonight. Got himself a righteous babe and she got herself a sailboat. Said for me to come over and party."

"No party here, friend. Unless you want to go a few rounds with my dog. He needs a friend."

"No dogs man. I'z just be leavin' then." The whole time he'd been talking, Jack noticed his left hand slowly moving toward his waistband. Along with a slow shuffle forward, he was inching his way toward Jack. With the residual light from the dock filtering into the cabin combined with the flashlight shining in his face, the man hadn't recognized what was in Jack's right hand.

"If you're leaving then stop the hand movement toward your waist and don't move toward me." Jack gripped his .357 Magnum revolver tighter and the laser sights came on. The red beam lit up a small circle on the man's chest.

"Hey, what's that? Don't go doin' nothin' hasty like. What's you doing, man?"

"I'm about to blow a hole in some jackass intruder. Nobody around here will hear a damn thing."

"You can't do that. They got laws in this city against you having anything like that. You'll be in a shit load of trouble."

"No trouble. No one hears it. You collapse where you stand. I wrap you up in plastic and when I'm out on Lake Michigan tomorrow and no one's looking, you take a swim with my spare anchor chained to your dead ass," Jack said. "A couple of miles further on I drop the gun into the middle of the lake. Simple."

"No man. You'z don't wanna to do that."

Jack let the man sweat. The intruder had stopped all movement and stared down at the laser dot on his chest. "Maybe you're right. Terrible mess. Blood everywhere. Take me all day to clean it up. And my ears would ring for a week."

"Yeah, that's right. Now you talkin' some sense."

"So, what do you propose then? Can't just let you walk out of here. You return with all your homies because I dissed you."

"No I won't. I swear to God. I'll just walk out of here like nothin' happened. We good?" The man started a slow backtrack toward the companionway.

"No, we're not good. Just don't move or it will be the last thing you do. We seem to have a Mexican standoff."

'But I ain't no Mex, man. Don't blame me for those dudes. Us folks have been here a long time."

What a dumbshit, Jack thought. *But what am I going to do with him? There was a risk of him returning with his friends to even up things. Or he could go to the cops and report me, a man with a gun on a boat. I don't need that hassle either.*

"Can you swim?" Jack asked.

"Yeah, I learned."

"Good. Now, we can do this the hard way or the easy way. The easy way is I shoot you where you stand and you spend eternity with the fishes. Your Mama never knows what happened to her sweet boy."

"That's the easy way? Christ, what's the hard way?"

"You lay down there on the deck and put your hands behind your back. I come over there and handcuff you. You move a twitch and I shoot you. We'll be back to the easy way."

The man immediately went to his knees and laid face down on the cabin deck. He placed his arms behind him.

"Now, just as a warning. I'm a cop and have done this many times. You might be thinking you're about to get the drop on me, but trust me, my finger pull is faster than any Kung Fu shit you can pull off."

"A cop. Shit."

Jack climbed out of his berth and hit the cabin lights. He placed the flashlight down and pulled some zip ties out of a draw. Standing in front of the intruder, Jack carefully moved up onto the settee and around the prone man, never getting close to the man until he was behind him.

"What's you goin' to do with me? You turn me in and you got some explainin' to do yourself."

"I won't be turning you in."

"You dumpin' me in the lake then?"

"Not if you act very nice and don't move." Jack reached down with his left hand and placed the zip tie around the man's wrists. As the man twisted his head to the side, Jack flashed the laser from behind into the man's eyes to remind him of the gun. He pulled the ties tight. Then he slid down to place another zip tie around the man's ankles.

"Hey, what's that for?"

"Added security. Now we go for a hop."

"What the fu..."

Jack helped the man to a standing position, keeping the gun away from the man's body. Police training had taught him never to jam a weapon into a perp's body. It lets them know where it is, making it easier to swing and try to knock it away.

Motioning for the man to hop up into the cockpit, Jack kept a grip on the man's bound wrists. He steadied the thug as he hopped up each step. From the cockpit, he had the man sit down on the gunnel.

Turning the man around so he faced the dock, he had him slip under the lifeline till his feet were on the dock. Jack climbed carefully off the boat, the laser trained on the man the entire time. He then had the man duck under the lifeline and stand up on the dock.

"OK, just hop on over to this pylon" Sitting him down, Jack retrieved another zip tie from his pocket and strapped the man to the dock.

"Hey, you can't do this."

"Any final words?" Jack asked as he pulled some duct tape out of his other pocket.

"You can't leave me here."

Jack stuck the tape over the man's mouth who began to struggle behind the gag.

"Now just settle down. The shipyard starts early so you only have a few hours to wait. They'll release you, maybe. Or they might call the cops. Either case, me and my boat will be long gone. And the good news is, you'll be alive to pillage another day. Take it from me, don't bother ratting me out to the cops. We made a deal. Your life for you keeping your mouth shut. I'd hate to come back and correct the situation if you renege on that deal. Remember, I'm a cop. Even in Chicago, that carries some weight."

With his guest trussed tightly to the dock pylon, Jack climbed aboard his Newport and cranked up the engine. The diesel sprang to life as Tree settled into his spot in the cockpit.

"Come on boy. Let's hit those city bridges early. We'll definitely avoid the morning rush at this hour."

Chapter 2

Lake Michigan

The wind was blowing at an official weather bureau-stated fresh breeze. Jack had one reef in his main sail because he had learned to sail the Newport flatter than normal. With less sail, the boat was slower but didn't heel over. A flatter sail meant things down below deck tended to stay in place.

After picking up the cabin numerous times, Jack had learned that it was easier to go slower. *Not as much excitement as having the boat laid over on its side*, he thought.

It was still late spring and the weather on the Great Lakes could turn quickly. The morning light was showing over toward Michigan as he kept the Newport on course along the Wisconsin shore headed toward Sheboygan.

He knew from his time in Oregon that he wanted to stay on the western half of Lake Michigan. Heading toward the eastern portion would put in on a lee shore. A lee shore was bad for sailors in that the wind wanted to push the boat into the land. Oregon was a notorious lee shore of the North Pacific and numerous shipwrecks on its hostile shore attested to staying away.

Jack had gotten used to handling the Newport singlehandly over the last eight months. A self-steering wind vane aided him on the open water stretches.

Starting late in the season on his 'looper' trip, he had dodged hurricane season along the East Coast. Wintering over near Mobile Bay, Alabama allowed numerous day trips on the Gulf of Mexico where he honed his ship-handling skills. He was now ready for the Great Lakes.

The wind kept increasing in intensity and Jack decided that he might want to look for a marina sooner than he planned. Leaving the self-steering to operate the boat, he went below to check his charts. A small marina was indicated a few miles ahead and he checked the chart for obstacles as he plotted his course.

"OK boy. We'll have solid ground in a little bit." Jack knew how much Tree loved getting off the boat. Doing his business on the forward deck just wasn't the same. *A marina meant sniffing time for my buddy. And grass,* Jack thought.

By the time the marina hove into sight, the winds had reached fresh gale strength. Jack had dropped the mainsail and rolled up the jib. Under diesel, the Newport plowed forward as the captain swung the wheel over to enter the bay. The waves crashed over the bow as the sailboat fought its way into the wind.

Reaching the harbormaster by shortwave radio, Jack was instructed to tie up in any vacant slip on 'A' finger. Learning that 'A' finger lay to starboard, he slowed the boat as he swung the wheel. With it still being early boating season, he saw a number of open slips.

Jack spied one slip with a familiar sight next to it. A Dufour 44 was already tied up and Jack slowed to line up his boat. Quickly throwing his fenders out, he put the boat's engine into neutral.

The forward momentum of the boat carried them toward their landing. As Jack readied his line to tie off to the dock, he saw a woman jump off the adjacent boat and motion to him. He threw her the line as the Newport slid easily up against the dock, its forward movement done.

Jack ran forward and grabbed his other dock line. By the time he was ready to jump onto the dock, the woman was waiting to take it from him. She bent down and wrapped it smartly around the cleat.

With her backside to him, Jack noticed the shapely figure she presented. *Not bad,* he thought. She wore Capri-style Lycra tights and a nylon windbreaker. While the windbreaker totally covered up her upper body, the tights certainly left little to the imagination.

The woman stood up and turned to face Jack. She caught him checking out her lower backside.

"Good job Captain. Nice work docking."

Jack recovered, looking up to the woman's face. She was tanned and fit. From her face and her backside, Jack knew that under the windbreaker was a matching set.

"Well, thanks for the help. Always appreciated. So we meet again," Jack said. The woman from the Illinois River locks smiled back. They hadn't had much time to socialize then as the lock master had kept them busy. But they had spent the whole day going through locks together and things got friendly as the chances allowed.

"What happened to you? We were paired up there for a couple of days. At least going through the locks. Once we hit that first one together, the whole mass of boats all continued together," she said.

She was referring to the small fleet of boats that had been rafted together. Once through the first lock, the boats tended to move up the river at the same pace to the next lock. The lock master would wait until all of them were gathered before letting them in the lock. It was a forced party for the couple of days that it took to travel the Illinois River.

Some days, boats would be missing but new ones arrived as people slept in or stopped along the river. But for three days the Newport and the Dufour were lock buddies. At least until Jack's bad diesel fuel had laid him up. Which had put her two days ahead of him. *I wonder what she's been up to that I caught up to her?* he thought

"Bad diesel. Took two days to clean the system out."

"Oh, I know the feeling," the woman said. "Got some bad fuel down in Missouri. Almost cost me an engine. Luckily my husband caught it in time."

Husband, she mentioned a husband, but I haven't seen anyone, he thought.

"I was warned about buying fuel," Jack said. "Told I should run it through a filter before putting it in my tank. But I thought that was for Mexico. I didn't think I'd have to do it in the States."

"I know," the woman said. "The place we got the bad stuff was a big marina outside St. Louis. You'd think they'd know better."

"Say, we never got formally introduced. I'm Jack Wesley. And my first mate's name is Tree. Coventry actually."

"Misty Duran. And my mate's name is Jackie. Pleasure to meet you both." The Jack Russell and the Airedale were already on the dock sniffing each other's body parts. They soon switched to other dock features as Tree began marking his territory. Jackie, being female, waited for her owner. "I need to walk Jackie. Care to join me?"

Jack reached inside his cabin and retrieved Tree's leash as marinas frowned on dogs running wild. The two boat captains headed off toward the green grass area behind the marina parking lot.

As they walked together, the two dogs made numerous stops to sniff. The humans waited patiently as their partners enjoyed solid earth.

"So, you mentioned your husband catching the fuel thing. Is he meeting up with you later?" Jack asked.

"Not likely. He passed away six months ago. Heart attack."

"I'm sorry. Didn't mean to pry."

"That's OK. He had a good life. No regrets. While we were together, it was special."

The two reached a wooded area that seemed appropriate for the dogs. They unclipped the leashes and sat down on a bench nearby, a memorial placard marking the bench. Obviously this spot meant a lot to someone in life. *Overlooking the marina and Lake Michigan, I can see why,* Jack thought.

Misty continued, "So, is there a Mrs. Wesley meeting up with you?"

Jack liked the forwardness. "Yes, there's a Mrs. Wesley but she's happily divorced and a long way from water in Colorado. I've been on my own for over ten years now."

"Didn't mean to pry either. But always curious what brings people to be solo sailors out here. Are you a 'looper'?"

"Yes, how'd you know?"

"I lived near St. Louis. Saw plenty of them on their journeys when they hit the marina we were moored in. They seemed to have something exciting about them. An adventurous allure."

"Sounds great. I didn't know I was giving off any allure. I thought it was just the lack of a proper shower. So, are you a 'looper' also?"

"Haven't decided yet. But after my husband's death, I decided I needed to get away. Thought some time on the Great Lakes would be a nice change."

Jack studied her as they talked. She appeared about forty years old. But I'll never say it to her face. *A man could get in trouble misjudging a woman's age,* he thought. *Widowed, with a very expensive sailboat.*

"Looks like the dogs will run all night. I don't know about you, but I'm starving. Would you join me for dinner tonight?" Misty asked.

Jack gladly accepted the invitation. With his quick departure from the Chicago area he hadn't had the chance to shop. His refrigerator was empty and his canned goods were getting low.

Returning to the dock, both dogs continued their sniff inspection of the area. Jack excused himself and climbed onto his boat. He did have a few bottles of wine he could provide for the hostess.

Asking permission to climb aboard, he stepped down into the Dufour's main salon. He was overwhelmed by the decor of the French sailboat. Where his Newport was utilitarian at best, the Dufour was luxurious. And with forty four feet of room, the passageway toward the bow offered more space.

"I only have red. I hope that goes with what you're making." He held up his bottle for inspection. He felt suddenly very common with his inexpensive wine amidst the luxury all around him.

Misty looked at the bottle and approved. *Being polite. She probably has bottles of wine on board that are worth more than my boat,* Jack thought. *And it isn't even my boat. At least my brother has money.*

"That will be splendid. I've got steaks for the barbecue. Excuse me while I go light it." She disappeared out the companionway to where Jack had noticed the stainless steel barbecue hanging over the fantail when he had climbed aboard.

He put his bottle on the counter and looked around at the pictures attached to the bulkheads. They showed a woman, obviously Misty, standing with an older man. Some were of a very much younger Misty standing with the same man, younger, but still old. *Her grandfather,* he thought.

He was busy staring at one of the photos when she climbed back down into the cabin. "Oh, I see your looking at pictures of my late husband."

Jack took a double take at the age difference. The man had to be forty years older than her. Misty noticed the stare and offered. "Yes, he was thirty-eight years older than me. We met when I was 25. He was 63 and a very successful businessman. He owned a financial investment business."

At 53, Jack had some experience with younger women after his divorce. But thirty-eight years was a big gap. He tried to look natural at the revelation. Misty pulled off her wind breaker and tossed it on the chart table. Now in a tank top, Jack could see what might attract any man.

"I see. He looks very happy." Jack kicked himself at his statement.

"We were. We had fifteen wonderful years together. He retired just after we married and sold his investment company. He set half the money up in a trust for his children. The other half of the money was set up in a trust for us. We just enjoyed ourselves. No cares."

"Well, you certainly have good tastes where boats are concerned. I've seen Dufours before, but never been inside one."

"My husband's choice. I grew up sailing Hobie Cats. I lobbied for a catamaran at the time but my husband had his heart set on this one. It's OK."

It's OK. Who is she kidding, he thought. "Well, compared to my Newport, this is something. Does it have air conditioning?" Jack asked.

"Yes, but only on shore power. But I don't think we'll need it tonight. The breeze pushed that hot air out. But last night the air conditioner was heaven. The boat got so hot yesterday sitting here."

"That's right, I was going to ask you. You got ahead of me from our lock buddy time. Anything hold you up while I was getting my tanks cleaned?"

"No," Misty replied, "I have an old friend in Milwaukee. I've been here for two days while I visited with her."

The rest of the evening went as expected. The steaks were cooked to perfection and the salad was fresh. Jack hadn't eaten such food for quite some time, nor had such a dinner companion for even longer. His wine was acceptable but he knew that she probably had a more discerning palate then him. The dogs also enjoyed each other's company and received the scrap steak for a treat.

"Thank you for a wonderful evening," Jack said as he stepped off onto the dock. His Newport looked decidedly proletarian in comparison.

"Will you be heading out tomorrow? My friend is taking me to see some sights but I'm free in the evening if you're still around."

"I need to restock. My food pantry is almost out. Why don't we plan on dinner on my boat then? I'll pick up something special."

Chapter 3

Lake Huron

The next two weeks were a constant dinner invitation between the two boat captains. Each day they would lay in their course for the next marina and then sail together during the day. The two solo sailors enjoyed each day sailing apart and each evening relaxing together.

Alternating evenings, one or the other would cook dinner. As the nights passed, each would return to their respective craft for a night's sleep. While they seemed to enjoy each other's company, anything physical escaped them.

The two sailed through the Mackinac Straits into Lake Huron. Now they were heading south along the Michigan shoreline. Jack had avoided any contact with Canada because of the revolver on board. Misty had been happy to comply with Jack's request that they stay on the American half of the lake.

Leaving their moorage in Thunder Bay, they set their course south. The wooded shoreline passed with only an occasional house or small community. Along the way, the State of Michigan had established numerous small anchorages in protected bays.

About half the time they chose to pick up a moorage in a protected spot away from any formal marina. These undeveloped spots allowed them to take the dogs on shore and let them run through the open woods.

This morning however, weather forecast called for gusty conditions as they pulled in their moorage lines. Jack looked up at the sky and noticed a slight red tinge to it.

"Are we sure we want to venture out today?" he yelled over at his neighbor.

"Red sky in morning, sailor take warning. Are you one of those sailors?" Misty replied.

"Just thinking. Wouldn't hurt to just stay put and see what happens."

"We'll miss Walleye Days in Bay City. My husband always wanted to be there. He was an avid fisherman and often talked about the walleye competition. He never made it. I promised myself I'd be there for him."

"OK. Just keep together in case we need help."

Misty gave Jack a grin as she scrambled to put the diesel into gear. Her Dufour started moving out onto the lake as Jack finished pulling in his line. Stowing the rope, he raced back to engage his engine. The Newport fell into line as it moved out onto the lake.

By midmorning Jack knew they had made a mistake. The storm clouds were building over

Michigan and the gusts bore down on them. The main sail was reefed as much as possible while the roller reefing on the jib had reduced the head sail to barely visible. The jib showed just enough sail to balance the main sail on the boat.

Up ahead, the Dufour struggled in the high winds. Misty showed too much sail as the big boat heeled over dramatically as it raced through the water. Making more speed than the Newport, the Dufour was steadily moving away. Jack didn't dare put on any more sail and decided that he would just follow along.

As the sky darkened, squall lines swept over them, the lead boat often disappearing from view. Then the rain hit. Jack scrambled below for his rain gear, unclipped his lifeline and pulled on his overalls. Throwing on his jacket with his safety harness on top, he clipped back into the harness.

Just when he reached the ladder to climb back into the cockpit, an intense gust hit the side of the boat. As the self-steering vane struggled to maintain course, the Newport staggered under the blow. Jack flew into the galley hitting the cabinets hard.

Hearing water rushing into the cockpit, he flew out into the cockpit. Standing on the side of the cockpit, he replaced the hatch to keep water out of the main cabin. He slammed the top glass and latched the two securely.

With Tree safely below, he grabbed the wheel as the Newport struggled to right itself. Jack threw the wheel over to bring the bow up into the wind and slowly the 36' boat came back upright. He spun the wheel the other way to put himself back on course.

His heart sank when he looked up at where the Dufour should have been. The rain obscured everything as he strained to catch a glimpse of the French boat. The wind-whipped white caps added to the maelstrom.

A break in the rain increased visibility but there was nothing of Misty's boat. He grabbed the binoculars from their secure holder and trained them on the water ahead. *She couldn't have gotten that far ahead of me,* he thought.

Then he saw it. Or what looked like something. But it didn't make sense. Something ahead rose from the water, but in the swells, he couldn't make it out. And it wasn't large and upright as a sailboat would display. He adjusted his course to intercept.

As Jack got closer, he recognized the Dufour. The sailboat laid on its side, water washing over the half submerged boat. Where the keel should have been, he could see a broken stump. A bright yellow arm appeared from behind the stern.

Jack reached for the ignition and the diesel fired to life. He hit the roller reefing and what remained of the jib disappear. Letting the main sheet loose, the boom fluttered free. He reached into a nearby locker and grabbed his rescue ring which was soon attached to the boom. A throw rope appeared in Jack's hand, ready to toss.

"Help!" the voice cried out across the expanse of water. A portion of a woman's head appeared over the gunnel. With the boat slowly sinking while laying on its side, Jack maneuvered around to the leeward side, avoiding the standing rigging now lying in the water. From this side he would avoid being pushed into the hulk by the intense wind.

Swinging the wheel around so his bow was into the wind, the Newport hobby horsed its way forward. Idling the engine so it held its position while the wind tried to push it backwards, Jack threw Misty the rescue rope.

Grabbing the rope on the first throw, Jack pulled with all his might. She leapt off the Dufour and disappeared into the froth. With the Newport now sliding away from the sinking boat, Jack pulled Misty around to his stern.

Jack lowered the rescue sling and Misty pulled it over her head, jamming it under her arms. The winch handle flew as Jack raced to raise her up out of the water. The Newport continued to struggle in the waves and it was all Jack could do to get Misty into the cockpit.

Finally, a very wet, exhausted woman collapsed on the deck. Jack pulled off the rescue sling and snapped Misty into the Newport life line. Then spinning around, he got the boat moving again.

Misty sat up in the cockpit and watched as the Dufour slipped under the waves. "I never did like that boat. Cheap ass construction almost killed me."

"The keel was completely broken off."

"When that big gust hit, it knocked me over. I was waiting for the keel to right the boat, but nothing. It just laid on its side. Then a big wave took out the hatch cover and filled the cabin. I knew it was over then."

"You were lucky that ..." Jack stopped mid-sentence.

"Go ahead, say it. You were right. We should have stayed in the moorage. I'm just glad you were with me. Thanks Jack." Then she remembered her dog. "My dog. Where's my Jackie? Oh my God, I forgot her."

The two stood, braced themselves against the boats violent action and scanned where the Dufour had gone down. Jack gunned the engine and swung the wheel as he searched the area for the missing dog.

"I had her down below. On no, she went down with the boat!" she screamed.

Just then, something caught Jack's eye. Something not water-colored was off the starboard side. Then he heard it. He swiveled his head so his ear could find the direction as he followed his intuition and steered toward the sound.

"There she is!" Misty yelled.

Jack saw the Jack Russell struggling in the water. The dog swam for her life as waves crashed over her. Jack adjusted course and idled the engine, letting the wind carry him down toward the dog.

He reached over the side as the Newport glided by the desperate dog. Grabbing her collar, Jack swung her aboard with all four legs still pumping hard. Misty immediately grabbed her dog in a hug.

"She must have swum out the broken hatch," Jack said.

"She's alive. Thank you. I can get another boat, but I could never replace my best friend."

Jack got both of them below, pointing to where the blankets were stored. Both the dog and her owner had taken on a bluish cast from their swims in the lake. Jack returned to manhandling the Newport in the heavy weather.

In all the excitement, Jack suddenly realized they had drifted over to the Canadian shore. The closest protected moorage was a small town located behind an island where the water would be protected from the fierce wind. He swung the wheel and increased his RPMs to make a safe passage.

"Misty, check the chart. See if there's anything to worry about getting into this town. We're on the Canadian side. I think it's Port Elgin."

Jack waited as Misty searched the charts for an answer. Finally a voice offered, "Looks straight forward. There's a buoy outside the channel. Just follow the range pole on shore."

The Newport turned at the buoy as Jack followed the shore range markers that delineated the channel. Once inside the harbor, calm returned to their lives. With the wind blocked, the waves gave way to a relatively calm anchorage. Jack saw the first open dock space and swung in toward the dock.

A man walked briskly out on the dock and helped with docking. "Mighty nasty to be out on the lake today."

"I have to agree with you on that. Is there any law enforcement about? We have to report an accident," Jack said.

"Oh. I can go call the constable. He can be right over," the man offered.

With the Newport secure, Jack scrambled below. Ignoring the shivering woman on the settee, he quickly dug out his revolver from its draw by the chart table. Jack climbed into the rear berth head first and crawled toward the stern. He had found this hiding place for this eventuality and quickly stowed the gun.

Jack pushed himself back into the main cabin and noticed a wide-eyed woman staring at him. He raised his finger to his lips to shush her to silence. By the time he was back on deck, the constable was walking up the dock.

"I heard there was trouble. How can I be of service?" the local constable asked.

"First, I guess we need to clear Customs since we started in the States this morning. Second, the woman in the cabin just lost her sailboat."

"What?"

"I just rescued her as it sank out on the lake. The keel broke off and it floundered. She's quite upset."

"As I'm sure she has a right to be. Let me come abroad and get a statement." The constable climbed over the lifeline and disappeared down the hatch.

Well, here goes, Jack thought. Canadians didn't like guns to start with and handguns were strictly forbidden. He would be in major trouble if Misty talked or if the constable conducted a thorough search.

Jack sat down in the cabin and listened as Misty related her story. The constable made notes in his official book and asked a few questions. When he was finished, he stood up to leave.

"Mrs. Duran, I can only say that I am happy Mr. Wesley was at hand. For your sake and your dog's."

He started to leave when Jack asked. "What about our Customs clearance or whatever needs to be done?"

"No worries, you're right. You've had enough excitement today."

Chapter 4

Cedar Point, Ohio

"Having fun yet?" Misty asked as Top Thrill Dragster cycled into position. Jack felt the restraining bars lock into position as he looked up for the expectant hill they would climb. Unlike a regular roller coaster, he saw none.

The only thing in front of him was a long straight track with a monstrous tower at the end. The tracks went straight up the tower, curled over the top and plummeted down to return them to their original start.

As he opened his mouth to say something, the car they were strapped to launched itself with a boom. Catapulted from zero to over 120 mph in 200 feet, the g-force pulled his mouth open, sucking in the wind. His body flattened against the back of his seat.

All around him he heard the screams of other people. The metal tower creaked and groaned as the car slammed into its base and rocketed vertically. The g-force of the switch from horizontal to vertical crushed Jack into the bottom of his seat.

His vision finally adjusted only to experience the rollover at the top of the tower, as the ride reached its maximum height of 420' above the amusement park. Jack felt his stomach revolt and he fought for control as the car performed a 180 degree turn sideways and plummeted straight down. Now he was weightless in the restraints as his body attempted to continue its journey straight up.

Just when he felt his stomach reconnect with the rest of his body, the car hit the bottom and the g-force once again slammed him into his seat as the car went horizontal. The ride's automatic braking system activated and their car jerked to a stop.

Misty jumped up as soon as the restraints were released, turning to look at the man struggling to regain his composure. Jack lifted himself carefully out of his seat and stepped onto the unloading platform. The safety gates closed as the now-empty car automatically swung around the track to gather its next victims.

How could anyone enjoy this? he thought. He hadn't minded the smaller roller coasters that were scattered around Cedar Point Amusement Park, but Misty had talked him into trying the big one.

"Was that great or what? Want to do it again?" she asked.

Jack just shook his head, looking around for a seat in the shade upon which to die, noticing several others doing the same thing. The park had been generous in providing park benches near the ride exit. *Obviously the designer knew what the reaction of many would be to this body torture machine*, Jack thought.

"I just need to sit for a bit," he mumbled out.

"Yeah, you don't look too good. Sorry, I should have noticed. You didn't exactly jump off that one," Misty offered. "I'll go find you a drink. That might help your stomach."

Just the mention of stomach brought waves of nausea welling up. Jack bent over and breathed rapidly to fight the urge to vomit on the spot. Misty soon returned with two drinks.

Jack sipped and felt the cold carbonation flow down his throat. Almost immediately his stomach settled enough so he could sit up.

"And you enjoy this?" Jack asked.

Before she even said a word, Jack knew the answer. Misty's smile showed it all. She beamed with excitement as the adrenaline from the ride coursed through her body.

"I've always had a thing for roller coasters," Misty said. "The bigger the better. And that one is one of the biggest."

Jack shook his head at her enthusiasm for what he felt was torture. He had endured taking his kids when they were little to Florida. When they were small, he enjoyed the kiddie rides. When they grew bigger, he had learned to beg off as they moved up to the super coasters. Luckily, his son and daughter had each other to ride with back then.

Today he was feeling a little obligated to be Misty's partner in fun. *Somehow the enjoyment is better if you have someone to share the experience with,* he thought. But he was thinking that the Top Thrill Dragster would be his last ride for the day.

"Jack, you've been a pal all day. I'll let you off the hook on the rest. Just walk with me. I only have four more to do and I'll have hit them all."

The two walked slowly over to the next thrill. Jack found a shady seat and held both drinks while Misty got into the solo rider line. She was back in what seemed an instant. She reached for Jack's hand and pulled him up.

"This is actually better. The solo rider line moves faster since there always seems to be a spare seat when the couples load up."

Misty quickly hit her target of hitting all the big rides the park offered. *At least the adult scary rides,* Jack thought. *If she'd been happy with the kiddie rides I'd still be out there with her.*

Misty announced she was starving from her workout and dragged a reluctant partner over to one of the food vending establishments. Jack excused himself and found a quiet table with an umbrella for shade, sinking into working on his two drinks.

Returning with a large helping of burger and fries, Jack scooted around so he was upwind of the tormenting smell. *How she could eat that after all those rides amazes me,* he thought.

As she squirted ketchup over the fries and took a bite of her burger, juice ran down her chin. She dabbed herself with a napkin.

"So, these rides don't get you excited?" she asked.

"Well, sure they do. But it's my stomach that reacts, not my heart. You seem to thrive on the adrenaline rush all those extra heartbeats give you."

"I love it. I spent as much time at Six Flags Over Mid-America as I could. It's just west of St. Louis. I'd drag my husband out there and we'd ride till they kicked us out at closing."

"So he enjoyed it as much as you?" Jack asked.

"Oh yeah. He was game for any of it. We always hit the parks wherever we went." Misty grew quiet. Jack knew from her look that she was remembering the times she and her husband had had together conquering roller coasters wherever they might be found.

"Sorry, I'm not much of a partner for you."

"That's OK. You're special to stay two nights at the marina so I could be here. I am a guest on your boat remember," Misty said.

That was true. I did divert my planned trip so she could be here, he thought. He smiled and she recognized his willingness to accommodate his boat guest. As Misty finished her gastronomic challenge, they decided to head back to the boat. Tomorrow would be an early day as they set out on Lake Erie on their way to Buffalo, New York, the Erie Canal waiting.

Tree welcomed them back to the Newport and Jack grabbed his leash to take him for an evening walk. Misty fell in beside them with Jackie as they headed along the promenade overlooking the lake. A short distance away the lights of Cedar Park twinkled in refection off the water. The night air was warm and pleasant as they strolled along, Tree sniffing and piddling the whole time.

Misty slipped her arm under Jack's and pulled herself tight against him. She rested her head on his shoulder.

"It's a beautiful evening. Can we just sit and admire the view?" she asked.

Jack was still not feeling one hundred percent from his close encounter with eternity, so he quickly agreed. They stopped at a park bench overlooking the lake and the amusement park. They sat and watched the lights before anything was said.

"Jack, I've been meaning to ask you something."

"Yes, what's that?"

"Your fanny pack. You take it everywhere we go. I've seen you take your camera out and take pictures. And I know you have your phone jammed in there. But can I ask what else you have in there?"

Jack looked at her to measure the seriousness of the question. Then he looked around to see how alone they were. Seeing no one nearby who would over hear them, he asked, "Why do you want to know?"

"It just seems heavy for just a camera and a phone. Just curious, I guess."

Jack considered the woman who was asking and why she was being so inquisitive. She had seen his revolver when he hid it from Canadian Customs. *But what was motivating her inquires now?* he thought. He had learned to avoid 'curious women' in his career in law enforcement.

"Misty, you've seen my revolver when I had to stash it from the Canadian authorities. How did you feel about that?"

"What do you mean, how did I feel about that? I didn't want you to go to jail, certainly. And I didn't want to go to jail if I'd been caught with you. Is that what you're asking?" Misty asked. Jack noticed a certain confusion.

"Oh yeah, those things for sure," Jack said. "But on a more broad view, what's your opinion of guns? Should I even have a gun on board my boat at all? Do you have an opinion on that?" Jack asked.

"My husband had guns. I grew up in a family in southeastern Missouri that hunted and fished, so we had guns around the house. My brothers and Dad went out all the time. I got to go shooting with them occasionally but I wasn't into hunting anything."

"OK. But what about handguns? Unlike long guns and shotguns, handguns only have one main purpose."

"Shooting people, right?"

"Well, people will say they have value in target shooting, but that's really just practicing for the real thing, which is personal defense," Jack said.

"I guess I never thought that much about it. People have a right to defend themselves. I'm all for that. Personally, I wouldn't want one on board my boat. But my husband did keep a shotgun on board. It's at the bottom of Lake Huron with the rest of my old life now."

"So, you sound ambivalent at best on handguns then."

"No, I support your right to carry one, if that's what you're asking?" Misty answered.

"Even after what happened in that Connecticut school recently?"

"That was terrible. So many little kids killed. Those parents lost so much, I can't imagine how they will ever move on in life," Misty said.

"And the laws that some states are passing in an attempt to redress that whole episode, how do you feel about them?"

"Well, I suppose something must be done. How many school shootings can we endure before someone does something?"

Jack sat quiet. *Those weren't the right answers to my questions. Can I trust this woman or is she one more misinformed liberal?* he thought. The silence between them intensified as the nearby screams of delight rolled over the water. The setting was one of happiness and joy, not of school shootings and death. *Maybe I should just drop the whole thing and just enjoy this woman's company.*

As the silence continued, a tension rose between the two. Soon it was apparent that the gun talk had stifled any further discussion. They stood and started the walk back to the boat. Tree resumed his sniffing.

After each had performed their nightly routine in the marina bathroom, they retired to their separate berths. Jack was settling into the V-berth when there was a knock on his small cabin door.

Opening the door, Misty stood in the doorway in her nightly attire: nylon jogging shorts and a loose T-shirt.

"Jack, can we talk? I think I said the wrong thing back there. I don't want to go to bed with anything between us."

Jack climbed out of his berth, his Big Dog shorts maintaining a sense of modesty between the two boat mates. They sat at the dinette table in the main salon.

Misty continued, "Jack, I'm just a typical female where guns are concerned. I want to believe the world is a safe place and that we don't need guns. But I know in reality the world is full of evil people. Like many females, I just choose to ignore reality."

"Thanks for your honesty, Misty. At least you admit it. Most women won't. And many men too. I was a cop for thirty years. I dealt with the evil side of society every day. I choose to go through life armed against those same people."

"So you were carrying in the park today?"

"I carry everyday of my life. Everywhere I go. And if I can't carry because some stupid state law prevents it, I don't go there."

"I understand where you're coming from. But don't you think we need to stop all these school shootings? You must agree that protecting children is a worthy goal."

Jack looked at her like the question was an insult. Misty recognized the reproach and held up her hands as a sign that she had gone too far.

"I dedicated my life to protecting the innocent. It's too bad that the politicians don't have the same concern toward their constituents."

"I'm sorry Jack. I shouldn't have said that. But something needs to be done. These people have too easy a time getting their hands on weapons for their evil deeds."

"Let me ask you a couple of questions then," Jack said. "Do you think we should have a law against someone buying a gun and then handing it over to someone the law doesn't allow to buy a weapon?"

"Yes, that sounds reasonable."

"Then you agree with a national background check system to prevent criminals and mental patients from obtaining guns?"

"Of course."

"How about a law that would send a felon to jail if he's caught by the national background check system just attempting to purchase a gun?"

"Again, reasonable."

"How about a law that sends anyone to jail for using a gun to commit a crime?"

"A no-brainier Jack. What's with these questions?" Misty asked.

"Because they are already in place. There are federal laws on the books against all of the above. With sentences of five years to life in prison for violating any one of them," Jack said.

"That's good then, right?" Misty asked. But there was a hesitancy in her voice.

"Let's just look at one of those laws; felons attempting to buy a gun for instance. During Senate hearings on more gun legislation, the Department of Justice offered evidence that more than 76,000 attempted purchases were denied. So, out of those many thousands, how many went to jail under that law?"

Misty thought for a long time before answering. "Half, thirty thousand."

Jack chuckled at her answer. Misty looked at him to attempt to estimate a number.

"Five thousand," she offered.

"Off by a factor of a lot. Try once more. Third time's a charm." Jack was suddenly enjoying this little late night soiree. *My stomach must finally be back with me*, he thought. He watched as Misty's expression showed she was refiguring her answer.

"Five hundred. They have to have gone after at least five hundred, right."

"I'll quote the hearings record, a few dozen. We can assume that would be less than one hundred" Jack stopped to let the number sink in. "Out of the multiple thousands of felons standing in a gun shop trying to illegally purchase a gun, they managed to arrest and prosecute less than one hundred."

The look on Misty's shocked face revealed to Jack that it had been worth enlightening her. If she had reacted differently, he would have stopped. *No point in beating a dead horse*, he thought. *But I see hope.*

He added, "The entire population of the United States of over 310 million individuals has to pay money and jump through hoops to exercise their guaranteed Constitutional rights to buy a gun. And the law that is there to supposedly protect everyone from the bad guys is used less than one percent of the time."

"But why have the law if the Feds aren't willing to use it?" Misty asked.

"Exactly," Jack said, "Millions of honest citizens are burdened by all these laws enacted to supposedly make us safer. But surprise, our wonderful Federal government does nothing, or next to nothing, in enforcing those same laws. But have a school shooting and those same Feds immediately start talking new restrictions."

"But what about gun shows? I saw on television that anyone can buy a gun there without any checks."

"First, most of the vendors at gun shows are gun dealers. They have a Federal license and all their sales are background checked. For the others, yes, you can buy a gun from an individual with no paper work," Jack said.

"That's bad right?" Misty was treading softly now in her conversation.

"It's what it is," Jack said. "Consider this. Say they decide to pass a law that all gun show sales have to be background checked. If I was one of those individuals selling my personal guns, I would just move my operation to the back of my pick-up truck out in the parking lot. I would be outside the gun show but have access to all their patrons."

"Aren't they talking about having all gun transfers require a background check?"

"So I want to give my adult son a rifle that I've owned for years. Right now, I just give it to him. But under that proposed law, I would have to go to gun dealer and have a background check done on my son. Then I could legally give him my rifle. But who's to say it isn't already his gun?"

"There's a list somewhere of the guns you own, isn't there?" Misty asked.

"I hope not. That's called gun registration. And a lot of people will forcefully resist the government knowing about every single gun they own. And where they've moved to gun registration, gun confiscation soon follows."

"That could never happen here."

"Don't be so sure what the ruling elite has for an ultimate goal in this country. Power is about control and the American people have clung tightly to their guns as the final arbitrator of that power. As long as the people are armed, the government has to be careful what it attempts to do."

"Jack, you sound like one of those . . ."

"That's because I am one of those. A person who believes in individual liberty. And I'm willing to fight for it, against all enemies, foreign and domestic. The Marines had me swear an oath to that effect when I joined long ago. Once a Marine, always a Marine."

"I see your point, and I agree with it. Maybe not as stridently as you, but individual freedom is high on my list. I just hope it doesn't come down to fighting for it in this country."

Jack looked silently at his boat mate. *She doesn't really understand what's at stake, does she?* he thought. *I think she'll be finding out sooner than later.*

Chapter 5

Albany, New York

Where the old Erie Canal begins its ascent away from the Hudson River, the old locks of the original canal had been preserved. New, larger locks were constructed on the western part in 1918 to handle the larger barges that were expected. But trains and long-distance trucks took the freight business away, leaving the Erie Canal to wither.

At least until tourism found the canal. Where the large barges disappeared, small pleasure craft moved in to replace them. By the 1960's, cruising the Erie Canal was a popular pastime of New Yorkers. As time went on, boaters from the Northeast found the relaxing enjoyment of floating along through history.

Towns along the canal soon learned the profitability of catering to the pleasure craft. Old mills were refurbished as trendy restaurants and hotels to cater to the tourists. Soon, non-boating tourists were enjoying the canal just for their historical nature.

Albany soon joined the redevelopment effort and made a major effort to reclaim the area along the Hudson River. Office blocks had taken over the old warehouses that lined the river. Daniella Martocci was one of those office workers who enjoyed the river view from her desk.

Overlooking the river, her window on the world held excitement each day. More so than her tedious job. She was the secretary to a psychiatrist who had her office in the old warehouse. It was a pleasant enough place to work. Shops and restaurants on the ground floor made it convenient on her lunch hour. Parking was provided in one of the non-river-side buildings. And it was all so historic. All her friends commented on what a fun place to work it was. *But they didn't have to put up with the boring job like I do,* she thought.

Daniella stared out the window as a pleasure craft headed north toward Canada. *Probably heading for Lake Champlain and the St. Lawrence River*, she thought. Canals connected both the lake and the St. Lawrence to the Hudson so a boat could do a loop around upstate New York if they wanted.

Montreal is such an exciting city, she thought. She and her friends went there often. Daniella thought Montreal more exciting than New York City. Though smaller, Montreal had that certain French character to it, giving it a European feel. Daniella had never been to Europe, but hoped to one day.

She had studied French in high school and enjoyed using it when she was in Quebec. *Anything was better than this dumb job sitting here*, she thought. I need to listen to my parents and head back to college.

At twenty-years old, she had struggled in one year of college. The party life had been too distracting and when her parents cut off financial support, work became a necessity. Luckily she had taken typing in school, so she easily passed that exam.

And she was good-looking enough to attract male patients for the good doctor to counsel. She knew that a lot of repeat customers were because of her. *Hell, they usually spent more time outside in the waiting room talking to me than they did with the doctor*, she thought. They even lingered after their session to talk.

"Daniella, I'll be leaving early today. Right after Mr. George's appointment," the psychiatrist said.

"OK," Daniella replied. *Oh great, that whack job George. I suppose he'll linger like the others. And no Doc to feign work to distract him*, she thought.

Ed George had been a patient of the doctor for over a year now. Daniella had learned to give the man a wide berth whenever he had an appointment. While almost all the Doc's patients seemed to be less agitated after a session, George left more animated. His wild-eyed look increased after each session. *Whatever he and the Doc discussed in their hour together, he wasn't one who seemed to be benefiting from the help*, she thought. But what did she know? She was just a twenty-year-old college drop out.

Daniella turned her thoughts to her job of filing. While all the confidential stuff remained securely in locked files in the doctor's office, her job consisted mainly of answering the phone and greeting the patients when they arrived. It was an easy job with lots of time to play Solitaire on her computer.

The door groaned as it opened and Ed George walked into the outer office. The wide warehouse floorboards creaked as he walked over to a seat and grabbed one of the magazines provided. *He always goes for "People' magazine*, Daniella thought.

Even as a woman psychiatrist, the Doc provided more manly magazines. 'Car and Driver' and 'Popular Science' were more typically perused by the male patients. Daniella kept her head down and looked busy so as to avoid any eye contact.

"Good afternoon, Ms. Martocci." Ed said.

Oh crap, I need to engage with the guy, she thought. "Good afternoon Mr. George. Have any plans for the weekend? The weather looks like it's clearing."

"That's what the weatherman said this morning. This rain we've been having has been miserable. I get all cranky when I'm stuck inside all day. How about you?"

I bet you get cranky you whack job, she thought. But today he seemed pretty coherent to her. "I do like the sunny days. Lifts my spirits."

"You can say that again. I'm just glad we're out of the winter weather. Each snowy season seems to last longer and longer to me," Ed said. "School will be out soon. I love it when those little kids are playing in the park. All their yells and screams just remind me of happy times."

Before she had to respond to that bit of conversation, the inner door opened and a male patient came out. The doctor was saying her normal encouraging words as the man held the door open for Ed as the two brushed past each other.

"Mr. George, so good to see you," the woman psychiatrist said as the door closed.

"So, Mr. Early, do we need to schedule another session for you?" Daniella asked the departing patient.

"Ms. Martocci, yes. The Doc said I need to come back in a month. We're making great progress. Are you ready for the weekend? Some romantic rendezvous perhaps?"

She hated the personal queries so many of the patients seemed to have. They all seemed to figure a young, good-looking single female had an exciting life. *In Albany, who are they kidding*? she thought.

And these middle-aged guys were the worst. Most were recovering from bad divorces and were always trolling for anything in a skirt, she thought. While she liked the attention, just once she wished a young guy would come through the office. *But then, if he was visiting the Doc, I don't want any part of him.*

"Nothing so glamorous I'm afraid. I've been looking for a newer car, so I suppose I'll be on the computer checking out the ads. Maybe I'll get a movie in with my girlfriends."

"Well, have a wonderful weekend. I'll see you in a month. You can let me know how the car hunt went."

As Mr. Early walked out into the corridor, Daniella sighed in relief. One more patient dealt with successfully. One more to go and she could kick back until quitting time. With the Doc gone after Mr. George's visit, she could spend serious time getting a head start on looking at the car ads.

As she played Solitaire the voices from the inner office grew louder. She couldn't make out what was being discussed, but whatever it was, Mr. George would be leaving more agitated than when he arrived. This seemed typical of his visits. *Pleasant and chatty arriving, sullen and morose leaving*, she thought. I'm not sure why he keeps coming back if this is all he's getting out of his sessions.

She braced herself for his exit as she watched the minute hand sweep relentlessly toward the top of the hour. Soon the door would open and she would have to deal with Mr. George. She shut down her card game and waited. Staring out the window, she saw another pleasure craft slowly drifting down the Hudson headed to New York City.

The door flew open and a wild-eyed George streaked out. As he reached the door leading to the corridor, Daniella risked his wrath.

"Mr. George, does the Doctor want you to make another appointment?"

Ed George stopped in his tracks and turned. Daniella shrunk into her seat as the thousand mile stare swept over her. Ignoring her while looking out the window, the pause frightened Daniella. The inner office door had slammed shut and she was alone with the crazy man.

"Mr. George, is everything OK?" she risked asking.

"OK? Everything's peachy. Just peachy." His grin was almost demonic. His stare didn't waiver one bit as he continued his focus on a point off in the distance. "And no, I'll need no more appointments. The good Doctor has declared me ready. The world will know of Ed George."

He was gone. A feeling of doom filled the office as Daniella shivered at the exchange. She had never experienced anything like it since taking the job. Before she could think of what she had heard, the inner door opened.

"Oh Daniella, you're still here. I'm leaving now. Since it's looking to be such a nice weekend, why don't you lock up? You can get an early start on

Friday. And don't forget, I'll be at that conference in New Hampshire all week. I won't need you."

"I have it written down," Daniella said. Her doctor seemed to have a meeting in New Hampshire every other month or so. She had never seen any paperwork on what the conference entailed, which seemed strange to her. *Usually those things have a brochure or something*, she thought. Then thinking about what had just happened, she asked, "Mr. George didn't ask for a new appointment for next month. Should I pencil him in for one and call him later?"

"No, that won't be necessary." The doctor returned to her office, gathered up her belongings and left without another word. *That was strange*, Daniella thought.

But she was happy to be off work early. She could catch up with her friends and get started early on relaxing. The car hunt could wait until Saturday.

Chapter 6

Pittsford, New York

"How about this place? It looks like it will have good food," Jack asked as he and Misty studied the menu posted outside the entrance.

"Looks good to me. And the view is nice," Misty answered.

The restaurant was located in an old warehouse right on the Erie Canal. Like most canal towns, Pittsford had joined the tourist clamor for re-gentrified buildings with food and microbrew beer available. The entire journey so far on the Erie Canal had been one trendy establishment followed by another.

Tonight's menu looked to be centered on Italian. Jack liked Italian better than the German food establishments they had encountered. While the beer was better, the heavy German fare weighed down his stomach more than his normal diet.

Part of him was missing his solo days aboard his Newport sailboat, eating simply, if more boring. He wasn't a gastronomic expert and while he enjoyed a good meal, he didn't base his life around it.

Misty, on the other hand sought out fine dining. She announced that her deceased husband had taught her the finer points of great cuisine. While

Jack had been the recipient of her culinary delights, he was beginning to miss his old bachelor diet.

The maitre d' escorted them to a table outside overlooking the canal. With a small lighted candle and night sky, the setting was worthy of the beautiful woman accompanying him.

"It's very romantic here, isn't it?" Misty said.

"Yes, quite. I wonder how their ravioli is here?" Jack asked. Whenever he ate Italian, he ordered ravioli. His great quest in life seemed to be to find the establishment serving the best ravioli.

"You know Jack, Italian cooking has other dishes. Some are very good. You might want to try one."

Ever since they had decided to team up and continue their journey together this had been the result. *She seems intent on changing my ways,* he thought. While he was a big boy and could handle the intrusions, it had grown a little old.

After reporting her Dufour sailboat lost and escaping the Canadian authorities before they became too nosy, the two sailors had decided to team up. Misty had always disliked the Dufour and wasn't sad to see it gone. That she lost all her personal affects bothered her some, but a quick shopping trip when they hit Detroit solved that problem.

Jack had found a marina safely located in the suburbs, and a taxi to the local shopping mall filled her needs. Misty had taken over the forward V-berth while Jack had the pilot berth under the cockpit. With separate doors, they each had their privacy. The Newport only had one head, though, so a little coordination was necessary with personal chores.

Things had gone well as they exited the Detroit River and sailed across Lake Erie. Reaching Buffalo, they had to have a crane lower the sailboat's mast in order to clear the lower bridges on the Erie Canal.

Having a second person on board to handle the lines as they worked their way through the locks was handy. Jack had grown tired of the solo lock work on the Mississippi River and the Illinois River. In fact, Misty often took the helm and Jack acted as deck hand just to break up the duty.

Things between them had been friendly for the two weeks it had taken to reach Pittsford, located just southeast of Rochester. While there had been the occasional gaffs with the use of the head and shower, no romantic inclinations had been raised. Both seemed content to be friends traveling together on a common journey.

Misty had placed an order for a new boat, one more to her liking. And with her inheritance from her husband's trust, one she could afford. While Jack wasn't privy to the cost of her new sailboat, he knew large ocean going catamarans weren't cheap.

As an old Hobie Cat sailor, Misty's choice to replace the monohull Dufour was a James Wharram-designed boat. Built in Great Britain of fiberglass, or GRP as the British called it, the Tiki 38 was a traditional Polynesian-designed two hulled boat.

Rigged with two masts for easy handling, Jack knew Wharram cats were famous for their quickness and seaworthiness. He read up on the Tiki 38 and the testimonials of those who had done ocean crossings confirmed the boats reputation.

The boat had been ordered but it remained to be finished and then sailed across the Atlantic before Misty could take possession. So she was enjoying the interlude taking in the sights of Upper New York until she could take possession of the new cat in Portsmouth, New Hampshire.

And she seemed in no rush. Misty Duran was content to linger along the Erie Canal enjoying the continuous gastronomic fare offered. While the two dogs were enjoying each other's company, Jack showed signs of being frustrated.

When the bread arrived, Jack sliced open the hot bread and offered the first slice to his dinner guest. He smeared butter on his slice and took a bite. Reaching for his glass of Chianti, he washed the bread down with a gulp.

Too much rich food and too much wine, he thought. And not enough exercise. His attempt to hold in his displeasure failed as Misty perked up to her partner's displeasure.

"We don't have to eat out every night you know. It can be expensive."

Jack was reminded of the income difference between them. His police pension was generous in comparison to the average retirement in America, but compared to Misty's monthly check, Jack could only imagine. The two had never brought up the subject.

I can certainly afford these soirees, he thought. Misty had been adamant that they split all expenses. Tonight would be her turn to pay, but that wasn't what was really bothering Jack. It was something else.

His sullen attitude contrasted with the setting as the other diners all seemed to be enjoying themselves fully. He pulled another portion of bread off and stuffed it into his mouth.

"It isn't my money is it, Jack? I forget sometimes that others around me don't focus on that. Where I came from, that seems to be what everyone is concerned with."

"How much do you have, anyway?"

Misty was taken aback by the suddenness of such a personal question. Her expression registered with Jack.

"I'm sorry, that's none of my business. Forget I asked," Jack quickly backtracked.

He swirled his red wine in his glass and watched as the liquid settled down the sides. He sniffed once and took a mouthful.

"No, we know each other well enough, and it's all public record, if you care enough to go look it up. When I married my husband, his children certainly brought all the tawdry details out when they only got half. I'm worth well over $50 million, Jack."

Jack almost choked on the bread he had just stuffed into his mouth. He cleared his throat with a slug of Chianti. He held up his glass at the waiter. The waiter recognized the signal and turned to retrieve another full glass.

"What! And you're out sailing by yourself? Aren't you worried?"

"About my safety? A little. But I refuse to be a prisoner of my wealth. I'm still young and I intend to enjoy life. I gave over my younger years to a man who made me very happy. I have no intention to sit in St. Louis doing fundraisers for the symphony the rest of my life. And don't forget, I have Jackie to keep me company."

"But, you have. . ." Jack was at a loss for words. His brother certainly had the trappings of someone who had been incredibly lucky in his investments. Jack enjoyed one of those trappings, but his brother was a piker in comparison.

"Freedom to enjoy life. And I intend to do just that. Ah, here's the main course."

The conversation was interrupted by the waiter bringing two steaming plates. A baked ravioli was placed in front of Jack and seafood fettuccine was Misty's choice. A new glass of wine arrived and Jack took another big swig.

Conversation slowed as both ate their entrees. The quiet only accentuated what had been said prior to dinner arriving.

"Jack, may I ask you something?

"Of course."

"Do you find me attractive?"

Now Jack was taken aback by the bluntness of the question. He had certainly noticed that his boat mate was a very desirable woman. And now he knew she was a very desirable rich woman.

He stammered slightly in his answer. "Well, yes."

"Do you have someone else in your life?"

"I did, but I think that's over."

Misty didn't respond but went back to eating. Jack looked at her in the soft glow of the flickering candle. The evening air gently rustled the tree's leaves lining the canal. Couples strolled arm-in-arm along the towpath nearby as they took in the wonderful night.

There was a certain flushness to her face as Jack watched her. *Maybe its the Chianti* he thought. He finally spoke. "Why do you ask?"

"All this time we've been together, you haven't made a pass at me. I was just wondering if something was wrong."

Something wrong? Hell, I'm struggling to maintain myself here, lady, he thought. Jack knew she was looking for something. He would have to provide her a good answer, and he searched for the proper response to the obvious statement.

"I just didn't want to impose myself. You've lost your boat. It just seemed that it would be bad manners not to be the perfect host while you where on my boat."

"Don't worry so much about that, OK?"

Jack nodded that he understood. *I'm not sure I do understand, but I'll agree to keep things civil between us*, he thought. *But what was that small impish smile that I just saw?*

As they finished the main course, the waiter asked if dessert was desired. Without even asking Jack, Misty ordered tiramisu.

Jack was working on his second wine and was enjoying the relaxed feeling it provided. The restaurant was generous with their large glasses and the effects were noticeable.

Misty was stirring her after-dinner coffee as both stared at the dessert. She picked up the two dessert forks and handed one to Jack. They had tended to avoid desserts in their restaurant meals. *I'm already stuffed, I'm not sure I need this*, he thought.

His dinner companion didn't wait for his opening but dug her fork into the tiramisu. She slowly lifted it to her lips and held it there. With her lips closed tight, she focused on Jack. He stared back at the intensity of the stare he was receiving. *What's this?* he thought.

As he watched, Misty slowly opened her mouth and moved the fork slowly in. The soft dessert parted her lips with some smearing onto both lips. She slowly closed her lips and withdrew the fork ever so slowly.

Placing the fork down on the plate without breaking eye contact with Jack, she slowly chewed. The tiramisu on the outside of her mouth moved up and down to her eating. When she swallowed slowly, she opened her mouth slightly. Her tongue flicked out and swiped the dessert slowly off her upper lip.

Then it returned and, even slower, gathered up the food on her lower lip. Jack felt his heart race and his groin twitch at the display. Misty picked up the fork and took another bite. She repeated the entire scene for Jack, never wavering her stare at him.

"Aren't you going to join me?" she asked. The words jolted Jack back to reality and he looked down for his fork. He took a forkful of tiramisu and raised it to his mouth. Unskilled in the seductive use of desserts in his foreplay, he shoved it in his mouth. His bad attempt at eroticism brought a smile to Misty's mouth.

Again she lifted her fork up and again very slowly smeared half the content on the outside of her mouth. A person watching her eating habits would have wondered if she was disabled by her lack of skill on getting food into her mouth.

But her table partner knew exactly what was being displayed, and it wasn't a disability. *I now know why her husband probably died a happy man,* he thought. My ex-wife had never done such a sloppy job of eating in her life.

Her tongue lingered as she cleaned up the dessert lingering on her lips. A stubborn piece had slipped down onto her lower lip. Her tongue slowly moved out of her mouth further and further until it gathered up the wayward morsel. Jack's blood pressure rose as he watched in mesmerized silence.

As he reached for another forkful, he jumped as he felt a foot run up his leg toward his groin. Never wavering in her stare, Misty smiled again as Jack's right eye registered the stimulation he felt over what had already been going on. Her toes worked their magic as she stared intently across the table.

Jack's right eye continued its twitch as his mouth chewed slowly on his dessert. Across the table, another bite of dessert made its way even slower to its target. The lips barely moved as the fork glided into the mouth. With dramatic flourish, Misty lifted the fork high and made a back and forth motion as if she had to work to get the contents scraped off.

As she did her fork motion, her toes worked their magic on Jacks lower body. She leaned forward as she placed the fork down. Her low cut top drooped open revealing her breasts. Jack shifted his eyes to the new view she was offering. Her toes moved and Jack twitched in his chair.

"Will there be anything else?" the waiter asked. Jack jumped at the intrusion to the erotic seduction taking place. He looked around to see if anyone else had noticed and was gratified that the dark setting and busy chatter from the other tables meant they had been unseen.

"No, I think we're done here," Misty offered. As the waiter left to retrieve the bill, she turned her attention back to Jack. "Care to retire to the boat, Jack?"

Jack reached under the table and took her bare foot in his hand, removed it from his groin area, pulled it lower on his leg and massaged it gently.

"I need a minute to recover. We don't want to embarrass the other guests," Jack said. His crotch was coming back under his control as he waited for the check. Misty pulled her foot back and reached under the table. She quickly pulled her sandal back on.

Paying the check, she leaned forward. "Ready?"

Jack discreetly adjusted his shorts and stood up. He took Misty's chair by the back and slid it out for her. She stood and turned, "Thank you."

She took his hand in hers as they walked slowly through the restaurant. The other guests paid them no mind as they stepped outside. Their pace quickened as they turned and headed to the Newport sailboat moored along the quay side a short 200 yards away.

Misty stopped Jack from fully entering the cabin. She placed the lower hatch door in the companionway as Jack stood on the lower step. With his shoulders and head protruding out the open portion of the companionway, Misty slid his shorts down. His naked lower body soon was being worked over by a discreetly hidden mouth below decks.

Jack tried to look casual as strollers walked by on the tow path a short distance away. The tree shadows dappled the lights nearby and kept the boat and its occupants secluded. Unknown to them was what was happening to him below decks. It was all he could do to not scream out.

Soon Misty's head appeared above the cabin roof. She pushed Jack's head down as she climbed up onto the cabin roof. Straddling the open hatch way with a blanket covering her lap, she slid her skirt up revealing a bare bottom. Now hidden in the cabin, Jack moved up to his target.

Misty leaned back slightly as the pleasure reached up through her. Careful to keep the blanket over Jack's head, she sat as if staring at the stars while below the waist her body shook with pleasure.

With the exhibition portion complete, both slid below decks to complete their lovemaking in private.

Chapter 7

Greenbush, New York

The next few days it seemed that the Newport 36 sailboat barely crawled along the Erie Canal. With the romantic dam broken, the trip down the canal took on an entirely different context. Dinners out now were ones of anticipation of what would follow. The exhibition portion of the journey took on almost legendary status as the hatch became a featured aspect of their time together.

They lost count of how many people unknowingly had walked by their love-making. Occasionally one of them would display too much emotion and draw a stare.

Soon the Erie Canal reached the long steps down to the Hudson River. The Waterford Locks were the finale to the 338 mile journey from the Great Lakes to the Hudson River. They had been lifted and dropped a total of 680' over the course of the trip. Now it was all downhill to New York City and the Atlantic Ocean.

For Jack, the Inter-coastal Waterway would take him back to the Chesapeake Bay via the Delaware Ship Canal. Washington D.C. lay at the bottom of the Bay and a return to his brother. His loop of the Eastern United States would be done. Part of him was ready to return to Wyoming and the wide open spaces of the West.

But part of him was sad. Misty's catamaran was due to arrive in Portsmouth in two more weeks. That would place them about in Wildwood, New Jersey.

The two had talked about traveling together to Portsmouth to receive the new boat. They would sail the Tiki 38 down the East Coast to Wildwood. Then the two of them had talked of cruising Chesapeake Bay together.

But first they had to complete the last locks and find a boatyard with a crane. The Newport's mast needed to be stepped. Once reinstalled, Jack would have to tune the standing rigging to make sure the wire tension was right for sailing.

An untuned boat risked snapping the mast in heavy weather. A badly tuned boat made a bad sailor as the sails would lack the proper shape to get every knot out of the wind. And for real sailors, even a partial knot speed difference mattered. There was a pride in having a fast well-trimmed boat. Misty handled the lines as they made their way down the final drop. Jack tied up on the Hudson.

"It's lunch time. Why don't we grab something here? The skipper we talked to yesterday raved about the deli," Jack said.

The two walked hand in hand across the river walk to a small deli. The small community of

Waterford had joined the other canal stops in catering to the boaters. Jack grabbed an outside table next to the Hudson as Misty went inside to order. The day was warm and the umbrella overhead kept their table cool.

* * *

The next day was busy as the Newport was lined up under the crane for its mast raising. The short float down the river to the small riverside town of Greenbush was uneventful the day before. The boatyard offered help in tuning the rigging and Jack gladly accepted.

His brother had a small library of nautical books on board and he had been reading up on rig tuning. While the author made it sound simple, in fact it quickly turned into an art form.

As Jack tightened one wire shroud, the other three would be knocked out of adjustment. When another adjustment was made, the three other ones were no longer good. It was the boatyard worker that showed him the fine points of slowly working all four wires into the correct tension. *That would have taken me a week of frustration by myself,* Jack thought as he thanked the worker.

"Boy, you're sweating like a dog. Are you ready for lunch? You've been working real hard. I have tuna sandwiches made the way you like them."

"Thanks. It's the humidity. I'm missing Wyoming right about now. I don't know how they take this heat back here."

"Jack, it's only 72 degrees," Misty said.

"Well the humidity makes it feel like 102. But food sounds good. And a big glass of water."

Jack had the boom attached with the main sheet shackled in. He'd thrown a tarp over the boom for shade from the sun and they set up lunch in the cockpit under the shade. Even with the shade the humidity made the day uncomfortable. Misty showed the effects with sweat beading up on her forehead.

"Hot down below? You'll be missing that air conditioner that's at the bottom of Lake Huron if this keeps up."

"We just need to move down to New Jersey. The ocean breezes will keep this heat down for us then," Misty said.

"Your new Tiki 38 doesn't have air does it?" Jack asked.

"No Jack. I'll be roughing it like you. No bourgeois boat for me. The proletariat will sail on," Misty joked.

"Well, tomorrow we can get an early start heading down-river. We should be able to cover the 150 miles to the city in five days."

"Not too fast. I want to see West Point. The Hudson School of Painting was one of the first

American art genres in our country. I'd hate to miss it."

"OK, we'll take our time Miss Art Connoisseur. I really think you want to enjoy it naked from the waist down sitting on your hatch."

"You know all my secrets. We've been together too long," Misty replied.

Jack wasn't sure what was meant by that, if anything. But he was content to enjoy the ride as long as it lasted. He know the new Tiki 38 would separate them physically. With two boats to operate, they would be solo sailors again.

Part of him looked forward to being solo. He and Tree had been together a long time. They had enjoyed many an adventure together. *I've been remiss in giving him enough attention lately. I'll get up early and we'll do an extra-long walk tomorrow*, he thought.

After dinner, the two sat in the cockpit enjoying the evening. Luckily the breeze offered a reprise from the few remaining black flies still about. Late spring ushered in the end of the black flies and the beginning of mosquito season. School was almost out and soon the river banks would be populated by families enjoying the summer.

"Jack, I haven't asked you this, but are you nervous having your revolver here in New York State? With those new laws they passed since that awful shooting at the school in Connecticut, guns seem to be public enemy number one."

Jack looked around to see if they had any neighbors before answering. Luckily they were still moored in the boat yard, the marina with other boats a short distance away. With the workers gone for the day, they were alone.

"Misty, stupid people have been using that tragedy for their own gains. All the laws that the states have passed wouldn't have prevented that school tragedy. They just impose draconian restrictions on law-abiding citizens," Jack answered.

"But you're revolver isn't legal here, is it?"

"If you're worried about getting in trouble, just act dumb if something happens. But I won't give up my rights as guaranteed by the U.S. Constitution because some self-serving state politician says otherwise," Jack said.

"But you're risking jail, aren't you?"

"Don't worry about me. That's why I never intended to travel east of the Mississippi River. It took some doing by my brother to talk me into this trip. And then he only showed up when I was in Mobile Bay for a few days."

"Well, it would have been kind of cozy if he'd shown up the last month, don't you think?"

Jack smiled at Misty's comment. *Yes, it certainly would have been real cozy with a third along for the open hatch romps each evening. Not that my brother would have minded,* he thought. *He is a red blooded American male who would understand such things.*

Misty continued, "So you've said that your brother was well-off. It's nice of him to loan you his boat for this trip."

"And his house in Jackson Hole and his collection of classic cars to drive. Yes, he's a good brother. Too bad he choses to stick himself in Washington D.C. Why he puts up with that snake pit is beyond me."

"He must enjoy it from the way you describe it. He has all the toys but chooses to stay and work. That's where my husband made a choice. He retired and enjoyed his toys."

I can see why he retired, with you as a new 20-something wife, Jack thought. Jack tried to imagine her twenty years younger. He had seen the pictures in the cabin on the Dufour before they went to the bottom. She was stunning then. At forty, she still held all the beauty he had seen in those earlier photos.

"Jack, I think we're alone enough here that we don't have to use the hatch trick tonight."

He looked around and the darkness was complete. The boatyard had no outdoor lights. The marina lights were too far away to reach their moorage. Jack slid over next to Misty and took her in his arms. Soon the small waves of the Newport's motion rippled out onto the main Hudson. They quietly dispersed before reaching any others.

Chapter 8

Greenbush, New York

The early morning light of a new day crept over the hills to the east. The Hudson River Valley was open near Albany but would soon close into the confines of the lower river. Jack rose with the light and carefully climbed past a sleeping Misty. The two dogs at the foot of the bed perked up at the human activity.

Dressing in the main salon, Jack strapped on his fanny pack. Grabbing two leashes, Jack slid the hatch open and stepped out onto a dew-covered deck. The two terriers followed close behind. Once on the dock, he clipped the leashes and set off through the boat yard.

A small unlocked gate lead to the marina and from there to the access road up the hill. Jack set a quick pace to fight off the coolness of the morning. *How I could sweat all day but be cold at night baffles me?* he thought.

The dampness in the air hung over him as he reached the top of the small rise overlooking the river. He turned left on the country road that followed the river and picked up his pace. The dogs happily kept out in front of him with the occasional sniffs to the side of the road.

Jack allowed no dog breaks as he kept their pace moving. The brush along the side of the road suddenly fell away and revealed a grade school that had been built along the river. *Nice setting for a school*, Jack thought. He increased his stride and the dogs joined the pace.

At about a half hour into his walk he spied the outskirts of Greenbush. It appeared to be another two miles further on, its church steeple announcing its location. Jack checked his watch and decided he would turn around. *If we're to get an early start down river, I can't be out walking too long*, he thought.

Letting the dogs have a quick break to mark territory, he soon got them headed back toward the marina. As he switched sides on the road so he faced the oncoming traffic, he noticed an increase in cars.

Approaching the elementary school, he realized where they all had been headed. Traffic was pulling in and depositing children. Reaching the school, Jack noticed the name: Chester A. Arthur Elementary School. *Named for a hack New York City politician that hustled his way into the White House*, he thought.

As he stared at the sign something caught his eye. Thirty years of police work had given him a sixth sense and now little bells started to go off in his brain that something wasn't right.

Sitting in a car in the parking lot was a man. But this man didn't look like a school employee. And he didn't look like a parent. The wide-eyed stare of the man told Jack to slow his pace and observe.

The dogs were only too happy at the chance to sniff and when Jack took up a discreet position behind a large maple tree, they busied themselves marking territory. Having walked past the parked wild-eyed man, Jack stepped off the road on the other side of the school. He could see the man's back, but from this distance couldn't tell what he was up to.

The cars with children ceased their delivery and a bell announcing the start of school rang out. The door opened on the car with the stranger. He stepped out wearing a trench coat. With long pants and the cool weather it didn't look unusual, but Jack's hair went up on his neck.

He reached down and pulled his fanny pack around to his stomach. Without taking his eyes off the stranger, he unzipped the pack. He felt for his 357 Magnum revolver. It was in its place for quick retrieval and, as he shifted his hand, felt the four speed loaders holding new rounds. He waited.

The stranger walked briskly toward the school's entrance. At the door, he pulled it open and walked in. Jack stepped out from behind the tree and slowly walked toward the school. He reached down with his left hand and unclipped the two leashes, his right buried in his fanny pack.

Just as he was in front of the school he heard the first shot, hitting him like a thunder clap. He dropped the two leashes and sprinted for the front door. More shots in quick secession reverberated through the building as the horrific noise carried outside. Jack ran faster.

He approached the front door from the wall and leaned around the corner to peer inside the foyer. Seeing no one, he opened the door and crept in. His revolver was up and ready as he sighted down the hallway. He allowed Tree to enter with him but kept Jackie outside as he knew his own dog had been trained for these circumstances.

Walking into the school he saw the back of a figure disappear into a doorway about thirty feet away. More shots rang out. Jack ran past the office to the right and saw the bloody bodies behind the counter. Multiple shots were ringing out as Jack reached the door where the figure had disappeared.

He shifted his head forward quickly to peer through the glass in the door. What he saw was a nightmare of violence. Standing over a prone teacher attempting to shield her kindergarten students was the stranger. His semi-automatic handgun was firing into the screaming children. Blood was everywhere as the teacher took hit after hit as she attempted to shield as many children as she could.

Jack flung the door open and, using the door jamb for cover, leveled his gun on the man's back.

His laser lit up a small dot between the man's shoulder blades. Tree moved beside him barking madly. Before Jack could even yell anything, the man spun around with his pistol and aimed at Jack.

Jack's screamed, "Drop it!"

The screaming children blocked out any other communication. Jack screamed louder. "I said drop it dirt bag!"

A round hit the door jamb opposite Jack's head in response. Before another one came his way, Jack pulled the trigger. The Ruger roared to life as the 180 grain bullet flew out of the muzzle. Hitting the man dead center in the chest, the small laser light was replaced by a large hole as the round hit with 524 pounds of pressure.

The man reacted violently to the first hit as Jack fired his second round. This one caught the man in the lower jaw just as he was falling backwards from the first hit. As his body succumbed to gravity, the second round that had been aimed at his chest missed the mark and hit his falling head.

The jaw flew off as blood splattered across the classroom. The screaming children increased their cries as the evil man fell among them in a heap. Jack left his protected position and raced to the children. The teacher was clinging to life as Jack took her head in his hand.

Blood was pouring out of her mouth as her eyes flickered the last bit of life. She convulsed and jerked. Jack knew she was gone.

Still holding his revolver, he slipped it into his fanny pack. Beside him were three obviously dead children. Jack had seen head wounds before and knew these children would not survive. He reached for an injured child. Two children were bleeding profusely, struggling to live.

Several more children appeared to be shot but none looked life threatening. From the screams it was hard to tell, but Jack knew these two needed immediate attention.

He reached into one small child's leg and could feel the blood pulsing out onto the floor. He squeezed the artery as best he could to stop the flow. Another child had a bad bleeder in the upper arm. With his free hand he pulled the child's belt off and strapped it around the upper arm. He pulled it tight with his teeth to form a tourniquet. The bleeder slowed.

He looked around for something to tie around the boys leg wound. The dead teacher had a scarf around her neck. Using one hand, Jack untied the scarf and swung it around the leg above the wound. With both hands, he cinched it tight and tied it off. Then he grabbed the dead man's semiautomatic pistol and shoved it in the tourniquet. He twisted the gun clockwise to tighten the scarf.

The pressure on the leg stopped the blood flow as the scarf did its job. He looked up at the other children to see if he could help another.

"Drop it now or die!" the command came from behind.

Jack hadn't noticed the sirens of the local police arriving but instantly knew he had probably multiple guns pointed at him. Not wanting to get shot in the confusion, he lifted his arms out and extended his empty hands.

"I'm a police officer," Jack yelled.

"Hit the floor or you're going to be dead mister," was the response.

Jack knew in the heat of battle that you always follow the instructions of the man holding the gun. Things could be sorted out later, if he was still alive.

He sank onto the floor with his arms extended out to his side. Instantly someone was grabbing his arms and pulling them behind his back. Handcuffs flew onto his wrists and were cinched down tight.

Two officers jerked him to his feet and pulled him over to a corner of the classroom. His revolver was quickly removed and bagged for evidence. A third officer was standing in the door way with a two-way radio, "Clear. Get those medics in here now."

Two EMTs rushed into the room and started attending to the injured children. Jack watched as one of the officers searched the dead man. More emergency personnel appeared as Jack could now hear the sirens as the entire area responded to the school shooting.

Soon the room was full of uniformed officers as the injured school children were treated and removed. Jack twisted to see the entire school being evacuated by uniformed officers, weapons drawn.

It didn't take long for all the children to be whisked away to either a hospital or safety. Activity in the classroom was slowing down when a New York State police officer walked in. Jack recognized the bars of a captain on his lapel. Jack knew things were about to change.

The State Police captain walked over to the dead man lying in his own blood. A local City of Greenbush sergeant that had been supervising the scene handed the captain a wallet that Jack had seen taken off the dead man.

Pulling out a driver's license, the captain said, "Ed George. Says here he's from Albany. Anyone ever seen him before?"

The entire local Greenbush force present in the room shook their heads. Jack knew he would soon be next. *Ed George wasn't about to tell them much*, Jack thought.

The State Police captain followed by the City of Greenbush sergeant walked over. They stood in front of Jack as he sat sprawled on the floor, his police guard by his side.

"And who the hell are you?" he demanded.

"Captain, first, can you have your man loosen the cuffs? They have them cinched up pretty hard. Sort of blocks out my answering question ability with the pain level so high."

The State Police captain eyed Jack. After a minute he nodded to the patrolman to ease up on the handcuffs. The relief was immediate.

"Thanks. I'm Deputy Sheriff Jack Wesley. Teton County, Wyoming. My badge is in my fanny pack along with my ID."

When Jack had retired from the Eugene, Oregon Police Department as a detective, he hadn't planned on a second career in a sheriff's office. But when his brother had invited him to sail his boat around the East Coast, Jack had balked. Jack avoided the East Coast like the plague due to its restrictive guns laws.

I don't go anywhere I can't carry, he had announced to his brother. Very soon after, he had been called to report to the Teton County Sheriff Office in Jackson, Wyoming. The sheriff was waiting with a badge and an ID making Jack a Deputy Sheriff.

When pressed for an answer to the uninitiated offer, Jack was informed that his brother made things happen in Wyoming. As Chief-of-Staff to Wyoming's only congressman, what his brother wanted his brother typically got. Now Jack had a legal right to carry a firearm anywhere in the United States.

Or at least that's what Jack had thought. Law enforcement officers had standing throughout the country to do their duty.

The captain reached into Jack's fanny pack and retrieved his badge and ID. Flipping it open, he examined both.

"You think this carries any weight here in New York?"

"I think most states recognize the legal right of peace officers to perform their duties. Yes captain, I think even in New York."

"Hrmmph. We'll see about that."

"Listen Captain, if you're not going to release these handcuffs, then I'll be asking for a phone call. I'm demanding my Miranda Rights as of now. You do recognize those here in New York?" Jack asked.

"Listen, Mr. Wise Guy. We got dead school kids here. We got a dead guy over there with his head almost blown off. And what I don't need is some Deputy McCloud, or whatever you say your name is, mouthing off to me. I would think you'd want to cooperate here," the captain said. "And is this your dog?"

The captain made a motion to kick Tree that sat guard next to his master. The Airedale went into defensive mode at the threat.

"I wouldn't if I were you. He might get shot for the effort, but he'll rip your throat out before your boys in blue here could draw a bead. And I believe I've cooperated by stepping in and stopping Mr. George over there from upping his body count. You can thank me later."

"Get Mr. Cowboy out of here. We'll see what his story really is back at the station."

The patrol officer pulled Jack to his feet. The handcuffs cut into his wrists as the officer led him toward the front door. From the hallway he could see the Albany television stations had already arrived and were setting up for a siege. Jack stopped in his tracks.

Chapter 9

Albany, New York

Daniella was looking forward to Monday off. With her boss gone to her conference in New Hampshire for the entire week, she would have time to enjoy herself. She wouldn't be getting paid for the days off, but time was more important to her.

The weather was looking nice for the entire week and she had called her girlfriends about heading up to Lake Placid. They would camp out to save money and see what summer thrills they could catch with the early vacationing crowd.

She fixed her breakfast as the television filled the morning quiet. Daniella always had it on while getting ready for work. *It helped fill the emptiness of my small apartment,* she thought, but she seldom paid much attention to it.

But something grabbed and shook her this morning. TV cameras were showing a school just south of Albany. The scroll on the bottom was on alert status. The yellow line said a school shooting had just taken place at an elementary school. No casualty figures were being announced, but Daniella made the quick assumption that there would be plenty by the amount of emergency personnel shown.

She sat down and watched. Police were shown escorting the little kids out of the school. All were crying and clinging to their classmate in front of them. Then more police ran into the building as emergency crews brought out victims on gurneys. From the camera's perspective she could see that they were covered totally.

Oh my God. Little children, she thought. The news reporter came on the screen and announced that police had just confirmed five fatalities. Two adults and three children. Daniella sat transfixed. *How could this be happening just outside Albany?* she thought. *They just passed laws to stop this kind of thing, didn't they?*

* * *

"Jack, where are you?" Misty called out. The boat was silent in return. Just the small chop of the river rocking against the hull broke the quiet. And sirens. Many sirens.

Something had woken Misty from her sleep. A popping sound followed by more popping sounds. It wasn't loud enough to snap out of her slumber, but enough to register in her subconscious.

The sirens woke her fully. She sat up and looked around. "Tree, Jackie," she called. The dogs weren't there to respond

There are those sirens again, she thought. She quickly pulled on her workout clothes and tied her running shoes. She shut the hatch up as she left and headed toward the main boat marina next door. Once through the small gate, she sprinted up the hill toward the sound.

Reaching the country road at the top of the small rise, she was almost hit by a State Patrol car screaming past her. He was all over the road as his speed kept him fighting for control on the high crowned pavement. She doubled her effort as she saw flashing lights just ahead.

Misty came up short as she cleared the brush and the elementary school came into view. Mayhem confronted her as emergency workers rushed children out of the building as frantic parents arrived, fear driving them.

More ambulances arrived and gurneys were wheeled into the school. Firefighters ran into the school for more victims as the ambulances screeched off heading toward Albany. A police officer stopped her from getting any closer as he quickly put up yellow tape across the front lawn of the school.

Frantic parents pushed past him as he lost his battle with crime scene control. As more parents arrived, the lone officer was finally assisted by fellow patrolmen and the crowd was held by the road.

As children were led out of the school, Misty watched in tears as parents lunged to their child.

How could this have happened? she thought. *And where's Jack?* That's when she spied Jackie. Her Jack Russell Terrier was dutifully standing guard at the front door.

Misty whistled and called her dog. The dog spun around to the call and ran across the lawn to Misty. She crouched down and hugged her buddy. *But where's Tree and Jack?* she thought. She waited through the chaos for an answer.

Television trucks soon showed up and the police motioned them to a spot in front of the school where they were out of the way of the emergency vehicles but close enough for their coverage. Misty watched as the cameramen jumped to their task of recording as the news reporters all tried to get someone to tell them what had happened.

The police on the line just stood mute. Their job was to keep the gathering horde at bay while the officials locked down the scene. The reporters were visibly frustrated at the decided lack of cooperation. Misty moved closer to the television crews in anticipation that they would get the first reports. *I need to know what happened,* she thought.

Just as she and Jackie took up a spot near one truck, all the cameras swung onto the front door.

"They're bringing him out," one of the female reporters yelled.

Misty turned to have her heart sink. A man in running shoes and shorts with a windbreaker over his head came out of the front doors. His arms were obviously handcuffed behind his back as he was escorted by two uniformed officers. Walking beside him was Tree. *What is going on?* she thought. *Jack's the killer? How can that be?*

As soon as they were out the front door, she heard a muffled command. Tree instantly began running toward the marina. Misty quickly ran to cut the dog off. She whistled and Tree changed direction and joined her.

She bent down to pat the dog. As she pulled her hand away she noticed blood on him. She immediately felt over Tree looking for a wound. Then she realized it was someone else's blood.

Pulling back in horror, Misty looked up and realized that the news crews were focused on the perpetrator and hadn't noticed Tree. She took his leash and blended back into the crowd, keeping her distance from the reporters.

Tree sat down with Jackie and waited. *That had been Jack who had been led away in handcuffs. I'd recognize him even with his head covered*, she thought. *What do I do now?*

"Excuse me. Are you the owner of this dog?" a small person voice asked.

Misty readied herself to leave instantly if it was a reporter. But when she looked up, she saw a small boy trembling holding his mothers hand.

"This is the dog that saved me Momma. He and the good man saved my life," the small boy said.

"I'm sorry to bother you," the mother said. "But my son saw the dog and wouldn't leave without thanking him."

Misty looked into the eyes of a traumatized little boy. "What's your name?"

"Riley. Riley Wood. What's his name?" Riley asked as he continued to hug Tree.

"Coventry. But we call him Tree for short. Was he brave today for you? He was trained to be brave."

"The most bravest dog I've ever seen. And the man, he was too," Riley said.

The mom noticed that they were receiving attention from the reporters now that the perpetrator had been taken away.

"I think we need to get out of here. The vultures are starting to circle."

Misty looked around Riley's small head and saw the attention they were starting to receive.

The mom offered, "I need to take Riley to City Hall so the police can talk to him. Will you and your dogs join us? I think Tree needs to add his story."

Misty didn't need to be asked twice as the reporters closed in. The mom scooped up Riley and all five made it to her SUV before being identified. Riley's mom quickly drove off.

"I'm Courtney Wood. Thank you again. Both your friends did something special today. I don't know how to ever repay them."

Misty sat silent in the passenger seat. She needed time to think. *If what this mom is saying was true and Jack was a hero today, why was he led out of the school in handcuffs? It doesn't make any sense,* she thought.

* * *

The news reports continued as Daniella sat watching. The scene had switched to Greenbush City Hall as more TV crews showed up to cover the event. The City Hall had been cordoned off as it became the headquarters for the investigation. It appeared that a news conference was about to take place on the front steps. Daniella turned up the sound.

"Ladies and gentlemen, I am sad to report that five people were gunned down today and killed. Two adult employees of the elementary school have died of the wounds inflicted. In addition, three kindergarten-aged children have been killed."

The bottom of the screen announced that the person talking was a captain in the New York State Patrol. He explained the situation in its basic description, leaving out most details. They would need to further investigate this terrible crime before they could offer more, he said.

Daniella had seen enough of these tragedies to know the drill by now. The world wanted immediate answers to unimaginable disasters. She continued to watch as the Captain finished up.

Questions from the reporters flew at him at the end. They were the normal questions asked as the reporters looked for more answers. She started to turn the volume back down when one question caught her. She gasped for a breath as she heard it.

She didn't even wait for an answer, even though one never came from the captain. She was in in a car headed south out of Albany. She had to get to Greenbush and find the answer in person.

Chapter 10

Greenbush, New York

"Who put this damn thing on his head?" the State Patrol captain in charge demanded. He looked around the squad room of the Greenbush Police Station. Located in the basement of City Hall, the entire building had been locked down as the school survivors were brought in for questioning.

A Greenbush police officer walked Jack to the rear of the station. He opened up the one holding cell and placed his charge inside. Removing his handcuffs, the officer then removed Jack's windbreaker off his head.

Jack slipped into the jacket and sat down on one the benches. It felt hard and unforgiving but he was focused on his wrists. The cuffs, even after being loosened, still had dug visible marks in his skin. He rubbed them to get the stiffness out.

The captain scowled at the patrolman as he locked the door to the holding cell. The officer ignored the State Patrol captain as he walked back to the desks in the front of the station.

"You think you're pretty smart, don't you?" the captain asked.

"I just didn't want to become the next Richard Jewel," Jack offered.

"Who?"

"Atlanta Olympics. Bombing in Olympic Park. Richard Jewel warned officials about the bomb, but then was accused of planting it. The press smeared his name and face all over the world. His life was never the same. It turned out he was actually a hero."

"Yeah right. So you think you're a hero in all this? Well, we'll just check out your story and see if this Wyoming Sheriff thing is legit."

The captain walked off and disappeared into an office to the side. Jack sat back and waited for someone to offer him his phone call. He knew that he might have a long wait. Police weren't always quick on offering anything. *And with this clown in charge, I'll probably find myself in Guantanamo before I get my phone call*, he thought.

Jack dozed from the adrenaline drop. Even the hard bench and wall couldn't keep him awake as his head sank to his chest. He was snapped back to reality with a clank on the cell door. Looking up, he saw the same Greenbush patrolman who had uncuffed him in the school. That had allowed him to remove his jacket and place it over his head to hide his identity from the press.

"What's up officer?"

"Thought you might need something to eat. Ham and eggs from the restaurant across the street. And coffee."

"Thanks. The food sounds great. But I'm not a coffee drinker. Hard to believe, I know. But English Breakfast tea if you don't mind would hit the spot," Jack said.

"I'll get over there in a couple. Anything else?"

"No, thanks again. Anything newsy on me getting out of here sometime?"

"The Police Chief is back. His wife was the principal. She was shot twice but they think she's going to make it."

Jack acknowledged the bad news with a nod that police officers recognize: a look of resignation at horrible deeds by bad people and a look of resolve to stop them in the future.

"I'm sorry I didn't pick up on the perp sooner. I saw him in the parking lot but wasn't sure. He had the look and demeanor."

"Hey, deputy. The town is grateful for what you did do. Things turned out a lot different than that school in Connecticut."

Jack took that as a sign that he had at least one local friend. He knew he was a long way from home and was a stranger here. *Not a good situation,* he thought. He heard more sirens outside the building but today was a day full of them. He paid them little heed.

Tea soon appeared. The ham and eggs had been long devoured so he handed off the paper plate.

Jack sat with his tea and focused on the comings and goings of the police station. From his holding cell, he could see most of the desks. Officers were busy working, some in suits. *Detectives,* he thought.

Jack knew the routine. He had carried the gold shield of a detective for twenty-five of his thirty years of police work. He knew that the small force that Greenbush employed would be supplemented by New York State and the Feds. Unil the FBI showed up, he was stuck with the State Patrol captain.

A man in a suit approached Jack's position. From the badge hanging from his suit pocket, he assumed the FBI had finally showed. Following closely along was the Greenbush patrolman who had been his companion since the school.

"Officer, please release Deputy Wesley. I'm sorry for any inconvenience," the man said. He handed Jack his badge and Teton County ID. "I'm afraid your service revolver is part of the investigation. It's been sent off to Washington. I'm sure your Sheriff can expedite another to you."

"Thanks, agent?" Jack asked, inquiring.

"Special Agent Frank James. No relation."

Jack smiled at the man's attempt at humor. Referencing the James gang of Wild West fame lightened the moment. "So, do I need to make a phone call?"

"Wouldn't hurt to let someone know you're OK. The New York State authorities seem intent on pursuing you for something." Special Agent James walked Jack over to a phone at a desk and offered him a seat. He stepped back a bit while Jack made his call. Jack spoke briefly and hung up.

* * *

"This is very unusual. We don't interview victims with other people present," the detective from the New York State Patrol said.

"And kindergarten children aren't supposed to be subject to the things they saw today, either. The dog and its owner stays or we leave," a visibly irritated mother said.

"I think it's OK, detective. I've been doing this kind of thing for years and if the dog helps, it'll be easier."

"OK Doc, it's your call," the detective said, backing off.

"Now, Riley. I'm Dr. Judith Skinner. I work for the State as an advocate for children who have been victims. I'm here to ask you about what happened today."

"Yes ma m'. As long as my friend can stay. He saved my life today." Riley clung to Tree. In response, the Airedale stood perfectly at attention, guarding his new friend.

"Yes, I understand Tree was a hero today."

"And the good man. He made sure the bad man wouldn't ever hurt me again."

"Yes, Tree and the good man. But can you tell me about the bad man?"

Riley gripped the dog harder as thoughts of the bad man came up. Tree stood his ground and provided needed support. Riley began telling his story. Misty and his mom sat behind him as he spoke. They held each other's hands as they heard the details of the attack.

When he had finished, the doctor said, "Your teacher was very brave. She tried to protect all the students when the bad man came into the room."

Riley shook his head in agreement. Tree swung his head around and licked the boy's tears. Riley pulled the dog in closer.

"And you said the good man saved your two friends. They were bleeding and he stopped the blood?"

He again nodded in agreement while burying his face in Tree's side. The fur muffled his words. "Are they going to be alright?"

The detective spoke up, "The hospital says that the good man saved their lives. They're in surgery right now but they'll be alright."

"He couldn't help my other friends. Their heads were . . ."

The mom reached for her son to stop the answer. "I think that's enough. We need to get him home now."

"Of course, Mrs. Wood. Thank you for your forbearance at a time like this," the doctor said. "Riley, you've been very brave. Thank you for talking to me."

"Just make sure the bad man doesn't come back, please."

"We won't let him come back, I promise," the doctor said.

Riley let go of Tree finally but was reluctant to leave with his mom. Misty assured Riley that Tree would be around and that they would come and see him soon. The mother and her son left the room. As Misty took Tree's collar to leave, she overheard the detective and the doctor talking.

"The legislature needs to finally act. They danced around the issue the last time. This will convince them guns need to be banned. Australia and Great Britain finally acted after just one of these slaughters. How many will it take to get the United States to finally act?"

Misty quietly closed the door on the two and their conversation. *What should we do about this type of thing?* she wondered. Watching Riley convinced her something needed doing. *That little boy will be scared for life. And he was one of the lucky ones.*

* * *

"What do you mean 'Thank you very much.'? That's all you're going to do about this?" Daniella was yelling at the Greenbush detective.

"Ma'am, you need to lower your voice. We have a big investigation to complete here. And we're just getting started. Your information has been noted and it will be in the file. Thank you for bringing it to our attention. We have your name and address if we have any follow up questions."

"Unbelievable!" The hot-blooded Italian turned in exasperation to leave. She almost tripped over the dog walking in front of her.

Misty apologized for Tree's transgression.

"Is this the dog that the cameras showed coming out of the school with the man they arrested?" Daniella asked.

"Yes, but that man didn't commit any crimes. He acted to save the children from . . ."

"I know. Because I know the whack job who shot those kids. And these people just seem to busy to . . ."

Misty cut her off. She took Daniella's arm and led her to a quiet place away from the police. "You said you know who did this?"

"Know him? I had to sit in the same room with him every month. The guy was crazy. But they won't confirm that it was him. When I heard the reporter ask if Ed George was involved, I almost fainted."

"Ed George, that's the guy?" Misty asked.

"And not only him. There's something else going on. But these folks are too busy reacting to this one. They don't have time to see if the next one is about to happen."

"Next one? What are you talking about? You know that another school shooting is about to happen?" Misty asked.

"Well, not exactly. I don't know for sure. But something is happening that the police need to look into."

"Can you wait here? I need to get my friend out of jail. He'll listen," Misty said. "Tree, Jackie, stay."

Chapter 11

Newfound Lake, New Hampshire

The lake compound was very secluded. Anyone wishing to see the large estate could do so only by boat. Located on Newfound Lake, the third largest in New Hampshire, the house with its surrounding acreage took up the northern shore of the lake.

While Lake Winnipesaukee dominated the Lake District area by its size, Newfound Lake was noted for its more urbane atmosphere. People on Newfound Lake felt their lake had a better clientele compared to the other nearby lakes. Well-monied people had owned summer places along the lake shore for decades.

Cottages were handed down through the generations and it was rare that one on Newfound Lake hit the open market. If it did, it didn't remain there long.

And on the end of the lake that held the estate, the truly wealthy of Boston hid away. The owner of the estate hosting the very select meeting was a Bulgarian billionaire. His billions had been made in currency speculation which allowed him to fund groups to his liking.

Already, his political action groups had made their mark on the country's elections. But this meeting was about something different.

"I guess we need to get started. Dr. Fisk appears to be running late this time."

"That's unusual. She's typically the first one here. She loves sitting by the lake waiting for the rest of us to arrive."

The five people gathered on the deck overlooking the lake all nodded. Dr. Fisk was typically very punctual.

"At least the news out of Albany is to our liking. It appears that her work was successful. Maybe that is why she's late."

* * *

Jack had become resigned to never getting to leave the Greenbush Police Station. As he waited for someone of authority to pass him officially out of suspicion, new sirens were heard in the distance. Suddenly, the entire office took on a seriousness that he imagined was impossible. *How could these people get any more serious?* he thought.

His answer came in the form of four very serious people walking into the squad room. One made a beeline toward Jack as the New York State Patrol captain pointed him out. *Oh great*, he thought.

"Deputy Jack Wesley, of the Teton County Sheriff's office?" the man asked.

Jack noticed everyone else in the room shrink into feigned obscurity at the man's presence. He thought he should know who he was talking to so he asked, 'Who's asking?"

The captain went ballistic, "He's the governor, you damn idiot."

Oops. Screwed that one up, Jack thought.

The governor recovered the snub. "May I have a word with you, please?" he motioned toward the Police Chief's suddenly vacated office after the captain opened the holding cell door. Jack headed in the direction offered.

Shutting the door behind him, Jack was alone with the New York State Governor. "How can I be of service, sir?"

"I don't know who the hell you are or who the hell you know, but I don't like being threatened. Do I make myself clear?"

Jack was taken aback by the instant broadside. "I'm sorry Governor. But I made no threats to you that I'm aware of."

"I just got off the phone with the governor of Wyoming. I was told in no uncertain terms that if you weren't released immediately and reinstated your proper Wyoming identification, the next ten drivers entering Wyoming with New York plates would suddenly find themselves incarcerated."

Jack smiled inside at the governor's rage. It paid to have friends in high places. *My brother had done his job, and quickly I might add,* Jack thought.

"My captain was going to charge you with carrying an unregistered gun. But under the circumstances, I suppose ten innocent New Yorkers would appreciate their freedom. But I don't like it one bit. Even if you're a duly sworn peace officer in Wyoming, it gives you no immunity from our laws."

Jack couldn't help himself, "So, interagency cooperation is not allowed in the Empire State."

"My ass. If you're working a case here in New York involving someone wanted in Wyoming, you report in first to the local law office. Only with their permission will you be doing anything in this state."

"OK, the next school shooting I stumble across I'll be sure to run to City Hall first. That would have been peachy today."

Jack thought the governor was about to explode at the comment. Instead, he turned and flew out the door, "Get that man out of my state now."

The Greenbush Police Chief walked in and closed the door. Jack had seen the man in the office but hadn't met him yet.

"I hear your wife will be OK. That's good news," Jack offered.

"Thank you. And thank you for what you did today. I know I'm not pulling the party line on that, but a lot of citizens are profoundly grateful. What those pinheads in Albany focus on is bullshit."

He is definitely off the reservation, Jack thought. *But reality only hits home when its your reality. The Albany politicians were insulated from the crimes they allow to happen. And letting decidedly crazy people walk among us is criminal.*

"You are free to go. My detective has your account of the story. Your gun will be returned when we're done processing it. I usually tell people not to leave town, but under the circumstances . . ."

"I'm sorry I didn't act quicker, Chief."

The Police Chief gave Jack a nod in agreement. He fought to hold his composure, "Oh, there's a woman who's been asking about you. She's out front."

Misty, I totally forgot. She must be frantic by now, he thought.

* * *

"Are you sure this is a good idea? I'm supposed to be leaving the state," Jack asked.

"We discussed all that in the car on the way over here. We'll just take a quick look around. And besides, Daniella has a key. It's not like we're breaking in or something."

Oh sure, easy for her to say. She doesn't have the New York State hounds of hell after her, he thought.

They had parked the car in the covered parking area and left the windows cracked for the dogs. Now standing outside Daniella's office as she opened the door, Jack looked over his shoulder to see if the authorities were already closing in.

The outer office had a desk and some chairs for waiting patients. *Nothing of interest here,* he thought. Daniella opened the doctor's office door. Jack saw the file cabinets. If what she was saying was true, there should be evidence stored in the files.

"Do you have a key for the files?" Jack asked. Daniella shook her head. Only the doctor had those keys. Jack sagged. He took out his wallet and retrieved two small metal devices. While Misty and Daniella watched, Jack worked the lock on the file cabinet. He turned the metal tools and the lock popped out.

"OK, you look through these. Your fingerprints can be explained," Jack said. Jack had warned Misty not to touch anything while in the office while he had grabbed one of the clean hand towels that Daniella kept for the more emotional patients.

Jack went to work searching the doctor's desk. He saw nothing of note that would confirm Daniella's story. He turned and saw she had come up with nothing in the files.

"Here's Ed George's file. There's nothing unusual in it. Nothing supposing that she was tormenting the guy into shooting up a school."

"In my experience people don't write those kind of things down. What we're looking for is any information about this conference she's at. As you said, it seems to be a pivotal aspect to our doc's life. You say that she seemed especially fired up whenever she returned from them?"

"That George character would really be agitated right after that. I was scared to be out here when he came out."

"Any other place to look? Have you been in her home? Does she have an office there?" Jack asked.

"That's right. I almost forgot about that. She has an office as you walk in the front door. I worked helping her with parties there a couple of times. She'd invite her colleagues over and they would do whatever psychiatrists do when they get together."

"Mostly talk, I'd guess," Misty commented.

"That's right. That's where I overheard her say what I told you. I was sitting below the retaining wall taking a break when the doc and another sat just above me."

"And you're sure they said 'We can make a difference. It's worth it even if some kids are killed'?" Jack asked.

"Those were her exact words."

"Then I guess we check the house," Jack said. "I suppose you wouldn't have a key for the front door do you?"

Daniella dug around in the Doc's desk. In the back under some papers she produced a key. She smiled as she held it up. Closing the outer door as they left, Jack turned to head back to the main staircase.

The old warehouse had been converted into an office and retail shop complex. An atrium had been built over half the building while offices lined a second story balcony.

The view from outside Daniella's office covered the entire length of the atrium. Jack didn't like what he saw. Entering the front doors were two State Patrol uniformed officers accompanied by two men in suits.

"Eh, we need another exit, now," Jack barked.

Daniella grabbed the two and headed south. A back staircase would lead them down, avoiding the arriving law enforcement. *Obviously they were coming to search the office,* Jack thought.

"We'd better hurray," Jack said "We may not have much time at the house, if they're not there already."

Daniella drove quickly southwest out of Albany. She skirted some small towns and finally arrived on a winding road that climbed a small hill. Halfway up, she pulled into a long driveway.

Located on a circular drive set back from the street was a 1930's Cape Cod house. At least a New York version of a Cape Cod.

A single car garage was on the left in a small add-on. This was offset by a small similar-sized add-on to the right. As Daniella unlocked the front door, the addition to the right held the home office. Jack went to work as Daniella searched for clues.

Misty, again admonished by Jack not to touch anything, wandered through the house. As Jack and Daniella were busy searching, a white-faced Misty returned.

"Jack, there's a car in the garage."

Jack turned to Daniella. "Does she fly to this conference?"

"No, she always drives. She says the time lets her think about something besides her patients. It lets her unwind."

Jack left Daniella searching and accompanied Misty to the door off the kitchen.

"You didn't touch the knob did you?" Misty held up a dish towel in answer. Jack took the towel and carefully opened the door. The garage was dark with no outside window for light.

He reached around the door jamb and flicked on the light. The doctor's car sat in the light with someone behind the wheel.

"Wait here," Jack walked over to the driver's side. Lying in a heap was a woman with her throat slashed. Dried blood ran down her front and soaked the seat.

"Jack, is that who I think it is?" He noticed the fear in her voice. Jack didn't want her any closer and held up his arm for her to stay.

A scream jolted him out of his study of the murder.

"Dr. Fisk! Oh my God. Who did this?" Daniella screamed. Jack hurried over and took both women into the kitchen. He shut the door to the garage.

"My guess is our friend Ed George ended his tormentor. She was probably ready to leave for her conference. When she hit the remote to open the garage door, Ed ran in and slit her throat. He'd probably been waiting for his opportunity outside."

"We should call the police," Daniella said.

"No, we won't be calling the police. We need to finish up searching her office and get out of here," Jack said.

The three redoubled their efforts in the office. Misty kept watch out the front window for arriving company.

"I think I have something," Daniella said. "It's a letter in her file marked 'personal correspondence'."

Jack took the letter in his dish towel hand and read it. "Yes, this gets us what we want. Fire up the copy machine so we can make a copy. But keep searching."

Daniella turned on the computer printer and hit the copy key. She made a copy and replaced the original. Jack handed her two more documents and they were added to the evidence.

But evidence of what? Jack thought. The proposition that Daniella had spewed was too incredible to believe. Sure, they had found some incriminating letters that could be shown to be a conspiracy, if they only could confirm the conspiracy.

Otherwise, the letters were just routine correspondence between two colleagues about rather vague stuff. They didn't exactly come out and say what they were doing, Jack thought. Most criminals don't. He'd seen the dumb ones do it. But these were highly educated people they were dealing with. They knew enough to write in code whatever it was they were doing.

But he had witnessed the supposed result of one of those conspirators. And if the Connecticut school shooting had been another result set in place by a co-conspirator, then the country had a problem.

There had been a rash of school shootings and Jack had even been part of one. Thurston High School in Springfield, Oregon had been a tragic recipient of a crazed teenage shooter. Located next to Eugene, Jack had assisted in the crime scene. He had been with the county deputies when they went to the perpetrators home in the country where they had found both parents shot dead.

What if this all went back that far? he thought. *How long has it been? More than ten years?* He couldn't remember. But he did remember that the mayhem was stopped when two National Rifle Association teenage members realized that when the bad guy stopped to reload that they could act. They tackled the kid and held him for police. *Their bravery had prevented even a worse tragedy that day,* he thought.

Finished in the house, the three joined the two dogs as they left the hillside home. Jack was lost in his thoughts trying to reconcile the whole day's events.

"Poor Dr. Fisk. Do you think she understood what she was unleashing on society?" Daniella asked.

"Lefty liberals never think through their actions. Ideology is supreme to them. 'The ends justify the means' I believe the saying goes," Jack added.

The three rode in silence as Daniella took the sailors back to their boat. Before turning into the marina, they drove by the school that had seen such violence a short ten hours before. Jack stared at the television trucks as the police continued their vigilance. He knew they would be there for quite some time. *A day late and a dollar short*, he thought.

He steeled himself. If what seemed to be happening was really taking place, he would be there. Somehow, he would find the answer to little kids dying and put a stop to it. And luckily, it meant leaving New York today. He might not make it out of the state by sundown, but it would be close.

Chapter 12

Washington, D.C.

"Ladies and gentlemen, we return to our live coverage of the Merrill Hearings in the U.S. Senate. We take you now to our Capitol Hill reporter. Chuck, what's been happening?" the television news anchor announced.

"Good morning, Peter. The Chairman of the Justice Committee has gaveled these proceedings open and we've had our first witness. With the tragic school shooting in New York State yesterday, these hearings take on more urgency. Let's listen in as the Senior Senator from New York grills the next witness."

Jack made a motion to turn the television off. They had been lying in bed watching the motel's small flat screen for the news.

They had left New York State late that night with Daniella driving. Stopping for the night in Great Barrington, just inside the Commonwealth of Massachusetts, they had tried to rest from their terrible day in Greenbush.

"Stop, Jack, I want to watch this."

"Assholes," was all Jack could mumble as he turned and went back to his shaving at the bathroom sink.

The television broadcast continued with a shot of the New York Senator looking over his glasses. He appeared to be looking down from the camera angle as he finished up speaking, "Thank you, Mr. Honeyman. Your organization, ENOUGH, has done an admirable job in bringing these important issues to the Senate's attention. I assure you we will place them in consideration when we draft our new laws to stop this senseless killing."

Jack turned to see a young man in a suit step away from the witness table. He froze when he saw the next witness step forward and raise his right hand. Jack wiped the remaining shaving cream from his face and joined Misty on the edge of the bed. The new witness finished swearing to tell the truth and sat down. He introduced himself and started reading a prepared statement.

"Well, I'll be a son-of-a -bitch."

"Friend of yours, Jack?" Misty smiled.

"Holy shit, what's he doing there?"

"I'm in the dark. Care to enlighten me?"

"I haven't seen that son-of-a-bitch in years and here he shows up in front of Congress," Jack said.

He watched the screen intently as Misty attempted to coax an explanation to who the son-of-a-bitch they were listening to really was. The line at the bottom of the screen identified the man as Phil Merton. Other than that, Misty was stumped.

The prepared statement ended and the time for questions started. Since Mr. Merton appeared to be an invited guest by one of the Republican Senators, that side of the political debate got the first question. Soon, it was the Democratic sides turn. The Chairman recognized the New York Senator.

Again the man looked over his half-glasses and down at the witness. Jack noticed the whole affect gave a certain superior feeling to the exalted side in the questioning. *Gives the public the television appearance of the ruling class deigning to mix with the riff raff,* Jack thought. And by his question, the Senator considered the witness as the enemy. "Mr. Merton, you come before this committee as a so-called public health expert. If that is true, then you seem to be at odds to the entire profession. They have all concluded that gun violence is a threat to public health. Even the CDC issued its report under the heading 'Firearms - Related Violence as a Public Health Issue', from which I quote, 'Violence, including firearm-related violence, has been shown to be contagious' unquote. Are you saying you disagree with the Centers for Disease Control, our nation's preeminent public health authority?"

"In a word, yes. I categorically disagree with the CDC," Merton answered.

"Seems a bit arrogant on your part, don't you think? Not only the CDC, but the National Academy of Sciences have weighed in on the subject. They seem to be in agreement," the senator added. "Are you telling me you have better science than these fine institutions?"

"Yes, better science. And Congress agreed with me when they outlawed the CDC from conducting any further 'junk' science studies on guns. That was seventeen years ago," Merton said.

As the testimony continued, Misty gave up waiting. "Jack, you know this guy?"

"Sshh," was all she got for a reply.

The New York Senator jumped right at Merton. "An oversight that our president removed with his Executive Order power. We can resume this most necessary study in order that we protect Americans from this dire public health threat."

A Republican Senator came to the rescue as he asked Mr. Merton to explain himself. Since his side had invited this witness, they would attempt to keep his credibility alive from the Democrat attack.

"Thank you, Senator. I'll attempt a simple explanation for all the Senators." Jack caught the sarcasm in the man's voice. "Public health is easy to define. If I stand on a street corner and a disease carrier stands beside me and I catch his disease through the air, that's a public health issue. If someone gives blood and I contract a disease from the blood, again thats a communicable disease and a public health issue."

"And if you catch a bullet as you stand on that same street corner, its a public health issue," the New York senator jumped in.

"Hardly, since I can't then pass that bullet on to the next person standing beside me. And they can't pass it on to the ten people standing beside them. But I can do all that with a truly contagious disease," Merton threw back. "The stray bullet is a social problem, not a health problem. The resulting wound caused by the bullet is a private health issue."

Misty had heard enough. She tackled Jack from behind. Once on top, she demanded answers.

Jack liked the position so didn't resist his confinement. But he did finally offer Misty an explanation.

Years before, Phil Merton had been a public health inspector in Eugene, Oregon. At a previous job, Merton had been involved with a religious cult bent on terrorizing a small Oregon town. Merton had helped solve what became known as the first bio-terrorist attack in the world.

The cult had grown Salmonella bacteria in their lab and then spread the results over salad bars in the local county seat. They hoped to throw the upcoming election in their favor. Over 800 individuals had been sickened.

Misty stopped Jack, "I remember that. Some guru from India and his followers."

"Right. I met Phil after he had taken his lesson of the attack and volunteered to be a reserve deputy. By the time I caught up to him he was still working on public health inspections, but he was a special deputy for the Sheriff Department."

"What happened?"

"Eugene held a logger's convention each year. Merton got a bad feeling about the event due to all the 'tree huggers' that call Eugene home. It's one of the most radical cities in the country between the University and all the old hippies still hanging out. Anyway, Phil took special interest in the loggers convention after a whole bunch of them got sick. He tracked down the culprit to one of the food handler's contaminating the meals in the kitchen."

"Didn't a bunch of people die? I remember that part."

"That was the next year. It seems that the new Lane County Public Health Director said he would have no deputies in his department. The whole 'head in the sand' approach. Phil moved on to another state if I remember. I didn't see him after our first investigation together."

It looked like the committee was almost finished with Merton when the two refocused on the television. Phil was holding up a paper and indicating he was going to read a passage from it.

"In closing, I'd like to enter into testimony Dr. Miguel Faria's comments. Dr. Faria served on the

CDC's Injury Research Grant Review Committee and had this to say about the experience, I quote, 'Suffice to say, that the work of gun control researchers in public health had a proclivity toward reaching preordained conclusions' unquote. Junk science in other words, ladies and gentlemen."

The Committee Chairman quickly gaveled the hearings adjourned for the day. Jack surmised that the Democratic side of the argument would have to re-bolster their argument after his old friend Merton's testimony.

Chapter 13

Cambridge, Massachusetts

The Cambridge Police Station sat on West Sixth St. near the Kendall Square MBTA Station. Police Lieutenant Lamarcus Lewis rode the subway to work each day from his home in Allston, a twenty-minute commute on a good day. If the Massachusetts Bay Transit Authority decided to do maintenance on the Red Line, then all bets were off.

Today was a good day and the train left Lamarcus on time at his subway stop. As he reached street level and daylight, Lamarcus took in the fresh air of a beautiful summer day. Next week was his planned vacation to Round Pond, Maine. His family had been vacationing there for years which was unusual for a family from Roxbury.

African-Americans typically didn't head down Maine for the summer. But his mother's grandparents had been shopkeepers and had invested wisely, including a cottage in Maine. They might have lived in the 'ghetto' of Boston, but Lamarcus's grandparents made sure their children got good educations.

His parents had moved out of Roxbury as soon as they could and Lamarcus had been raised near Quincy. Traditionally a white town, upwardly mobile blacks had moved into the suburbs. When his father left the family, Lamarcus's mother took her family to live with her parents in Quincy. His father's brother in Mattapan kept the male role model going in Lamarcus's life.

Growing up to be a large man, the 6'4" Lamarcus earned his place in the community by excelling at athletics at his high school. A stand-out football player, Lamarcus was still remembered in the community.

After a stint in the Marines, Lamarcus had returned to start a career in law enforcement. He had worked his way up through the ranks from patrolman to his current slot as lieutenant. In charge of the gang unit, Lamarcus had his eye on a captain position.

The whole black Harvard professor incident involving the President of the United States had moved his career path forward with the Cambridge Police Department. Lamarcus wasn't above using whatever means the people upstairs offered. *They might call it 'affirmative action', I call it good for the home boy,* he thought. *Yes, things are looking up.*

Stupid people making stupid decisions for the wrong reasons and I'm the guy to reap the rewards. He knew he'd be able to move up to an ocean front cottage in Round Pond when he made captain.

Lamarcus walked in the front door of the police station a confident man.

"Hey Lieutenant. There's a call for you. Line three," the sargent working the day shift for the gang unit called out.

"Who is it?"

"Didn't say."

Now, who would be calling me and not offering a name? he thought. He had trained his people to screen his calls better than that. He'd talk to the sargent after the call.

"Lieutenant Lewis. What can I do you for?"

"You can hit the deck and give me fifty, you old swab."

"Jesus Jack, where the hell did you come from? This is a bolt from out of nowhere. I haven't heard from you since you retired. Too busy hanging at the beach chasing pussy to call an old war horse."

"Lamarcus, sorry. It's been too long. Buddies don't forget each other. I should have called earlier. But I was chasing a little, if that helps."

"Makes all the difference. Never one to stand in the way of a jarhead on the hunt. So how goes it?" Lamarcus asked.

"I'm on the hunt, all right. But not for the sweet stuff."

"What's you saying? You back doing the Lord's work? I thought you were through hunting bad guys."

"I did to. These bad guys sort of fell in my lap, I'm afraid. Did you watch the news yesterday? The school shooting in New York," Jack said.

"That was you? Shit. I watched them take that guy out in handcuffs with the coat over his head. I said to the boys, 'if I didn't know better, that looks like a buddy of mine from the Corps'. You're shitting me."

"No bullshit. That was me. Took the governor of Wyoming to get me out of there, too."

"Don't tell me they done run you into the Bay State? I'm not sure the state can handle the both of us at once."

"Well move over. I'm on the Mass Pike outside Worcester. And I need your help. Something bad is going down. I'm fixing to stop it and could use some local help."

"Christ Jack. I got my Maine vacation planned next week. The kids will be disappointed."

"Marcus, I didn't hear anything about the wife being disappointed in there."

"She'd only be disappointed if I get killed in the line of duty and the alimony checks stopped coming. On second thought, the department's generous survivor's benefit might go her way. I think I forgot to change the beneficiary when we divorced."

"Sorry to hear that, buddy. But things will pick up. I can attest that things certainly can pick up.

134

But I'm really in a bind. And when you hear the details, you'll understand. Hell, your kids are all grown up. What do they need the old man for to head to Maine?"

* * *

When Jack had announced at the boat what his intentions were, he was surprised by the response from his crew. Misty and Daniella had no intention of being left behind. The boat yard would be called and instructed to redo the bottom. Jack's brother had been complaining that it needed repainting and Jack would arrange the work.

The dogs joined the three adults as they quickly packed the few things they would need. Daniella announced she'd buy whatever she needed as they went. They were out of New York State before 10 PM.

Hitting West Stockbridge on the Mass Pike, they had stopped for the night at a local motel, Jack springing for two rooms. He and Misty took long hot showers before climbing into fresh clothes. Jack's blood-stained clothes landed in the trash.

The morning found them heading east refreshed and energized after breakfast. Using Misty's replacement cell phone, Jack placed his calls. The first call was to the boat yard.

He was anxious for the next call but it would have to wait. He needed a new service revolver shipped overnight to Massachusetts but it was too early in Wyoming. Catching Lamarcus on the way into work, Jack had convinced the subordinate to put the call through anonymously.

Just like Lamarcus, he thought. *Insulating himself from the extraneous stuff.* Jack recalled that Lamarcus had the same attitude when they were in the Marine Corps together. They had spent basic training working out their respective differences. Lamarcus was a big city black kid with a chip on his shoulder while Jack was a small city white kid with a chip on his shoulder. Both chips had eventually been knocked off, first by the DI during basic.

Any bad feelings between the two was finally erased when both pulled the same outfit. They had served most of their four-year hitch together in the 3rd Marine Expeditionary Brigade. Floating around on attack transports in confined quarters resolved things one way or the other.

For Jack and Lamarcus, they had become fast friends. They each watched each other's backside when the going got tough which enabled them to be an effective sniper team.

Growing up hunting in Oregon, Jack had an instinctive ability to hit targets. The Marines recognized Jack's expert marksman skills and teamed him with Lamarcus. Sometimes spotter, sometimes gear grunt, but always backup, Lamarcus and Jack developed into a very effective killing team.

Jack's only complaint about his friend was his ability to disappear when the work was being handed out. *Seems he's continued his Semper Fi ways in civilian life,* Jack thought.

* * *

"I can tell you where to get this stuff," Lamarcus said as he held up the scribbles Jack had made. Meeting in a roadside rest area along Route 2, Lamarcus had driven out to meet his buddy after work. "But this other stuff? Jack, are you planning World War three? Man, this is hot stuff in this state. You know what Mass thinks about any of this. You get caught and you won't see the light of day again."

"I know," Jack said "But I'm not sure how serious these folks are about going to jail. If they have the resources to pull this off, they could have some heavy hitters protecting them."

"Sure, but . . ."

"Look, I don't need it right away. You can sit on that list. But the other stuff I need right now."

Lamarcus instructed Jack where he could fill out his first list. As they finished, Lamarcus took Jack's arm, his voice showing the seriousness of the situation.

"If what you told me is true, who knows what you're up against? Maybe we should go official. I can call . . ."

"And tell them what? No, we need to get more facts as to who and where before we call the men in blue. And when we do, I'm not part of this. I don't even want a hint of my breath anywhere near this. It will be all yours. Hell, you'll make Mass State Police Major with this."

"Or dead and buried out past Killeen, Texas with the real Kennedy assassin. If we run into those boys, we could . . ."

"I know, my friend. But our kids are grown, our ex-wives will cry no tears and the young ones we've yet to meet will never know what they missed," Jack said.

Lamarcus smiled at the thought of him and his friend going to war again. "Two guys out kicking some serious ass. Semper Fi."

"Semper Fi."

Chapter 14

Harvard, Massachusetts

Dr. Hillary Sumner arrived at her office in the small town of Harvard. She had her practice in Boston but she kept her suburban office open two days per week. She felt like it allowed her to remain connected to people better.

The Boston clientele were rather aloof. They expected a professional distance be maintained between psychiatrist and patient.

But living in Harvard, she knew some of her patients personally. She even considered some of them her friends and she liked that.

Although she had never married, her career had taken to much time, she wanted a family. The small exclusive Town of Harvard offered as much of a family as she could expect. She even accepted some less-than-affluent patients from the old working mill towns that scattered the area.

The mills were long gone, but the inexpensive housing attracted the less fortunate. And Hillary Sumner would be remiss if she only helped the rich. She had been raised by a very successful Boston family to respect all people. The Sumner's had been part of Boston's social fabric since before the Revolution.

"Good morning Margaret. It's a lovely Tuesday morning out there. Thank God that humidity is gone."

"I'll say, Dr. Sumner. I sat at Crane's Beach yesterday and did nothing. But the sky was sure lively last night with the front pushing through."

Margaret was a middle-aged woman who only worked the two days a week when Dr. Sumner had office hours in Harvard. As a divorcee, she was content to earn a little extra, but was careful not to earn too much. Too much would risk her alimony check.

"Well, we have a full day today," Hillary said. Tuesday was her day for the less fortunate. Thursday was her day to make money helping the privileged locals. *The people who paid the bills*, she thought.

Hillary looked out the window before retreating to her inner office. She had tomorrow off, like every Wednesday. *It was a good schedule,* she thought. Two days in the big city and two days with a short one-mile commute, followed by Wednesdays off. Time to work in her garden with no distractions.

The intercom buzzed announcing the arrival of the first patient. She settled into helping the mentally compromised live a normal life in society. *Thank God the days of state hospitals for all these people are over,* she thought. *Society had progressed, but not far enough.*

* * *

Jack put his binoculars down and studied the street in front of Dr. Sumner's office. He wasn't used to such a slow community. Any surveillance in such a small town was going to stick out like the proverbial 'sore thumb'.

Another approach would have to be devised. He climbed from the back of the windowless van into the driver's seat. Starting the motor, he watched a Harvard police cruiser slowly drive by. *No, we need to do this differently,* he thought. He drove off heading south on Route 70.

Reaching the Town of Hudson, he pulled into the small motel parking. Two women waited for him in the room when he opened the door.

"We need to go to Plan B," Jack said.

"But you said Plan B was more dangerous."

"Not in Harvard. I stuck out too much. I won't last a day sitting there watching."

"Do we go tonight?" Misty asked. She had already gotten into the cloak and dagger stuff in a big way. The last three days were spent getting all the supplies they needed for the first part of their job. Misty had been in charge of procuring a van in which they could do their surveillance.

Checking the on-line ads, she had withdrawn money from her ATM account. Paying cash, she had quietly purchased a very plain windowless Ford

141

E-150 van that would blend in with most areas. *Just not in Harvard*, Jack thought.

But at least now they had a vehicle with local tags. Daniella's New York tags stuck out and would never do for undercover work. The owner of the van had provided the required paperwork, Jack would just be slow on hitting the DMV to change ownership. He figured by the time they were done, he'd be leaving it on a street corner in Roxbury with the keys in it.

"Not tonight. I don't know if this Sumner has an alarm system or not. I'll have to get inside and see what they have for security," Jack said.

"That's dangerous. They may ID you later. It would be safer if I went," Misty offered.

"You don't know what to look for."

"Excuse me. I was living in secured homes not so long ago. Remember who my husband was. I can spot most anything they would have in Harvard," Misty threw back.

They agreed that a woman inquiring about counseling would be less obtrusive than a man. And with the offer of cash for services, a tone of anonymity would be established.

They called for an appointment and found out that Wednesday the doctor was unavailable. But the secretary announced that they had just gotten a cancelation for Thursday. Misty could have the time if she was available. Misty gladly took the appointment and gave a fake name. She hung up the phone and was all smiles.

"How do we know for sure that this Dr. Sumner is part of the conspiracy?" Daniella asked.

"Her name was on both letters we found in Dr. Fisk's home," Jack said. "They seem to have developed a personal relationship at these conferences. Their correspondence refers certain events the two women wrote about in their letters."

"And we have no other name to go on," Misty added.

* * *

The Thursday appointment arrived and Misty dressed like the rich suburban housewife she was supposed to be. Jack watched her get ready in the motel room they were sharing and realized she didn't have to play act much. Until recently, she had been a rich suburban house wife.

Driving Daniella's car with the New York tags on it fit the scenario better than the van, Misty worked up a cover story if anyone asked. It entailed her sister visiting from New York and Misty's Lexus was in the shop.

Her initial session with Dr. Sumner went like so many other counselor's she had met over the years. Misty had been a rebel in her youth and her parents had spent considerable amounts attempting to keep her from falling through the cracks of society.

It had partially worked. She had gotten out of high school without any diseases or babies. Misty had tried college but lacked the focus that studying required to complete much of anything. Her future husband had discovered her working as a waitress in a popular country club near St. Louis.

Misty had known enough about life to charm her customers and with her good looks, she became a success story. Her parents had initially been taken back when she announced she was marrying a man 38 years her senior. But as the marriage seemed to settle their daughter, they came to embrace their son-in-law.

The main thing that had bothered Misty was that her parents and her husband were contemporaries. He was actually older than they were, but their world view was very similar. She learned to dread home visits because the three of them would be recounting events she had never experienced. It made her very aware of the age gap.

"Jack, it's a piece of cake. She doesn't even have motion detectors. And no window contacts. Totally unsecured from what I could see," Misty reported.

"I thought it might be the case. Harvard seems the type of town that hasn't experienced much of the 21st Century yet. Now Daniella, it's your turn."

Jack referred to Daniella's role in the surveillance. They were going to need a location to park the van close to Dr. Sumner's office during her office hours. One of them needed a job near by as an excuse for the van to sit all day. Jack would just have to invest in a portable toilet since he couldn't be seen leaving the van.

Daniela had a job the next day. A young voluptuous Italian body, combined with her open personality, got her hired at the corner coffee shop. She would start the next Monday which meant Jack had to get into the office and plant his bugs over the weekend.

"I don't think either night will be especially wild in Harvard," Jack said. "I'll go early evening when there's still activity around. Early morning I'd probably attract every dog within a mile of the place."

Daniella offered to drive and wait in the van. With a radio and ear set, she would warn Jack of any threat. If questioned, she could explain that she was a recent hire and was just getting the feel of Harvard before her first day.

Friday evening arrived and Jack and Daniella drove out of Hudson headed north. Their conversation limited by the steps they were about to take, the ride to Harvard rose the tension. Breaking and entering would be serious in a small town like Harvard.

"You've done this before, right?" Daniella asked.

"Hundreds of times," Jack said.

Daniela drove along Route 70. *Cops didn't break into buildings,* she thought. *At least honest cops. But I know what has to be done and with no security it shouldn't be difficult. As long as the local police don't come by and see me lingering, we'll be all right.*

A short distance from Dr. Sumner's office, Daniella pulled over and Jack slipped out of the passenger's seat. He had a small backpack on with his tools. She drove on as he walked down the sidewalk. When she looked in the mirror, he was gone. The bushes and trees melded with the darkness to keep his presence hidden.

Daniella pulled into the nearby coffee shop parking area. It was closed and the lot empty. She wheeled the van around so it faced the office and slipped into the back of the van. The dark interior hid her from any prying eyes, yet she could see the entire downtown area. She clicked on the radio and pushed the transmit button three times.

Without speaking a word, the message was received. Somewhere Jack clicked back two static-charged answers. Sitting on a folding camp chair they had purchased, she waited and watched.

Daniella figured a half hour had passed when the Harvard police cruiser drifted through town. She noticed no change in its direction as it kept moving up Main Street. She tapped her button four times. Two static cracks on the radio gave her an answer.

Jack is still out there, she thought. About fifteen minutes later the police cruiser came back through town. This time it slowed and she could see the officer looking her way through the faint light. She picked up one of the disposable cell phones they had purchased and dialed 911.

"911, what is your emergency?" the operator asked.

"This is Mary Newberry out on Redstone Hill Road. I just heard breaking glass from the front of my house. I'm in the bedroom and I've locked the door."

"Just stay where you are, I'll have the police there shortly. Please stay on the phone."

But Daniella wasn't about to cooperate. As soon as she saw the blue lights flash across the town common, she hung up. The cruiser streaked by her parked van headed to an address and a real Harvard resident they had found just for this purpose.

OK Jack, that will keep them busy for at least twenty minutes. Time to wrap it up, she thought. In ten minutes she received her signal. One click followed by three clicks was her signal to head back to their drop off spot to pick him up.

She climbed back into the driver's seat and started the van. Putting it into gear, she pulled out onto Main Street and turned left. A quick left again and she saw him walking along the sidewalk on her side of the road. She slowed to a stop and Jack jumped into the passenger's seat.

She accelerated slowly away, leaving the downtown area. The street lights disappeared and the dashboard was the only illumination in the cab. Turning toward Jack, the expression on Jack's face said it all.

As Daniella drove the long way back to Hudson, she didn't dare ask. She waited until all three of them were together to hear the answer.

Misty saw Jack's expression and asked, "What is it?"

Jack dropped the backpack on the motel bed and took one of the chairs. Misty and Daniella remained standing, too nervous to sit down.

"Sit. The news is bad," Jack said. The two women slowly sat on the bed. Their stares grew more intense as they awaited the bad news.

Chapter 15

Boston, Massachusetts

The early morning light filtered through the high rise buildings that sat sentinel over the northeast corner of Boston Gardens. The famous swan boats that took the tourists around the small lake in the center of the Boston Gardens were quiet. Soon the summer throngs would be descending on the city and the boats would start their rounds.

The real swans of Boston Garden floated contentedly across the pond. They knew that people would soon arrive, many with bread crumbs. Easy living for swans, as long as the ducks stayed away.

Ducks were the bane of swans. They never learned their place in the pecking order of winged water fowl. Swans were bigger and prettier and deserved their place at the top of the food chain. People came for them, not common ducks. They could see and feed ducks anywhere.

An intent man walked by the swans lost in his thoughts. He had no knowledge of the power struggle in the water fowl community. He was focused on the raging power struggle in the human world. And he was convinced that events around the country would finally tip the power his way.

While he and his organization had been making steady progress toward their goal locally, it was nationally that drove him. The entire country must be shown that his way was the correct way. Today he would push his agenda. He knew the time was ripe.

The man crossed Charles Street with ease. The traffic this early was limited mostly to delivery trucks heading to the restaurants along Boylston Street. He slowed as he climbed Beacon Hill. *I must work out more. After this month, I'll take some time. Maybe go hike part of the Appalachian Trail,* he thought. He used to do such things, but the cause had taken him away from all that.

He didn't miss the women, though. The earth muffins he used to spend time with out of doors were a bit much sometimes. Hairy arm pits and body odor weren't at the top of his list. The groupies he attracted now were more urbane and sophisticated. An office on Beacon Hill attracted a more cultured class of woman and he liked the change

Both groups of females were similarly inclined toward recreational sex. It just was more pleasant with the selection he enjoyed now. *But I do miss that open air nakedness,* he thought. *I'm sure one of my present partners was an outdoor type sometime in her past.*

He made a mental note to make inquires as to who in his office had been into the outdoors. Some might still take the time for such exploits. *Soon I can relax and relish in what I've accomplished. And the rewards,* he thought. His boss was famous in his generosity to his underlings for successful accomplishments.

The man daydreamed briefly about having the money to travel to exotic locales and have his way with some of the local females. That would be a reward he could get into for all the hard work he was doing.

As he reached his destination, a woman who worked in his office approached him from the opposite direction. *She rides the Red Line and gets off at Park Street*, he recalled. He racked his mind for her name. *Jamie-something. But what was it?*

As she grew closer, her smile radiated at him. She was ten years younger and in spite of the rather dour way she dressed, he knew that naked, she would be hot. *The way she was smiling at me she might be ready for some personal attention. But what was her name?* he thought.

"Ms. Jamison, good morning. You're here early." he said, finally remembering her last name. With so many female staff and volunteers coming and going, he had a hard time keeping up.

"Elizabeth please. I'm here early because I knew this was a big day, Mr. Honeyman."

"Darren. Mr. Honeyman is my father." They both laughed at the director's small joke. He opened the heavy door to the building. The large brass plaque on the brick facade next to the door read, ENOUGH. Below the large letters in much smaller ones was 'Every Noxious Owner, Ur Guns History'. Below the words was the logo of the group, an antique dustbin.

Darren Honeyman was director of the largest, best funded anti-gun group in the United States. The dustbin logo hadn't been his idea but relegating all guns to the dustbin of history was certainly something he could get behind. Unfortunately, most people had no idea what a dustbin was or had been. Most thought the logo looked like a condom.

It really didn't matter to him. He had turned ENOUGH into the preeminent lobbying machine in the nation. His arch enemy, the National Rifle Association, stood on the opposite side of the issue, and the NRA had been steadily losing to Darren's skill at turning political tricks.

Being funded by one of the nation's richest man certainly helped since politics was all about money, who had it and who gave it away for the right reasons. And Darren had access to a lot of his benefactor's millions.

Along with the preeminent political organizing group, BRIDGEIT.org, and the influential media watchdog, NEWSCREWS, the Bulgarian billionaire had put together a trifecta of powerful game changing pressure groups.

I can't believe I landed this job, he thought. *I get to change the world in profound ways and get my whistle cleaned regularly by hot driven females.* He concluded life was good as he stepped inside his group's headquarters.

"So, Elizabeth, remind me, are you working here or a volunteer? With so many helping our cause I have a difficult time keeping up on everybody."

"I'm a volunteer, but I'd love to get on here. It's such an important thing we're doing."

The two walked into the brick townhouse that held ENOUGH where Darren's office was on the second floor overlooking the Boston Common. The three floors above him held the multitude of people getting the work done. The first floor held the reception area and two conference rooms with a break room in the back for all the workers.

Downstairs held the printing and mailing staff. Darren had spent many a night down there getting mailings out in the early days. He recalled some of the dalliances he had had with those young women. Doing important work and receiving pleasure at the same time. *Yes, I'm a lucky guy,* he thought.

"Walk me up to my office, why don't you," Darren said. "We should see what we have coming up for positions. I'm sure we can make room for one more." Following behind as she climbed the stairs, Darren's imagination added much to this view from behind. The positions he could get into with this woman filled his mind. "Tell me about yourself."

"I did my undergraduate work at Dartmouth in Environmental Design. Then I was accepted at Boston University, their Master's Program in Public Administration. I've finished my course work. I just have to write my Thesis."

"Oh really. What's your topic?"

"Gun deaths in America in comparison to Australia. I'm working on the effects of Australia's ban on guns after the Tasmania massacre."

"Well, you're working in the right place," Darren realized his mistake and corrected it. "Oh excuse me, your volunteering in the right place."

The two sat in his office as they laughed again at the director's small joke. As their laughter slowed, an awkward silence came between them. They stared at each other, each seeming to be waiting for the other to speak. Elizabeth lowered her gaze, slightly embarrassed.

"So, Elizabeth, Dartmouth, eh? Do any hiking in the White Mountains while you were there?"

The volunteer perked up immediately. "Oh Mr. Honeyman. We used to go out every weekend. Even in winter, we'd put on skis to get into Dartmouth's huts. They have a wonderful Outdoor Club, you know."

Darren didn't really know that but he liked her answer. *I will have to take a special interest in this one for my adventure* he thought.

"It's been great chatting, Elizabeth. I'll see what we have in the way of permanent positions for you. If you'll excuse me now, I have to get ready."

"Of course, I'm sorry for taking up so much of your valuable time." She shifted in her chair to leave. The short skirt she was wearing opened up and reveled most of what was underneath. Darren stared at the exhibition presented to him. As she stood up, he looked up at her face. Her smile said it all. *Yes, this one will do nicely,* he thought.

He nodded his approval as she left, then bent to the task at hand. Greater things needed to be accomplished than one more female conquest. But he did linger his gaze on her back side as she closed the door behind her.

The Massachusetts State Legislature was voting on the final act of what he had spent the last year working for. Although it didn't appear so, guns in Massachusetts were about to be banned. *Not directly, but this final piece of legislation would so encumber gun owners, they would have little recourse but to give up their guns. Or move out of the state* he thought.

That fact didn't bother Darren one bit. *People who were gun owners shouldn't even be around decent people,* he thought. *Let them head out west where the*

Neanderthal types still clung to their belief in the 2nd Amendment. If things continued to work my way, even the Western states would succumb.

He knew the West would never change on their own. Only getting the Federal government to ban guns would end the violence. Darren firmly believed that once all guns were banned in America, the country would take its rightful place in the civilized world.

He looked out the window and saw his lieutenants at work. A large demonstration was planned today in front of the State Capital Building. He was scheduled to give the main address. Of course his political allies would have their time in front of the cameras, but his mission was bigger than the Bay State.

ENOUGH wanted the entire country disarmed. *Massachusetts was just a willing patsy to get the ball rolling,* he thought. NewYork State had come close after the Connecticut school shooting. Now that New York had suffered its own school attack, maybe their Legislature would finally react.

Kill enough school kids and eventually the politicians would succumb to the rage of the voters. That was the plan, and Darren sat back and relaxed. The deal was coming together nicely. Just keep the fires burning today in his speech and it would all turn out right.

Chapter 16

Hudson, Massachusetts

"Hey you two, get in here quick. You'll want to see this," Daniella said as she stuck her head out the motel door. Jack and Misty hurried the dogs along toward the door to Daniella's room.

Grabbing a towel from the bathroom, Jack sat down and wiped the sweat from his face. He looked over at Misty who looked cool as she stared at the TV set. How she could withstand the humidity and not perspire was beyond him. They had given the dogs a good workout along the old rail line that ran out of town.

The TV news reporter explained the reason for the rally on the Statehouse steps. The news feed that crawled along the bottom explained the other details.

"I've heard of these clowns," Jack said. "ENOUGH. Good thing they aren't out in Wyoming. Don't think they'd like the reception out there."

"Quiet Jack, these people are serious," Misty said. "And they seem to be winning the battle. The people I had to associate with at parties were big supporters of these guys. They have billions backing them."

"I know. My NRA magazine keeps me up to date on the anti-gunners. ENOUGH carries a lot of weight in liberal states," Jack said.

"That's right," Misty said. "If they get enough of the liberal states on board, the conservative states will get rolled. The Feds go for a gun ban and its toast for everyone."

"I can't believe the American public is buying this guy's crap. Whatever happened to the Constitution and the Bill of Rights? Someone forgot that the law of the land says otherwise."

"Come on, Jack, don't live in a dream world. Washington has been running rough shod over the Constitution before the ink was dry. Hasn't stopped them on anything else they wanted to do."

"Quiet, you two. I want to hear him," Daniella broke in on the heated discussion taking place. The two shut up and stared intently at the screen. The Director of ENOUGH was coming on.

"Ladies and gentleman, today marks a historic day for the citizens of Massachusetts. Finally reason has prevailed in this state. Your legislature is about to embark on the most civilized of behaviors. I can only hope the rest of the nation is watching."

"Yeah, watching this state shoot themselves in the foot," Jack injected. "Stupid bastards if they buy this guy's line of bull."

"Shhh."

"The recent tragic events in New York State only reminds us that guns cannot exist in our society anymore. They have outlived their usefulness in this country and need to be placed in the dustbin of history."

The reference to ENOUGH's logo got the large animated crowd going. The crowd started to chant.

"Enough, enough, enough, enough."

The man at the microphone raised his hands and the crowd settled down. "We have had enough. Enough killings, enough injuries, enough crippled children." He stopped for effect. "Enough innocent children killed in their classroom. I say enough. It's time to get rid of the guns. History's dustbin is waiting."

The crowd roared its approval. The man backed up and was joined by a cadre of Massachusetts politicians as they all clasped hands and raised them over their heads. Pumping their arms in solidarity for the victory they expected.

"When is the vote supposed to take place?" Misty asked.

"This afternoon. That's why their rallying the troops," Daniella answered.

Jack sat in a funk. He had a low tolerance for stupid people. And right now he was finding himself in a state of stupid people. He knew Massachusetts' reputation. Every gun owner knew about the draconian gun restrictions the Bay State politicians had imposed in their attempt to drive guns out of people's hands.

"Eventually a people get the government they deserve," he said.

"What's that Jack?" Misty asked.

Jack repeated his favorite quote again, but louder. *I just want to get this over with and get back out West,* he thought. *I love the fierce independence Westerners display in their daily life. They would never tolerate such clowns representing them.*

"Jack, you're not getting it," Misty said. "If enough kids are killed and maimed, then even reasonable people will be calling for change. And people like ENOUGH have the answer. At least the one the media presents. When was the last time the NRA was on prime time TV to answer these questions? And when they do have them on, how many 'gotcha' questions do they have to fight through? The public sees what the media wants them to see. That is if they turn their sets onto such programs. Most are too lost in football games to know what's happening to them."

"I didn't know you were so passionate about this. On the boat you seemed ambivalent about me and my gun. You seemed to just want it out of sight. Leads to out of mind, doesn't it?" Jack said.

Misty grabbed Tree and hugged the dog. Jackie came over looking for affection too.

"That was before I met Riley Wood, one of the kindergarten students that you saved. And when I came up with blood from Tree's fur. - someone's blood in that awful room, some little five year old's blood - it makes you think a little more clearly," Misty answered.

"That guns should be out lawed. Then we'll all be safe," Jack's sarcasm was thick.

"No Jack. That more people should be allowed to carry them. The honest people of this country. The ones who go to work each day and make it the best country they can. The people who live in states that don't allow that now," Misty said.

"Tomorrow we will see if the information we have is correct," Jack said. "If it is, you may get your wish. Discrediting these gun grabbers by exposing what they've been doing will set their agenda back."

* * *

Jack squatted over the portable toilet and relieved himself. He had been in the back of the van since 7:30 AM non-stop. It was Daniella's second day of work in the coffee shop. The van was parked nearby and Jack worked hard to keep the movement from showing to any passerby.

But as the afternoon sun beat down on the roof, the temperature rose suddenly. Daniella had picked a spot under a tree, but unfortunately the sun moved and the van was now in direct sun. She had left the windows in the front cracked but not enough to compensate for the heat Jack was suffering.

He pulled another water out of the cooler and settled back into his camp chair. The listening devices he had planted in Dr. Sumner's office were working splendidly. He was already tired of the morning discussions of mothers hating their daughters.

And the vitriol some people laid on their supposed partners. No wonder divorce consumed half the marriages in America he thought. *I'm glad none of these hags is in my life.*

But the patient they were waiting for hadn't surfaced yet. Being Tuesday, it seemed to be the indigent day of whining. And Jack had assumed that some loser would be the target of the good doctor.

As the sun moved behind a large maple tree, Jack finally felt some relief come over the interior of the van. He used the facilities again. *I'm glad Misty didn't insist on accompanying me today. The body functions I have to perform in close quarters would have been less than romantic with her here*, he thought.

As he listened, he could tell Dr. Sumner was getting ready to leave for the day. He looked at the coffee shop and saw Daniella dragging through her 9th hour of slopping coffee. She had volunteered for extra hours, stating she needed the money.

The proprietor had hastily agreed as he had seen a boost in business from her first day on the job.

Jack had noticed that large gravel trucks were stopping at all times of the day *I don't remember these the other day I was staking out things,* he thought. *How did the word get out so fast?*

That most of the dump trucks had Italian company names on their doors escaped Jack's attention. He was distracted by the phone ringing over the bug as he hit the tape recorder's on-switch.

"Yes, Dr. Sumner here."

Unfortunately, Jack hadn't bugged the phone itself. Only the office had a microphone to pick up the conversation. The oversight caused him to only hear half the conversation.

"I see. Well, he'll be here on Thursday. I think he's ready. He has been more and more delusional lately. I've done my best keeping him agitated without going over the edge."

More quiet time interrupted by some 'ah huh' and some 'I sees'. Jack was really kicking himself now. He wanted to know what the other person was telling her. And maybe who was speaking.

"I'll do my best. I understand how important this is. Yes, I know, school is out in a week. And yes, I got the word on the meeting next week. I'll be there." She hung up. Jack stopped the tape.

Whatever had been discussed, Thursday seemed to be the trigger point. He needed to get a hold of Lamarcus. Jack felt like things were about to happen and they had to be ready.

* * *

"Jack, you look awful. What happened?" Misty said, shocked at Jack's condition.

"Nine hours in the back of an overheated van, that's what. Whoever said police work was exciting never did a stake out."

Daniella rolled her eyes and held her nose. She made a fan motion with her other hand in front of her face to indicate the condition of the van.

"I'll clean it out tomorrow. And empty the toilet. But right now I just want a hot shower and some clean clothes," Jack announced. "And thanks Daniella for stopping at Kimball's. The shake went great with the burger and fries. Nothing like ice cream and junk food to kick start an old cop."

Daniella acknowledged Jack's compliment and excused herself to her room. Jack knew she had had a long day serving truck drivers. At least he didn't have to return tomorrow like she did. *I figure by Thursday the gravel trucks will be parked end to end through Harvard buying coffee. Should make the town fathers blanch,* Jack thought.

Alone with Misty, he headed to the bathroom for part one of his rejuvenation. He had dreamed of a long hot shower for most of the afternoon. As the sweat streaked down his back in the hot van, he couldn't wait to get back and relax.

The hot water tore at his flesh as he let the spray bring some feeling back. Sitting in the chair was tolerable, but on about the sixth hour, his body had begun to complain. Now he was getting his reward.

Suddenly a hand with an arm attached appeared through the steam. He retreated.

"Jack, how can you take that spray? It'll take your skin right off."

He turned to see a vision of Misty floating in the vapor. She was naked and was looking longingly at the shower. Jack reached around and dialed back the heat and volume.

"That's much better," she climbed in and ran her hands over Jack's back. "Your back is all red. Does it hurt?"

Jack just shook his head. He wanted to wash all the bad thoughts off of him. The dead children he hadn't been able to save in New York. The injured kids that he hadn't gotten to quickly enough to prevent their pain. He wanted it all washed off, and the hotter the better.

Misty picked up the soap and lathered his back. She rubbed sensuously across his body with a smooth slippery motion. The tension left his body. She reached around to his front. Her soapy hands worked their magic on his chest while her breasts pushed into his back

Dropping lower, her hands lathered up his lower body. Soon, he turned and took her in his arms. Tears were flowing down his cheeks as he ducked under the shower head and let the spray clear off his face.

Reaching up to his face, she cradled it in her hands. Their lips met and he kissed her hard. The magic continued and eventually moved to the bed. Jack wanted to forget for a minute what they were involved with.

Those thoughts were too horrible. He wanted the softness of this woman around him. Even for a few minutes, he could forget. But his thoughts of the children's blood splattered on him returned. Even the attention of a beguiling woman couldn't make it leave forever.

* * *

The Town of Harvard was not a trucker kind of town. He was sure that a week of such attention and the coffee shop owner would be getting a visit by the movers of Harvard. *Business of that kind wouldn't be tolerated,* he thought.

Which, if what they found out on Thursday was he hoped they would, they wouldn't need Daniella as a decoy anymore. She could escape the fine attentions of half the Italian truck drivers in eastern Massachusetts.

Thursday came quickly and Jack was back in the van. The weather had turned rainy and he was glad of the change. Rain pounded on the roof in downbursts all day. He sat content in his dry listening post as the patients came and went.

Today's problems seem to revolve around ingrate kids of rich parents. The whining continued as mothers complained to the doctor about kids that didn't appreciate all the things they were doing for them.

Jack was concluding he enjoyed the problems of the poor people on Tuesday more than the rich. That's when he heard a male voice enter the room. It was the first male voice he had heard all day. Women were not noted as mass shooters so he had been relaxed listening until now.

He hit the digital recorder. Daniella had purchased the high-tech recorder and showed Jack its operation. Jack was old school. But knew he had to get with the times and tape machines were out of date.

Jack heard the doctor greet her patient, calling him Winthrop. *Who the hell names their kid Winthrop?* he thought. *No wonder he's a whack job.*

But the conversation got interesting very quickly. Jack had experienced a couple of shrinks over the years both on the job and in his failed marriage. He thought he knew what counselors were supposed to do to help their patients.

After listening to two days of conversation between Dr. Sumner and her patients, he had realized quickly what her style tended to be. Suddenly, it was like a totally different person talking.

While Winthrop listened, Dr. Sumner fed him a line of crap that stunned Jack. *She's baiting this poor bastard,* he thought. He could tell by the broken short responses from the poor guy that he was taking every bit to heart.

As the conversation went on, Jack sat stunned. *At this rate, I'd go out and whack an entire community too,* he thought. He was impressed at the doc's ability to manipulate the poor sucker into doing her bidding. But she never exactly came out and told him what the target was. The innuendo was there, but Jack wasn't privy to the previous conversations.

The doctor kept referring to his past in broad terms and how he had sought out revenge. *Whoever and wherever his tormentors had been, someone was about to get it big time,* he thought. Jack knew he needed to follow this guy and see if he led him to any clues.

Jack picked up the disposable cell phone and called Misty. He explained what she needed to do and that it needed to happen right now. He hung up and scanned the main street.

As predicted, the composite of gravel trucks idling without drivers had grown exponentially. He looked in the coffee shop and couldn't see Daniella for the mass of drivers lurking. As soon as one would leave in a roar of diesel smoke, it seemed two more would pull in. The rumble of diesel engines had overtaken downtown Harvard.

Jack noticed the local citizens driving about with scowls on their faces. Their routine life had suddenly been overwhelmed by noisy commercial behemoths. *Yes, one more day of this and Daniela will get her walking papers,* he thought.

As he watched, Daniella strode into view in the shop's window. Her choice of dress had become slinkier and slinkier as the week progressed. By now she could pass for a Hooter's graduate. *Harvard wouldn't be the same,* he thought. Jack chuckled to himself. *Well, if she doesn't want to return to Albany and look for another job, she can certainly open up a coffee shop around here. The other shops might just pay her off to stay out of the business.*

As he watched, two large trucks with 'Ballidino Brothers' on the door pulled out onto Main Street. The extra heavy black smoke belched skyward as the drivers cut off an elderly lady pulling out of the Post Office.

Immediately, the police cruiser hit his lights and siren. The two trucks backed off the accelerator and pulled over to the side. Air brakes hissed as they set the parking brakes. The diesel engines of both continued their global gas contributions.

On the end of the hidden microphone, Dr. Sumner was saying goodbye to Winthrop. He didn't respond but Jack thought he heard a grunt. *Where was Misty? She was supposed to be here by now.* he thought. *I need to follow this guy now.*

There was no telling what Winthrop intended after the talk he had just received. They would have to watch him day and night and be ready for when he acted.

Jack looked for a car with New York plates. *Still no Misty,* he thought. *I have to do something.*

Chapter 17

Boston, Massachusetts

The previous two days had been a nightmare. The State Legislature had again been taken over by the forces of darkness in Darren's mind.

The western representatives with rubes for voters around Pittsfield had worked hard against the gun measure. Boston controlled the power in the Bay State. Whatever the Hub City wanted, eventually, they got their way. But on occasion, the more conservative, if such a thing existed in Massachusetts, politicians out in the western part of the state banded together with the politicians from around Worcester to achieve a blocking position.

And Monday they had jammed their block right up Boston's ass, Darren thought. The gun ban measure had gone down to defeat in the House by two votes. *Two stinking votes stopped my allies and me from finally obtaining a state worthy enough for decent people in the country.*

At least that's the way he had described it to his disappointed employees and their volunteer compatriots. The only personally consoling event that came out of it was one of his researchers had quit in disgust. Her feeling, loudly expressed on her leaving, was that ENOUGH hadn't worked hard enough. She announced that she was going to go find an organization to work for that took this matter seriously.

Which left Darren with a decision to make. He found Elizabeth Jamison and asked her to stop by his office at the end of the day. He had something to discuss with her.

It was past six o'clock when there was a knock on his door. He had been busy with revamping his strategy to return to the Legislature with another bill. Defeat only meant he had to redouble his efforts.

He looked up to see Elizabeth walk into his office. She shut the door behind her. He gazed as she sat down in the chair opposite him, her short skirt once again sprawled open as she sat. His gaze watched intently the show she provided. He looked up at her stare and smiled.

"You wanted to see me, Mr. Honeyman?"

"Darren, please. If you're going to be one of my employees, I pride myself on the close relationship I have with everyone."

"I'm sure you do, Darren. It was a shock today when Martha quit. She seemed so dedicated to the cause. I don't know where she'll find a better place to reach her goals."

"I'm glad you feel that way. That is one of the hallmarks of ENOUGH. Dedicated people willing to put themselves on the line every day. Are you willing to do that, Elizabeth?"

"Why, yes. Working here has been my dream since high school. Everyone I met then was more interested in sports or hooking up. Diversions I call them. But here, everyone is so focused. I know we'll achieve our goal soon."

Darren listened to the woman, but really he was listening for noises in the building. After such a defeat, he had told his people to take the rest of the week off and go rejuvenate. He had instructed them to be ready to hit it hard on Monday.

He was expecting good news by Monday. News that he had specifically made sure would happen. News that would pay back some of those negative votes he'd gotten from Central Massachusetts. *They needed the full wraith of ENOUGH to change their minds*, he thought

But now his thoughts were drifting to what was before him. He stood up and walked over to his door. He gently turned the lock. He walked back and stood behind his volunteer. The sun was still bright outside, but the lights were out in his office. The darkness added to the mood.

"So, Elizabeth. Do you think you're ready to take over Martha's job? It's a little more than our new hires typically get. But I think you might be the person that can fill the bill." His hands massaged her shoulders as he rubbed his legs against her back. Her head leaned back.

"I know I'm the one. Maybe you need some persuasion?"

I thought you'd never ask, he thought. She stood up and hiked her skirt up. She backed up to his desk while taking his hands in hers. Sitting down on the desk top, she pulled his head down. He followed her lead as the two pulled at his pants.

He leaned into her and kissed her. Her tongue immediately found his mouth as one hand pulled him onto her. They fumbled with removing articles of clothing that were in the way. Soon, they were both on top of the desk as Darren's work landed on the floor. *I think she got the job,* he thought as he was consumed by the Ivy Leaguer beneath him.

* * *

Jack picked up the cell phone and dialed Misty. He instructed her to pick up Daniella as he was busy following their prime suspect.

He swung through a rotary as he kept Winthrop in sight. It was fairly easy, even in a big Ford van. Winthrop was not a particularly good driver, and with the agitation that the doc had added to his head, it made him worse.

If he's not careful, some patrol cop is going to stop him, the way he's driving, Jack thought. *I'm not sure that would be a healthy event for Winthrop. With the added juice running through him from the psychiatrist playing mind games on him, he was likely to explode at any time.*

Jack turned left as he kept his target in sight. *Any reasonably aware person would have picked me up tailing them by now,* he thought. He had tailed plenty of people in his thirty years of police work. Some were easy and some weren't.

This guy was about to get the prize for being the most clueless he had seen. But Jack was happy. It made his life easier that the perpetrator was so out of it. Jack sped up a bit as Winthrop seemed to be gaining speed. Winthrop's thoughts seemed to have congealed on something, and now was in a rush to get there.

Another right and Jack saw the next town announce itself. "Lancaster," Jack said out loud. "Established 1689." *Boy, things are a lot older back here than out west*, he thought. *It took them 69 years from landing at Plymouth Rock to settle out this far and incorporate as a town. Interesting, considering it's only about 50 miles from Plymouth to here. Figure a mile per year. At that rate Rochester, New York would be just getting started. Good thing the pace of western growth had picked up.*

All manner of thought raced through Jack's head as he took another intersection at speed. *If this boy isn't careful, the local police will be grabbing your ass. How will that be for old Dr. Sumner?* he thought. *Think she'd bail out her little bad boy so her little chore can be completed.*

Suddenly Winthrop braked hard and Jack had to react quickly to keep from running into him. Jack focused on the surroundings to determine what was of interest to the psycho. There it was, an elementary school on the left with school buses loading up kids for the ride home.

Winthrop was barely moving and Jack could see his head turned studying the school. A crossing guard blew his whistle and the car lurched to a stop, Jack pulling up behind his target. Five little kids, their backpacks dangling and papers in their hands, ran across the street. The gang split up, some turning left toward the houses, the others right.

Lancaster's downtown was just ahead and they got the signal from the guard to move on. Winthrop accelerated but looked over his shoulder at the school as he left. Jack was glad that no traffic was in front of him as he would have rear-ended anyone from his lack of attention to the road.

Jack followed Winthrop across the town boundary into a place called Clinton. The housing took a decided turn for the worse. *Obviously Clinton was a lower income community than Lancaster,* he thought. The houses had been large and well maintained, but in Clinton most of the large homes had been turned into apartments.

When he hit the downtown area, Jack knew Clinton had fallen on hard times. The empty mills and the weed-infested train tracks attested to a prosperity that had left the area. *Gone overseas*, Jack surmised. *Hudson had the same problem but seemed to be recovering better than Clinton.*

The small area towns appeared prosperous. Jack had noticed the surrounding small towns were robust in comparison to the larger towns. Suburbia had reached out from Boston along with the high-tech companies lining the freeway roads around Boston. People had sought out the safety and quiet of small New England towns to the detriment of the old mill towns.

And it appeared that Winthrop had seen a similar demise over his short life. That he or someone he knew had the money to pay for a high price psychiatrist in a swish town like Harvard meant that he had been connected at one time.

From the look of his living quarters, he obviously wasn't paying for the doctor visits. Sandwiched in between High Street and Main, Winthrop parked and walked into a very run-down building. From the looks, it was a former commercial building, at least downstairs. Now it was just boarded-up glass.

Apartments above the commercial portion looked lived in from the open windows. One or two windows had air conditioners rattling away in an attempt to cool the interior. Jack parked the van in a spot across the street and reached for his phone. He needed to get things in gear if what he was thinking was about to happen.

Chapter 18

Cambridge, Massachusetts

Lieutenant Lamarcus Lewis had been dreading getting the call. But it arrived in spite of his trepidation. He flipped open his buzzing cell phone.

"Jack, I know I should be glad to hear from you, but I was hoping."

"We found him. And from the tape I've got, things are about to go down. You know the drill," the phone went dead.

Jack and Lamarcus had worked out ahead of time what would happen when the perpetrator was discovered. He just never figured it would happen so fast. *Or maybe not at all,* he thought.

The whole idea was too much to contemplate. If it had been anyone other than a Marine Corps brother, Lamarcus would have laughed in their face. People just don't do those kind of things. *America hadn't succumbed to that level yet. Or had it?* he wondered.

The reports he had received from another source seemed to confirm things. His friend was the State Police Liaison Officer at the State House. A fellow lieutenant, they had earned their strips together in patrol cars. Each had saved each other's life at least once from the bad guys.

Lamarcus trusted the man with his life, literally. But what he had heard disturbed him. After the gun control legislation, or ban, had been defeated, his friend had picked up rumblings. And not good rumblings.

It seemed that some of the losing politicians were promising revenge on their opponents. And unlike the normal give and take of legislative matters, this seemed like a personal vendetta.

His friend had commented to Lamarcus that over the years the relations between political parties on Beacon Hill had grown more vitriolic. Any semblance of bipartisanship had vanished from the Massachusetts political scene and his friend decried that it had become a 'blood sport'.

But Jack's call shook Lamarcus from his worry over the State Legislature and what they were attempting. He suddenly had a more urgent matter to see to.

Lamarcus checked himself out of the office as he grabbed one of his gang control patrolmen. With a squad of officers assigned under his command, Marcus had ready backup for any occasion. And he was feeling he needed backup for what he was about to encounter.

* * *

The stakeout of the potential shooter continued in Clinton, Mass. Jack had been ensconced in the white Ford van now for 12 hours. His food supply had run out and as the early morning light grew in the east, he decided he'd risk a quick food run.

Misty would be relieving him soon so he could return to the motel in Hudson and grab some sleep. She would monitor the suspect in the interim. Daniella would provide shuttle service so the van could maintain its parking spot. It provided a clear view of the suspects car and doorway to the apartment building.

Jack cringed at the mess the van had become. And the smell, he didn't know what to do about the smell. Using a portable toilet so he didn't have to expose himself outside the van left the interior rather rank. *She will have to endure the odor until we can break off our surveillance,* he thought *But food first.*

He looked at a donut shop just across the street and down a few steps. At this time of morning, he could quickly grab some muffins and coffee and be back hidden inside unnoticed.

Checking for any signs of life around him, Jack opened the van's passenger door and stepped out. He stood for a minute and just stretched his legs before moving across the street. Lacking any other customers in the shop, his transaction went without interruption.

As Jack walked back carrying his bag of food, he checked that the suspect's car was still parked were he had left it. *Good, no movement,* he thought. He walked around to the passenger door side of the van and reached for the door handle. That's when things went dark.

* * *

Misty Duran finished her makeshift breakfast. Oatmeal cooked in her motel room microwave with some raisins thrown in fit the bill. Compared to places she and her husband typically had stayed, it wouldn't have rated one star.

But her life had changed back in Greenbush. Holding Jack's dog and having little kid's blood on her made her mind focus. Sitting with little Riley Wood as he explained how the good man saved him from the bad man had galvanized her determination.

She would endure any hardship to get the people that could do such heinous crimes. If eating oatmeal in a lowly motel in Hudson, Mass. was called for, she was ready.

As she arrived at the allocated exchange spot, she quickly had second thoughts. Daniella dropped her off nearby and Misty walked quickly to the white van. Using her key, she opened the passenger door and climbed in. She moved to the rear before anyone outside noticed.

What's that awful smell? she thought. Between the chemicals in the portable toilet and the human waste deposited, the smell almost made her gag. *But I can do this,* she thought.

Her disposable cell phone rang. "Misty, this is Daniella. Where's Jack? He wasn't at the designated pickup."

The three had worked out how they would conduct their switch so as to not draw attention to the white van. Jack was to leave just before the appointed time and walk to a corner where Daniella would pick him up. But Jack hadn't made it.

"He's not here. I don't know where he is," Misty said. "Take another lap around and see if you spot him. He might have ducked into some place for a toilet break."

That was all Misty could think of from the smells attacking her nose. She put her coffee down. *No more liquids till I'm out of here. I'm not using that portable toilet even if my life depends on it,* she thought.

* * *

Jack had lost all thought of the smelly portable toilet. As he slowly regained consciousness, the smell of rubber overwhelmed him. That and some other foul smell that he couldn't recognize.

His head hurt from where someone had struck him from behind. He focused on the pain until his mind cleared totally. Coming fully awake, he started to move but found his hands and legs strapped together. A gag had been placed over his mouth.

In the darkness, he heard road noise and the smell of exhaust. *I'm in the trunk of a car*, he thought. His eyes fully open now, he attempted to focus on something in the dark. A slight glow cut the darkness as the taillights allowed sunlight to filter inside the trunk.

The car continued its journey. Eventually thoughts of the portable toilet came to mind as Jack's body announced its needs. He shifted slightly to help with the pressure in vital areas. *No telling when I'll get a break, if at all,* he thought.

As the agony grew in his bladder, the car slowed and Jack felt the turns the car was making. After several stops and starts, Jack surmised that maybe they might be reaching their destination. A sound like a garage door opening and a quick forward movement by the car announced an arrival. Jack waited to see his abductors.

A key in the trunk and a swoosh of fresh air announced the lid opening. Jack blinked to adjust to the subdued light of an enclosed garage. Standing over him were three men holding guns, each aimed at him. *Not good*, he thought.

"Get his sorry ass out of there," one of them said. Jack marked him as the leader.

The other two tucked their handguns in the waistband of their pants and reached down to grab him. They roughly pulled him out of the car's trunk. Standing upright, they lifted him slightly and drug him across the garage to a doorway. A basement room with small windows near the ceiling held a single chair. They plopped Jack unceremoniously into it.

Jack winched from the pain in his bladder. He held control barely as the two thugs stood back and stared. The leader walked up and punched Jack in the side of the head.

"That's from your friend in Chicago. He wanted to announce himself personally but you'll have to wait for that."

Jack's mind raced. *Chicago, who do I know there?* he thought. His mind processed that information when the other side of his head pitched sideways from a savage blow. One of his handlers stepped back, rubbing his fist.

Jack attempted to speak but the gag kept him silent. The leader reached over and untied the rope in his mouth.

"Something on your mind asshole?" the thug asked.

"If you don't want me soiling your floor, you'll let me use the toilet," Jack said.

The leader nodded his head at the other two to take their charge to the bathroom.

"Any bullshit, and I'll waste you right here, in spite of orders," the leader warned.

Jack was lifted and drug to a nearby toilet. The two guards froze when they realized that their captor couldn't relieve himself tied up.

"I'm not touchin' nothin'"

"Don't look at me," the second one offered.

"Look guys, there's no window in here so I can't escape. Just take the cuffs off my wrists. I can't run away with you two standing here can I?" Jack said.

The two looked around the small bathroom and then out the door at their leader. With a nod to each other, one reached around and uncuffed Jack. Both stepped back and pulled out their guns. *I guess privacy would be too much to ask for*, Jack thought.

Jack unbuckled his pants and started to pull them down. The two guards realized what was about to happen and grimaced.

"We'll be right outside. We'll shoot you dead if you try something," one said. They slammed the door shut.

Jack finished and called his captors. Feeling much better, he held his arms behind his back as the guards reattached the handcuffs. They picked him up and drug him back to the chair.

"So, your mind a little clearer now? Remember anything about Chicago, asshole?"

"Only thing that comes to mind was a brother I left strapped to a dock," Jack offered.

"He ain't no brother of yours, honky. But he was a brother to someone important. And blood runs deep. He put the word out to find you and return your sorry ass to Chicago where you about to learn some respect."

All three laughed at the last comment. Jack knew respect in this instance wouldn't be good for his health. *But how had they found me so fast?* he thought. He had no idea how long he'd been knocked out or where in the trip back to Chicago he was. He decided to try and find out.

"So, the brother I dissed. He's important eh?"

"His brother is. You mess wit' the wrong blood and it comes back to bite your ass," the leader laughed. His two associates joined in.

At least the conversation keeps their fists from my head, he thought. "So how long before I get my respect lesson?"

"Be awhile. We need some sleep before we continue drivin'. Be there tomorrow. Lookin' forward to it."

Tomorrow huh. That would put me somewhere in up-state New York, Jack thought. Not that the information helped his situation much. But he still wondered how they had found him.

"You know, I thought I was being respectful of the brother by leaving him alive on the dock. I gave

187

him the choice of being dropped on the bottom of Lake Michigan. Kind of wish I'd done the swim lesson for him now."

A fist crashed into the side of his head and Jack pitched sideways. The chair tipped over and Jack landed on the floor. A boot immediately hit him in the back. Then another one went for the groin. Jack instinctively pulled himself into a fetal position to protect his vitals.

"Stop. They want him alive in Chicago," the leader said. The blows stopped but not before a hand swiped him across the face. The sting registered as pain wracked his body.

"I have a question though. How did you boys ever find me? I'm pretty below the radar. You must have a good network," Jack asked

"Man, you don't know who you messin' wit'. We got brothers all over the East Coast. Word goes out from Chicago to find a white dude on a sailboat. We had the name and make of your boat. Easy to spot in New York. Then a little inquire and we find a Daniella Martocci has gone missin'. Police looking all around for her. We just have a better network to find her car before the cops do. She just leads us to you, white boy."

Jack had known taking Daniella with them would be a risk. She was part of the police investigation of the New York school shooting. They might not miss an outsider like Jack, but Daniella was a local. They would miss her and alarms would be sounded. He was stupid for not seeing that fact.

As he admonished himself, the two guards grabbed his arms and slid him across the floor. Taking out another set of handcuffs, they attached one end to his wrists. Then they pulled on his arms and snapped the other end of the cuffs to a ring on the wall. *Obviously I'm not the first person to be held here,* he thought.

The three men left him lying on the floor and closed the door behind them as he heard footsteps on stairs. Jack looked around the room. He was now alone, firmly attached to the wall. He looked for an escape but couldn't see any options. He was stuck and tomorrow would learn some respect.

Chapter 19

Hudson, Massachusetts

Misty woke with a start. She was alone in the motel room while Daniella maintained watch in the white van. She scanned the darkened room before getting up. *This was the day. She just knew it*, she thought.

She didn't know much about the psychological patterns of mass shooters, but the suspect had been quiet all day yesterday. She had sat in the horrible smell watching and saw no movement. When Daniella had come to relieve her that evening, Misty had returned to the motel. A long shower still hadn't removed the smell from her nostrils.

As she contemplated her next shift in the van, the phone rang. Daniella reported that the suspect was on the move, announcing that she would follow in the van and would keep the cell phone ready.

Misty hung up and dialed the number Jack had provided her. She passed on the message that the suspect was moving. She hung up and quickly got dressed. She wanted to be there when it happened this time.

* * *

"Larry, we're out of here," Lamarcus said to his backup as he hung up his phone.

The two Cambridge city cops had visited the Lancaster grade school the day before. Their recon completed, they received the word that the suspect was moving. It was a short drive to the school from their motel room in Leominster, a town next door.

Lamarcus had brought his personal car so that any suspect wouldn't be tipped off. The unmarked police cars would be too visible in the school parking lot with their antennas.

"Like we planned Larry, you hang back in the parking lot while I go in the school. Don't let the perp see you, but follow him. I may need your backup if he's determined to go down shooting."

"You got it," the patrol officer said.

The two arrived at John Quincy Adams Elementary School just as the first teachers were arriving. Lamarcus climbed out of the car and adjusted his suit. Dressed in civilian clothes, he was fully armed. A semiautomatic handgun on his right hip as well as two backups, a revolver in an ankle holster and a second compact semi-auto in a holster in the small of his back. Nothing would be left to chance today.

Larry was similarly armed but had a Cambridge patrolman uniform on. He slid down in the passenger seat of Lamarcus' Buick sedan to keep his uniform out of sight. He held a small police radio in his hand while Lamarcus wore a discreet earpiece.

"Good morning. I'm Lieutenant Lamarcus Lewis of the Cambridge city police," he announced as he walked up to the front counter. He held up his badge and ID to the school secretary. The school principal stood nearby and walked over.

"Yes Lieutenant, to what do we owe this visit?"

"Ma'am, I'm in charge of the gang unit for the Cambridge police. We have credible evidence that we are about to have a gang-related incident here this morning. I need your full cooperation."

"Certainly, but shouldn't we call the local police and lock down the school?" the principal asked.

"No Ma'am. That would scare him off. We need you to act like today is like every other day. I'll just take a seat over there by the front door. Just pay me no never mind."

Lamarcus walked over to a metal chair that had been left by the office and grabbed it. He carried it over to a spot inside the front door but unseen from outside. He sat down to the stares of the two women.

"Now please, like nothing is going on. I'm counting on you both."

The two women looked like two guilty suspects as they mechanically went about their duties greeting the other staff members as the children started drifting in. The noise level increased as the grade schoolers all walked by the stranger in the suit.

As a black man in a mostly white community, Lamarcus received the normal stares from everyone. Used to the behavior, he just smiled at each child. Outside the big cities of Massachusetts, the rural parts of the state were still very white and moderately conservative. Lamarcus knew conservative was a relative term in Bay State. Compared to Wyoming, real conservatives didn't exist in the state any longer.

His earpiece updated him on the comings and goings outside. Larry reported each bus arrival along with each parent dropping off their child. With almost exclusively woman teachers at the school, no lone male had driven into the parking lot. Lamarcus waited.

His cell phone suddenly rang with Daniella reporting that the suspect was approaching the school. She hung up.

Lamarcus reached into his suit pocket and double clicked his police radio. Outside, Larry would get the message and be ready.

"Suspect getting out of his car now. He has a trench coat on. I repeat, suspect is in the parking lot," Lamarcus' earpiece squawked. Lamarcus stood up. He looked around and the halls were free of children.

School was about to start and they were safely in their class rooms. He looked over at two wide eyed women manning the front desk. He carefully motioned them to go into the principal's office.

"Suspect entering front of school now. I repeat, suspect in school now."

Standing out of sight to the side of the front doors, Lamarcus could see the outside door open and a figure walk in. Grasping the inside door, the suspect swung the door open, a semiautomatic handgun swung up into firing position. The suspect walked in the door ready to fire.

Instead he was met by a gun shoved into his cheek from the blind side and the command, "Drop it or die."

The shooter froze at the sudden appearance of someone else, a gun ready. He hesitated, not sure of what to do. Lamarcus stood to the side and slightly behind so the shooter couldn't see who he was dealing with.

"I said drop it, shithead. Give me an excuse to blow your brains all over the wall, please."

The threat was enough to unhinge the shooter. He dropped his hand and began sobbing. Lamarcus stepped around him and grabbed the gun out of his hand. Larry was right behind and arm-twisted the man to the floor.

Handcuffs swiftly incapacitated the shooter. Lamarcus rolled him over as he searched him.

Underneath the trench coat the man had a shotgun with its butt stock cut off. The scatter gun was tied to a piece of rope that went over the man's shoulder. On the other side of his coat was a semiautomatic carbine.

Larry pulled both guns off the shooter and tossed them to the side as Lamarcus continued the pat down. At the man's ankle, a revolver was pulled out and added to the weapons pile.

"Clear," Larry yelled to indicate that the man was now disarmed.

A scream brought Lamarcus back to his surroundings. He looked up as the school principal stood gaping at the man and the pile of weapons.

"What is all that? Why is a gang member here to shoot up our school?" she asked.

"Ma'am, you can call your local police now."

* * *

As the Director of the anti-gun lobbying group, ENOUGH, Darren would typically arrive at work whenever the mood hit him. He put in enough hours each week fighting the good fight that he didn't need to justify his time to anyone.

But this morning he had arrived before anyone else. He was anticipating good news on the battle to rid America of its scourge of guns. School was almost out for the summer and with that went the school children. School shootings wouldn't happen again until the fall.

And with summer's arrival, the state legislatures around the country that had been so carefully manipulated over the last year would be leaving on recess. Momentum for action against guns would be lost as each legislator relaxed with their families. Things had to happen now or the time spent preparing would be wasted.

Not that they couldn't reestablish gun mayhem at the turn of a switch. It had almost become too easy to kill school children. Even copycat killers had taken up the cause in a vile attempt to outdo the last school shooter. There seemed to be almost a body count contest at hand and the media was expert at manipulating the news to generate more shootings.

It's almost not fair how easy it is, he thought. *Kill some more kids and the law makers all fall in line.* He actually started to feel sorry for those assholes over at the NRA. They had to fight the politicians, the anti-gun groups and the media just to get their word out. And now they had been so scapegoated he doubted anyone would listen to them ever again.

Yes, today just might push the whole enchilada off the cliff for good, he thought. And good riddance. America could finally take its proper place among the other civilized unarmed peoples of the world.

He switched on the TV in his office and waited for the expected announcement. As he sat, staff members walked by his office, each looking in as they went. *No doubt wondering what's up,* he thought. Darren was excited that he knew what would be coming and how their reaction would spur them on. *Shock, followed by rage, as more innocent children fell in the raging gun battle,* he thought. *So predictable, it was like shooting rats in a barrel.* Darren laughed at his own little ironic metaphor.

Suddenly the screen switched to a news alert warning. *Oh good, here it comes,* he thought. A live screen came on just as his new assistant walked in and sat down. He and Elizabeth had been living together since their hard-charged fling on top of his desk a short time back. *She seems to think that she could just stroll in her any time now.*

"Bad news?" she asked.

If she only knew, Darren thought. "I don't know. The news alert just came on. Turn it up,"

"This is Channel 8 News outside an elementary school in Newark, New Jersey. Initial reports says a lone gunman has entered the school. So far we have twenty-two confirmed dead. New Jersey joins the long list of states suffering through school shootings. We turn now to our anchor for more information."

The screen flipped to the anchor in the studio. The network had file tape of previous school shootings ready to roll. The anchor woman introduced the segment and the taped segment started.

"This is awful. Another one. And so soon after New York," Elizabeth exclaimed.

Darren's office suddenly filled with staff members as the word spread through the building. They all talked among themselves recounting their past emotions over such events. To some, the routine of it all was noticeable in their almost surreal non-response.

One of those was Darren. He sat mute as he watched the feed from New Jersey. *It's not suppose to be New Jersey this time,* he thought.

"Turn the station. Is there any news from Massachusetts?" he asked. One of the staffers dutifully went through all the news networks. Nothing but news from New Jersey came through.

I'm sure it was Massachusetts that was next, he thought. *And what's the deal? Those are all black kids they're hauling away in ambulances. That's not suppose to happen.*

A woman staffer flipped the channels from the national news onto a local Boston station. The New Jersey shooting dominated the local news as more information came through. The body count was now over thirty children and five staff members. It was turning into the worst school shooting in the nation's history.

As Darren watched, the local Boston anchor came on the screen. He announced, "In other news, police in Lancaster have arrested a would-be school shooter. Stopped with four guns as he entered a primary school, his attempt at adding Massachusetts to the growing list of victims has been thwarted."

Darren jumped out of his chair and screamed at the screen. "What! No, that can't be."

The staff in the room all turned toward their boss. Like stunned mullets, they stared at the man screaming at good news. Suddenly Darren realized the scene he was making and sat down. He collected himself before speaking.

"I just can't believe that someone in this state would dare attack our children. I thought we had successfully gotten guns away from anyone like that."

"We just need to work harder," one of them said. The entire group nodded in agreement.

Good, yes, work harder, but leave the thinking to me, he thought.

Chapter 20

Upstate New York

Jack was awoken by a boot in the side. He reacted instantly by curling into a ball. No other abuse followed and he relaxed. He ached all over from his beating the previous day. He'd slept fitfully on the hard floor while handcuffed to the wall. His body screamed in its need for a bathroom again.

The guards already knew what needed to happen as they uncuffed his arms from the wall and lifted him to his feet. Dragging him to the nearby bathroom, they freed his wrists.

"Same shit, different day asshole. You screw with us and we shoot you," one of the thugs said. They stepped outside the room, leaving Jack alone. After he announced he was finished, they recuffed him and dragged him to a waiting chair.

The leader walked into the room muttering. "Jesus, all those black kids dead. I bet we got some brothers with family down there."

The three men all started talking among each other. Jack quickly surmised that there had been another school shooting. And this one sounded bad from the way they were talking.

"I can't believe a brother would do such a thing. Man, its like the white man's disease is spreading among the family."

"Yo, did you see those kids? Not right, it just ain't right."

Jack wanted to join the conversation but was reluctant to try. He looked at each of the men for an opening.

"What you lookin' at, fool?" the leader barked at Jack.

"Sounds like a bad school shooting. Where was it?" Jack asked.

"What you care? Just a bunch of poor black kids shot dead. Happens all the time in the cities. You white people don't do nothin' about it, why you care now?"

"Newark," one of the thugs added. The leader gave him a scornful look. But the man added, "I'm from Newark. I got family there. Could be my kid sister who's dead, man."

"Dead now or dead when she's 18 from getting pimped out. What's the diff?" the leader said.

"Makes a big difference. Get an education and the world opens up. Lots of opportunities out there," Jack decided to work on the guy from Newark. *I see a spark of humanity there,* he thought.

"Well, who asked you? You going to Chicago soon and you can stop worrying about all those little black kids. You'll have your hands full for sure," the leader and one thug laughing at Jack's fate.

But Jack saw the look on the third man. He was generally worried about his family back in New Jersey. He had to play his card now.

"Terrible things, these school shootings. I was there at the one in New York."

"What you saying? You there? No way," the leader said.

"How do you think I hooked up with the Martocci woman you tracked down? She was part of it too. That's why the police are looking for her. Her boss was killed by the same guy," Jack said.

"You a bystander. Anyone can be a lookin'," the leader chimed.

"No, I stopped the guy. I was walking my dog when I saw him enter the school. I ran in when I heard the gun shots and stopped him."

"Then you got a major set of balls mister. You stop him barehanded?" the leader taunted.

Jack wasn't about to announce he was a deputy sheriff or that he had been armed. If they hadn't found that information out so far, he would leave that alone.

"I have a black belt in Taekwondo. I came up behind him and took him down."

"You a karate man? Bullshit. The reports said the guy was killed," the leader said.

"We struggled. His gun went off and he shot himself. That was when I figured out that maybe the school shootings weren't such a random event," Jack lied.

"What you sayin', karate man. Some secret society like, is gunnin' kids down? Why they want to do that?" the guy from Newark finally joined the conversation.

"'Cause the Man wants to control you. That's why. Kill enough kids and America will give you control to make it safe." He emphasized 'man' as he said it. This was is only chance to avoid a trip to Chicago.

"What you know about the Man, karate man? You not lookin' like you from the 'hood. The Man good to you," Newark answered. *The leader is falling back, good,* Jack thought.

"Then why am I living in the back of a van when you picked me up? I was watching the next person the Man was sending out to kill. You see any reports from Massachusetts today?" Jack hoped that Lamarcus had done his job.

"Yeah. They says a school shootin' was stopped by the local blue. Had four guns and lots of ammo on him when they sacked his sorry ass. You in with that?" Newark asked.

"That was my main man. See a big black Cambridge city cop on the news that was in on the arrest?" Jack asked.

"Yeah, there was a brother talkin' to the reporters. He your main man, then?" Newark was carrying the conversation now. The other two only stood and watched.

"We go way back. Brother in arms. We were in the same gang together."

"Yo, which one?"

"The U.S. Marines."

"Woo, the man be a devil dog for sure. Well, karate man, me and the brothers need to talk. You just sit tight, now, hear?" Newark said. He nodded his head toward the door and all three left the room.

* * *

In the living room of an older home in East Providence, Rhode Island, a war veteran watched the day's events unfold. He shook his head in disgust at what had become of his country. *Is this why all those men had died?* he wondered. Over the thirty years he had spent in the Marines, he had known plenty of good men that weren't with him anymore.

The front door opened and a woman walked in. She was a little younger than the veteran but looked decidedly healthier. She placed her parcel she had been carrying in the kitchen before returning to sit down.

"Any more news on that school shooting Salvatore? It's just horrible what goes on now," she said.

"The body count keeps going up, but nothing else. I don't know why these crazy people get to run around free to do this crap. We used to lock them up in institutions," the veteran said. He shook his head in disgust as the television reporter announced another attempted school shooting.

Both he and his sister sat straight up as the screen switched to the news conference being held in Massachusetts. The lead investigator walked up to the microphone to make his announcement.

"Isn't that..." the sister started to say. She was cut off by Salvatore before she finished.

"Corporal Lewis. That's him alright. A few pounds heavier and more gray hair, but that's sure as hell him."

They both listened intently as Lamarcus Lewis described the apprehension of a man bent on adding to the school shooting list. No one had been injured due to the quick reaction of the local police the TV announced.

Salvatore's sister looked over as her brother doubled up in pain.

"Hang on, I'll get your medicine." She ran to the kitchen and retrieved a prescription bottle. Running some water in a cup, she returned and handed him two pills. He drank them down.

The pills quickly did their job and he sat back in his recliner. His face showed relief from the pain as he closed his eyes.

"You need to see someone," she said.

"Who, the priest? You know what the doctors have all said. Inoperable pancreatic cancer, Sis. 'Go home and get your affairs in order,' they said," Salvatore said. He looked at the tears in his sister's eyes, reaching over to take her hand. "Thanks for taking an old dying jarhead in. I know its a burden on you, but I didn't want to go through this alone in that apartment in North Carolina."

His sister squeezed his hand as tears flowed down her cheeks. "I just think maybe someone somewhere has an answer. You're too young."

"Every day after I put on that Marine uniform I was ready to die for the Corps. That I survived the thirty years was pure luck. My time with the Marines is satisfaction enough, the rest is just so much waiting."

"You shouldn't talk like that. People love you and will miss you."

"Sis, I never married and I never had any kids. At least ones that I know about. My life ended when they retired me from the Corps. It was all I ever wanted, and I got to do it for thirty grand years. Just let an old vet die in piece," Salvatore said.

They continued to watch the Massachusetts press conference in silence. When it was completed,

Salvatore turned to his sister. "Give me the phone, please. I need to make a call."

* * *

Jack Wesley tried to stand up. But being hog-tied with his hands behind his back made standing difficult. The hood over his head didn't make the task any easier. But he fought to get up off the ground.

He had been summarily dumped by the side of a road somewhere. His abductor's had reached some sort of decision to let him go. *Had they believed my hunt for the mastermind of the school shootings or something?* he thought. *I have no other clue as to why they were letting me go.*

He was just wishing they had left him with some of his clothes. While he couldn't see the highway, he could hear cars streaking by close. And it wasn't a busy road since the frequency between vehicles had big gaps.

A naked, hooded man standing tied up by the side of the road would certainly draw someone's attention. He just had to hop toward the sound of the cars.

His bare feet felt the clutter on the ground. He had no idea what was surrounding him, but from the feel, there must be trees about. He could feel the twigs and small branches cutting at his feet.

Jack moved a couple of hops and ran into a tree. Almost falling over, he leaned against it for stability. A car swished by. From the sound, Jack figured he was about fifty feet off the road. He hopped some more, the rocks cutting his feet. A large bush stopped his progress and he had to maneuver around the impediment.

Soon, the gravel of the edge of the road announced itself through his feet. He stopped and waited. He could tell it was day time from the light filtering through the hood. But he didn't want to stumble out into the roadway and get hit. He would just hope he was visible on the roadside and that someone would call the authorities.

A short burst of siren announced that help had arrived. The tires of the cruiser crunched to a stop not far from him. The sound of a car door followed by footsteps before a voice announced itself.

"Son, you look like your friends done you wrong."

Jack saw the Massachusetts State trooper smiling as the hood came off his head. His hands were undone before Jack's ankle restraints were removed.

"Hey thanks," Jack finally offered. "It's been quite a day so far."

After some questioning at the State Police barracks, Jack was allowed to call Misty for a ride and some clothes. The wool blanket the trooper had provided at the scene was replaced with some surplus clothes at the barracks. Jack wasn't sure who had worn them prior to him and was anxious to get into his own clothes.

After Misty's arrival, the drive back from Western Massachusetts seemed extra long.

"Tell me again, who abducted you?" Misty asked. She couldn't believe that some Chicago gang had put a 'hit' out on Jack. Jack went through the story once more.

Misty enquired when he had finished, "And they let you go after all that? Why?"

"I'm not entirely sure myself. But when those black kids were all shot down in Newark, their attitude definitely changed. Especially the one that was from Newark. He seemed to sense that everyone was at risk with what is happening. And when he found out I was the one who stopped the New York school shooting, something registered," Jack said.

"Well, leaving you gagged, tied and naked by the highway wasn't especially friendly of them."

"Better than the alternative," Jack added. "I know the Chicago crowd wouldn't have left me alive."

"How were they going to show up in Chicago empty handed? I'm sure they had notified someone when they captured you."

"They said something about another hit they had to do. Said that whoever it was would be shot in the face so there wouldn't be much to recognize."

"And you went along with that?" Misty asked.

"It wasn't a democracy. They didn't ask my opinion. I was gagged and being stuffed in a trunk at the time when I overheard them say it."

The ride after that was quiet for some time. As they exited the Mass Pike onto Interstate 1-290, Misty stopped and paid the toll. Accelerating onto the freeway, she merged into the heavy traffic headed toward Worcester.

Jack finally spoke up, "So we stopped the crazy guy from shooting up the Lancaster school. At least you guys stayed on top of things."

"Yes, Lamarcus was great. He was there waiting when the guy walked in the door. Never knew what hit him."

"So, where are we at now? Any surveillance get done on our friendly Dr. Sumner?" Jack asked.

"Daniella went back to work. The coffee shop owner was glad to have her back. The heat he had gotten from the truck drivers when she wasn't there outweighed the town fathers' concern over the truck traffic."

"And you figured out how to listen in on Sumner's office? Enjoy the portable toilet?" Jack asked. He smiled as he said it.

He received a scowl in return. "Yeah, once I'd spent all day scrubbing it down with bleach, thank you very much. It's rather pleasant now. Just so you keep away from it."

"Fine with me. Surveillance is all yours now. Like I'd miss the eight-hour days stuck in a windowless van."

Misty continued along I-290, headed toward Northborough. Their motel room in Hudson was just to the north as Daniella's car hummed along with the two dogs in the back seat. Their heads rested near the half-open windows as they sniffed their way across Central Mass. Tree had been glad to see his owner emerge from the police barracks. Now he was content.

"No news on the Dr. Sumner front means we need some indication that whoever is behind all of this is having a meeting. We need to get a wider net out so we can stop the next shooter. We missed that guy in Newark," Jack said.

"We did hear Dr. Sumner discussing that on her phone. I got the impression that wasn't one her little group had sent. From the one-sided conversation I think it was a copycat."

"I was afraid of that. Put as much news coverage out there as these school shootings generate and every crack pot will want to join in the contest of who can kill the most. It's sick."

"It's the weekend coming up. Maybe you should pay a return visit to our dear doctor's office and bug her phone. Then we can hear both sides of any conversation," Misty offered.

* * *

Jack pulled Daniella's car into the parking lot and turned off the engine. The two women climbed out of the car with the two dogs right behind them. They snapped leashes on and proceeded to walk the dogs toward Walden Pond. Jack stood by the car with New York tags on it. He was expecting someone.

Jack had received a call the day before and set up this meeting for Sunday. Walden Pond State Park was chosen as a convenient spot midway between Hudson and Boston. No mention was made of the content for the meeting, but since it had been Lamarcus calling for a meet, Jack assumed it concerned the case.

Jack observed a car pull in and he noticed the Rhode Island plates on the front. He didn't pay the driver any more notice. When the six New England states as well as New York State were all less than a two hour drive, random out-of-state plates didn't raise much suspicion.

Jack studied the next cars as they entered the parking lot as he leaned nonchalantly on the front fender of Daniella's car waiting. Suddenly a hand jabbed him in the back. Jack jumped in reaction and twisted to see who had snuck up behind him. After his run-in with the Chicago abductors, he was extra jumpy.

"Ha ha ha. You're losing your edge Corporal Wesley."

Jack's mind flashed through ancient history to place the now-aged face to the voice. His memory was failing him until Lamarcus stepped out from some trees behind his antagonist. Then it all registered.

"Sal, you old son of a swab. What the hell are you doing with old Corporal Lewis here? I thought you were down in North Carolina. Couldn't drag yourself away from Camp Lejeune." As soon as he had said it, he saw the pain in Sal's face. It was a pain from both his loss of the Corps and the loss of a fight with life.

Sal reached into his pocket and pulled out a prescription bottle. He unscrewed the cap and flipped two tablets into his hand. He threw them into his mouth and swallowed hard, waiting for their numbing effect to take hold.

Lamarcus walked up to his old friend and offered him some water from a bottle. Sal took a long swig. "Let's walk," Lamarcus said.

The three veterans headed for the pond and found a secluded spot with a park bench overlooking the water. Trees dappled the water with shade and kept the three men out of the direct sun. It was a pleasant place to discuss unpleasant business.

"Sal called me last week when he saw me on the news on that school shooting. Or non-school shooting thanks to you," Lamarcus said, looking at Jack. "If you hadn't dug up this whole thing, who knows how many kids would now be dead in Lancaster?"

"Yeah, but we missed that one in Newark. And who knows what they have planned next? School is almost out so they have all summer to plan a big surprise for the fall," Jack said.

"Look Jack, Lamarcus has filled me in on what you two are up against. I think you need a good squad leader on this. You know, you two guys were always skipping out on details that required hard work. I could never find you when I needed something done," Sal said.

Sal had been their sergeant when they were the squad's sniper team. Jack bristled at the sergeant's implication that he was a slacker. "Ah, that's not how I remember it. Seems like a certain Corporal Lewis was the one . . ."

Lamarcus interrupted his old partner, "That's an old story, told too many times to repeat now. What do we know about our target now?"

"Well, I've been busy this weekend and we should have better intel coming our way on Tuesday. I wish I could get into her Boston office but I'm afraid their security is a little more sophisticated than out in Harvard. We'll just have to hope that she uses her phone to set something up. If we can find out where and when the whole group meets, we can be ready for them," Jack said.

"And I want to be there when they do. Any bastards doing this to my country need to be dealt with harshly," Sal interjected.

"Sal, we talked about that," Lamarcus said. "With your condition, it's just not feasible. We may need to move fast and hard and you're just not up to it."

Jack looked at his old partner and then at Sal. He'd seen the pain register and watched the sergeant pop some pills. Beyond that, he was clueless.

"Corporal Lewis, as we have discussed, this is one mission where you won't be leaving me behind. You got that?" Sal tried to impose his former rank on his friend.

"Sal, I'm in the dark here," Jack said.

Lamarcus filled him in on Sal's condition. As they were talking they didn't notice the three women walk up behind them.

Lamarcus finished describing Sal's terminal condition when Misty spoke, "We've been talking to Sal's sister. We met over there while we were all sitting watching you boys argue. We introduced ourselves when it was obvious that we were all watching you intently. We say Sal goes."

Sal's sister added, "I don't know the details and I think I don't want to know. But my brother has one more mission in him for the Corps. Let him go out as the warrior he has always been, please."

The five others all remained mute at the request. Jack was the first to break the silence.

"Sergeant Salvatore Pelayo, report for duty. Your squad needs you."

The dying sergeant perked up at the command and sat up at attention. "It's a pleasure to serve," he responded.

Chapter 21

Boston, Massachusetts

Darren Honeyman, Director of ENOUGH, lay in bed looking out his window at the river. With a third story apartment on Back Street in the Back Bay, he had a commanding view of the Charles River Basin. Already sailboats were tacking back and forth as the Sunday morning flotilla went about their summer regatta series.

It seemed that the sailboat races never ended. With MIT and Harvard University having boat houses along the river, they were constantly engaged in either rowing competitions or sailboat races. Along with Boston University and Northeastern University, the Charles River attracted all sorts of students and professors bent on relaxing. Add in the other hundred colleges and universities in the greater Boston area, and beautiful Sundays in the summer were a bee hive of activity.

But Darren was more intent on just relaxing. It had been a busy six days and he had pushed the staff at ENOUGH hard to get as much mileage out of the Newark school shooting as possible. Summer break was upon them and the kids would be safe for a while.

But Newark combined with the New York tragedy was sufficient to get some action out of a number of state legislators before they disappeared for summer holidays. Already Colorado had continued its slide into becoming an anti-gun state. Darren had recognized Colorado's action after the Connecticut school shooting as monumental.

As the first western state to enact strict gun control measures, Colorado would hopefully be the wedge that would force the other states to act. Everyone knew the northeastern states were anti-gun, along with California.

The South was hopeless and Darren recognized the futility of getting those rednecks to put any restrictions on guns. He would have to wait until the Federal government finally acted. And with Colorado tipping the scales toward more control, other states would finally force action at a national level.

Minnesota and Iowa had introduced measures similar to Colorado's and reports showed their passage seemed certain. Iowa surprisingly had joined in the exodus from the gun culture along with Florida. With those four states on board, Darren felt the weight of political pressure would move the Federal government to act.

Actually, it was the House of Representatives that was the hold up. The U.S. Senate was firmly in control by the gun control crowd. It was the House that had blocked any type of action against guns. The pro 2nd Amendment crowd and their allies were bent on stopping anything related to tighter gun control.

Darren continued to debate policy matters in his brain when he felt a surge of energy hit his lower body. As the sheets rustled slightly, a mouth found the right mark and began to entice him to activity. He rolled his eyes back as the sensations increased over his entire body.

He reached out and ran his hand up the leg of his antagonist. She parted her legs as his hand reached its target. The reaction resulted in more sensation streaking through his body.

Ever since he had met Elizabeth Jamison, this had been his diversion. She was insatiable. Whoever had taught her the ways to excite and satisfy a male had done a magnificent job. Her skills at love-making were only surpassed by her tight athletic body.

Once Darren had removed her rather mundane dress, he had discovered the gem that had been hidden beneath. *Why did these earth muffins all want to dress like they were frontier women crossing the Oregon Trail?* he thought. While some of his female employees dressed in revealing Lycra tights and skimpy tops, most wore what seemed like sack cloth, long dresses or big baggy cargo pants. *And the tops, they were nothing short of hideous*.

But Elizabeth had discarded all that for a more bourgeois look. And once she had left the earth muffin realm behind, Darren felt like he could assign her more and more responsible tasks.

Not only was she a master in bed, but her organizational skills were top notch. That she could take over each task he had assigned her with such energy amazed Darren considering how she spent her evenings. There were mornings he could barely crawl out of bed from her tender attentions the previous night.

Maybe it's the redhead thing after all, he wondered. Darren had never been with a redhead before. At least he couldn't recall a redhead in his past. But if they were all like this one, their reputations would be safe. And he could attest that she was a natural redhead since his face had been close enough to see any deviation.

As the two fell back on the bed exhausted from their Sunday morning tryst, Darren drifted off. When he fully awoke, breakfast was arriving on a tray. Elizabeth placed the tray on the bed and climbed in naked. Her breasts shook as she crawled up beside Darren where he sat against the pillows. She placed the tray over his lap and sat cross legged to eat.

Jesus, does this woman ever stop? he thought. *She's sitting there with everything hanging open for all the world to see. Unless someone is across the river with a telescope, I'm the only recipient of Elizabeth's exhibition.*

When they finished breakfast she placed the tray out of the way. Leaning into her bed mate she whispered in his ear, her breasts hanging down and rubbing on his arm. She swung one leg over his lower body and lowered herself down to meet his. She rotated her hips slowly as she talked.

"Maybe we should pack a picnic and go out in the country. I bet you'd love some attention out in the fresh air."

Darren could only mumble in response. His manhood had risen to the occasion and she gyrated her body to stimulate more. He finally slapped her bottom to get her to behave.

"If we're heading out, then we need to get dressed and moving," he said. He shocked himself as he said it. *That is the first time I've ever pushed away someone who was definitely looking to get it,* he thought. His age difference suddenly hit him. *Am I getting to old for all this?*

As they drove north on Route 3 toward New Hampshire, Elizabeth reached over to keep Darren focused on their mission. He almost side swiped a pick-up truck pulling a boat when her hand ran up his leg. He pulled back into his lane.

"Jesus, stop that. We could have run off the road with you doing that."

"Doing what? You mean this?" Elizabeth redoubled her efforts in his groin area. Darren swerved into the next lane at the distraction. Luckily no one was immediately beside them but he received a horn blast from the driver he had cut off.

"Cut it out," he admonished her.

"I don't think you'd like me to do that. No cutting here. But you need to get to that spot you mentioned or I might have to bite something off." The mischievous smile told Darren her intentions. He pulled into the passing lane and floored the Subaru Forester to make time. He had to get this woman satisfied or she'd never leave him alone.

Finding the secluded spot on a lake that he had discovered many women ago, they quickly hiked into his favorite seduction spot and stripped naked. Darren barely had time to spread out a blanket before Elizabeth attached herself to him. He dropped onto his knees as the two wrestled for position.

Afterward, they lay quiet looking up at the trees overhead. Darren brushed the perspiration off his forehead. It was a warm afternoon and like most New England summer days, humid. Elizabeth suddenly stood up and announced she needed a swim to cool off. She walked carefully over to the lake edge and stepped into the cool water.

Darren sat up and watched her back side as she stepped slowly into the water. When she was hip deep, she dropped under. She burst to the surface with a scream. He quickly looked around for intruders. The spot on the lake was secluded, but there were others that would be using the lake. He didn't need any people investigating loud screams in the uninhabited cove.

He stood and walked out to join Elizabeth. The two embraced and tipped over. Clinging to each other under water, the couple explored each other's cold skin. Floating to the surface, they kissed a long tender kiss.

"Darren, when we first got together, you asked me if I had done much outdoor stuff at Dartmouth. Did you have something in mind?" her smile showed her inquisitiveness.

"I used to get out a lot before I became ENOUGH Director. I miss it. I've been thinking I need to get back out there, that's all," he said.

"Well, most of the state legislatures are leaving for their summer breaks. Why can't we get away. You've been going day and night trying to get answers to all these school shootings. You need to go out and get reenergized."

"I know. I feel so much better after I've been out doing something physical," he said. He wished he hadn't because Elizabeth immediately took it as a challenge. She reached down and coaxed a reluctant Darren back into action. They found a large rock by shore and carried on their outdoor fling.

Again satiated, the two returned to their blanket. Darren tried to continue his discussion, "As I was saying, I need to make plans to do something. Maybe hike the Long Trail." The reference to the trail that ran the length of Vermont's Green Mountains perked his companion right up.

"I've hiked parts of it, but never the entire length. Can you take that much time off?" she asked. "A shorter hike but more spectacular would be from Franconia Notch to Mt. Washington. You get the high country with the magnificent views. The Long Trail is in the trees most of the way."

"Yeah, that sounds better. I've hiked the Franconia section, but I've never done the Presidential Range. I can definitely get the time off for that," he said.

Elizabeth waited beside him in silence. He hadn't offered a spot to her on his adventure. Darren felt her body pull closer looking for an invite. *There are other work plans coming up about the same time*, he thought. *I could combine both, go hiking and then attend my meeting. They're both in New Hampshire he thought. But what about Elizabeth? She isn't privy to the meeting and I've never taken anyone with me before.*

"Would you like to join me?" he finally asked, deciding to take the chance. She was turning out to be a good worker at ENOUGH and it might be critical that someone else at the organization knew the scope of its operation. *I'm not getting any younger,* he thought. *And this woman has the energy level of five people. Maybe I'll make her my assistant.*

Elizabeth's answer came in the way of a kiss. She rubbed her body vigorously against his. *I just hope I can last hiking each day and who knows what each night,* he thought. *I can only imagine what's she like after a couple of days in the outdoors to be energized. Dartmouth sure must be missing her.*

* * *

Jack held tight on the two dog leashes as he walked along the old railroad right-of-way. Starting not far from their motel, the rail to trail led out of Hudson heading east. The long-abandoned rail line attested to the changing dynamics of New England.

The old mills that had left long ago were soon followed by the railroads that had serviced them. Now New England enjoyed the recreational potential that the old rail beds offered. All over the six states, towns and cities opened up trails for the local population. And like the now-familiar faces he saw each morning, Jack was one of the converts.

Tree and Jackie fought their restraints as they sniffed their way from Hudson to Maynard. The two-hour walk they took each day gave them plenty of ground to discover the other dog purveyors of the open trail. Jack just enjoyed the fine New England weather if not the insect count.

But the black flies had died off and the mosquitoes were mostly a torment in the evening. By the cool morning sun, an occasional deer fly was the biggest nuisance. Tree snapped at one as it buzzed around the dogs. Jack was impressed at how frequent his Airedale would successfully catch one. *Must be deer flies in England* he thought. *Its in the dog's gene pool.*

He had trained Tree in many things but capturing and killing insects hadn't been one of them. Coventry, as Jack's daughter called him, had attended obedience school after his daughter had followed his ex-wife to Colorado. Alone with his son Carl, he had searched for things to do with his son. Dog training had been his choice for the two of them. Carl had chosen Taekwondo.

In the end, he and Carl had reestablished a bond that had been missing due to Jack's police work. While each of them worked their way up to black belt standing in the martial art, Tree had become a very accomplished guard dog. He could take non-verbal commands and had distinguished himself many times in tight situations.

But today, Jack was letting the women do the heavy lifting. He was still recovering from his run-in with disrespecting black culture. Or at least the gang banger culture.

The kicks and punches he had received from his captors were still sore. Misty had discovered how sore he was when they were together that first night. Her advances were announced with cries of pain as Jack had asked politely for a rain check. Misty felt bad and had been an angel administering comfort to Jack ever since.

She was now ensconced in a hot white windowless Ford van listening to the bugs he had planted in Dr. Sumner's office. Daniella was close by working the gravel truck driver crowd and bringing home huge tips. Jack was afraid he might lose Daniella as she became the object of desire to numerous Italian truck drivers.

Hopefully we get news soon Jack thought. His disposable cell phone in his shorts pocket waited for Misty's call. It was Tuesday and Dr. Sumner's Harvard office day. Misty had called earlier to announce that the doc was conducting office hours today. He had been afraid that she might head out on vacation after her botched Lancaster school shooting.

He pulled hard on the two leashes to get the reluctant dogs to move past one decidedly aromatic spot on the trail. *At least aromatic to dog sniffers*, he thought. *To us humans, its was just another bush along the trail. Must be some old arthritic dog with a bladder infection to gain that much interest from these two.*

Jack's cell phone rang and he pulled it from his pocket. He flipped it open to Misty's voice on the line.

"Jack here." Before he could get another word out, Misty took off.

"Jack, we hit it. We've got time and place. And it sounds like the main man will be there. We can bag the whole crowd in one spot."

She hung up just as quickly. He never got to ask a single question. He would be in the dark until Daniella and Misty returned from Harvard that evening.

Jack turned the dogs around and headed back toward Hudson. Today would be a shorter walk as he suddenly had work to do. The second list of items he had sought from Lamarcus needed filling now, the list that Lamarcus had balked at. The list of things that could get him thrown into a Massachusetts prison for a long while. And after driving by Concord State Prison on Route 2 numerous times over the last few weeks, he had decided he would avoid such incarceration.

But the bad guys had to be stopped. And if it meant the good guys risked prison for their action, so be it, he thought.

Chapter 22

Mt. Washington, New Hampshire

The hut shook from the wind as the tired hikers lay in their bunks. It would be a long night as the noise from the intense weather outside mingled with the snores of those who could sleep through the racket.

Elizabeth rolled over in her bunk and bumped into Darren. The two had been hiking for four days now and had arrived at Lake of the Clouds Hut below the summit of Mt. Washington late in the afternoon. The weather had been miserable, sideways rain lashing them as they emerged from the forest.

Located above tree line, the hiker's hut was about one thousand feet below the summit of 6,288' Mt. Washington. As the highest point in New England, Mt. Washington was more noted as the windiest spot on earth.

With a weather observatory cabled down onto the top of the mountain, the highest wind speed ever recorded on Earth took place on April 12, 1934. While tonight's wind didn't match the 231 mph wind of long ago, Elizabeth felt as if the cabin they were in was about to join the other debris that had whistled by them as they reached the safety of the hut.

Shedding their rain gear, the couple had joined the other hikers eating and drinking in relative warmth. The wind had increased through the evening and it took the hut staff's assurance that the building would survive and that sleep was possible.

Now she was glad of the distraction. The communal sleeping arrangements meant the open bunks two levels high were packed with hikers. She and Darren had grabbed an end spot on the upper level. Another couple had grabbed the two bunks immediately to the side of them.

The snoring and other body noises were drowned out by the wind battering the side of the hut. Whistling caused by obstructions on the building added to the eerie feeling in the low light of the room in which thirty people were packed.

"Are you awake?" she whispered in Darren's ear.

"Yes, who could sleep through this?" he whispered back.

This was their first hut experience of their hike. The previous nights had been in the trees with the small tent they carried. It allowed privacy when needed and independence on where they spent each night.

But the Presidential Range of the White Mountains consisted of two days hiking above tree line. Camping in a tent wasn't even allowed in the fragile alpine habitat.

Communal living interrupted their non-stop sex romp through the White Mountains. It had been one spot after another as the two young hikers enjoyed daylight open-air exploits followed by close evening time in their tent. Elizabeth was certainly enjoying herself but noticed a certain lag in Darren's energy as they went. She was determined to keep him interested. *And I'm not letting this communal thing slow me down*, she thought.

She slid her hand into Darren's sleeping bag and ran it down over his stomach until it reached her target. He flinched at the intrusion.

"Elizabeth, what are you doing?" he whispered, a little high pitched. The man sleeping beside him rustled in his sleep. Elizabeth stopped her activity to make sure he remained asleep.

With a snore returning, she began her manipulation again. Darren moaned slightly at the action while she grabbed his hand and pulled it into her sleeping bag. Directing it down to its target, she gently pushed his hand where she desired it. He complied as his fingers stroked her.

As the two faced each other, their hands did their work. The snoring next door continued not two feet from Darren's back. Obtaining satisfaction, the two closed their eyes. Sleep came over them as the wind continued its determined attack on the hut.

By morning, the wind had abated and blue sky announced a grand day for hiking. Darren was a little slow getting out of bed as Elizabeth left him alone in the sleeping room and headed to breakfast. Hot oatmeal with raisins had been prepared by the hut staff and she sat down with the couple she and Darren had been next to in the night.

As she ate her breakfast she noticed the two eyeing her curiously. She tried to engage them with trail talk but they were decidedly cool toward joining. When Darren finally arrived with his oatmeal, the two excused themselves and quickly departed.

"What was that all about?" Darren asked.

Elizabeth leaned close and whispered, "Maybe they weren't totally asleep last night."

She watched as Darren grew red in embarrassment at their nighttime activity. Elizabeth just smiled.

"Just think, we have to stay in the Mt. Madison Springs Hut tonight. Maybe we'll get them as neighbors again. If they are, I'll try to be more energetic," she added.

After breakfast, they finished packing and headed out. The trail led up and over Mt. Washington. Darren was taken aback as he reached the summit to find a parking lot full of cars. The toll road built in 1861 took adventurous drivers up a winding road. As the hikers kept moving past the summit, the cog railroad to the top came into view.

"I knew it was touristy up here, but I had no idea," he said.

"Then let's get out on the range where the tourists don't go. There's a nice secluded spot behind Mt. Jefferson that has a view to die for."

Elizabeth didn't elaborate how many times she had been to this secluded spot and with whom. But the way Darren looked at her, she knew his imagination was working hard. They reached her favorite spot by noon time and dropped their packs. Pulling out water and food, they sat on a rock and took in the view.

The northern portion of New Hampshire lay at their feet as they stared toward Canada. Elizabeth pointed to the northeast toward Sugarloaf Mountain in Maine. The valley that held Conway, New Hampshire sat far below them.

As they strained to see the Town of Conway, Darren spotted two naked people just below their perch. He pointed them out to Elizabeth who dug in her pack for her small binoculars. Training her gaze in the direction that Darren was pointing, she gasped slightly and handed the binoculars to her hiking partner.

As he lifted them to his eyes, he stopped mid-breath, "Is that who I think it is?"

"Looks like Mr. and Mrs. High-and-mighty from this morning. They seemed upset about our nighttime activity but here they are, naked as jaybirds and going at it like rabbits," she said.

Elizabeth took the binoculars back from Darren and refocused on the couple. "Yep, that's definitely them. She looked much bustier this morning. Maybe it's the binoculars," she added.

They took turns sharing the binoculars as the naked couple continued their amorous hiking stop. It continued on as both Darren and Elizabeth pulled on wind shirts as they cooled down.

"We shouldn't be watching, should we?" Darren asked.

"Why not? They sure seemed put out by our romp last night. Oh look at that, I've never seen that done before. And in the mountains at that, I'm impressed."

Darren grabbed the binoculars away from Elizabeth and trained them on the couple. He whistled when he saw the acrobatic moves being performed. Suddenly he froze. The wind had carried his whistle the distance to where the couple was engrossed in non-hiking chores. The couple stopped in mid-movement and turned to where Darren and Elizabeth sat.

Darren put down the binoculars when he saw their faces turn toward him. The couple continued their gaze as Darren and Elizabeth quickly put their packs on and hiked off around the mountain.

"Well, that takes it. I miss out on any fun at my favorite spot," Elizabeth complained.

Darren kept quiet and moved a little faster down the ridge, the Mt. Madison Springs Hut coming into view tucked into the notch between Mt. Madison and Mt. Adams. They arrived earlier than planned for their night's lodging so the hut staff told them they could leave their packs and do a short hike near the cabin if they wanted.

Elizabeth jumped at the chance to get her daily session in spite of her interruption on Mt. Jefferson. Darren fell in dutifully behind her.

* * *

Lamarcus lifted the trunk lid to his sedan. He was meeting Jack at a quiet spot in Ayer, Massachusetts to exchange a few things. And he didn't want any prying eyes seeing the transaction. His career as a Cambridge Police Lieutenant was at risk as it was.

If what he was about to do got out, he would be joining Jack at Concord State Prison for the rest of his life. And he didn't relish missing out on his move to an oceanfront cabin in Maine when he landed his Captain slot on the force.

Sal had remained with Lamarcus after his sister headed back to Rhode Island. Lamarcus was now realizing how dicey it was having Sal on their investigation. The few days he had seen Sal convinced him that he was in a terrible way. Sal's cancer was advancing and all he could do was suck down pain killers.

Lamarcus would be passing off Sal as well as his car trunk contents to Jack. Maybe when he saw how sick Sal was, Jack would reconsider this whole adventure.

"I got what I could on the list. The rest is up to you. I've given you the best places to get it, but be careful, all of that stuff is dynamite here in this state," Lamarcus said.

He lifted a large case out of his trunk and carried it to the back of the waiting white Ford van. Except for his dog. Jack had arrived alone. Lamarcus flicked the latches holding the case shut and pulled back the lid to reveal the contents.

"Holy shit Lamarcus. When you said we could be sent away for life, you weren't kidding," Jack said.

Sal walked up behind the two former Marines and whistled. "Where did you get that? That's not standard U.S. issue even."

The three men stared down at a STG-44, the first assault rifle in the world. It had been developed by the Nazis in the early 1940s and entered service in 1944. Fully automatic, the rifle fired a 7.92 mm round from a 30 round magazine.

"This thing should be in a museum. It must be worth thousands," Sal added.

"Many thousands in fact. One of these guns in the news lately was estimated at $20,000. Some lady tried to turn it in at a gun buyback in Connecticut. Someone recognized the historical value of the gun and convinced her to seek out a museum for it."

"Well, it's worth twenty to life if I get caught with it. I'm assuming its not registered with the Feds," Jack said.

"Ah no. My daddy brought it back from the war along with a whole trunk full of memorabilia. We didn't even know the gun was in there. He kept the trunk locked in the attic and would only pull out the top stuff to show us kids. It was after he left home when we get to discover the things at the bottom," Lamarcus said.

"You never said anything about your father being in the war all those years we were together," Jack said.

"I was mad at him when I was in the Marines. My Momma was his second wife and he had me late in life. Alcohol caught up to him by then and he wasn't ever home. When he was, it wasn't pleasant. I'm sure he had Post-traumatic Stress Disorder all those years before they really knew what PTSD really was," Lamarcus said.

"So he fought in the war?" Sal asked. He knew that many 'colored' troops, as they were called then, had been in logistical support. Truck drivers and ammunition ship loaders seemed to be their main duties. But toward the end of the war, some black troops and airmen got into the fight.

"He was part of the 761st Tank Battalion. In fact, Kareem Abdul-Jabbar wrote a book about the outfit. Kareem's father was a sergeant in the unit with my daddy. It saw heavy fighting against the Germans during the Battle of the Bulge with Patton's Army."

"Well he knew how to pick war souvenirs. Why didn't you give this to a museum along with his other memorabilia?" Jack asked.

"What, in this state? There's a movement to remove any warlike artifacts from the museums around here. They'd sooner melt this down into scrap than display it to the public," Lamarcus said.

"Well, at the end of all this, I'd be glad to take your father's belongings to Wyoming. They have a veteran memorial museum in Laramie, the state Capital. I'm sure they'd be proud to display all of it and tell the story of your dad's outfit," Jack offered.

"A colored outfit getting a display in Wyoming, are you sure?"

"Listen, Wyoming along with other people out West don't care about your color as much as they care about your politics. If black folk went off to fight for their country, that suits Wyoming just fine, I guarantee it. They'd do your dad proud," Jack said.

"OK, it's agreed. If we live through this and aren't in jail, you can take my daddy's collection out

West," Lamarcus said. The two old friends shook on it then turned to face Sal. They suddenly realized that their other old friend wouldn't probably survive. Sal grabbed each of their hands and shook anyway.

Lamarcus held back his emotions as Jack closed the lid to the German gun.

"So, do you have any ammunition for this thing?" Jack finally asked.

Lamarcus was already carrying a large crate marked with the correct ammunition out of his trunk. He dropped it in the back of the van with a thud.

"You expecting World War 3? Must be two-thousand rounds in that thing," Jack said.

"Two thousand four hundred to be exact. Minus about one hundred rounds I fired last week to make sure this baby still worked," Lamarcus said.

"Obviously it still works. Cleaned and ready? Extra mags?" Jack asked.

"Would I leave a weapon any other way? And there's six magazines in the carry bag here, along with a modern red dot scope that fits. I had to finagle some to get a modern combat scope to fit on this thing, but it all works," Lamarcus said.

"Then we're set. Sal has his AR-15 and you're bringing your M-14. Plus side arms and knifes, we should be set," Jack said.

"We aren't involving the women in this, are we?" Sal asked.

"Misty volunteered to drive us to our insertion spot and pick us up after," Jack offered. "Daniella will be monitoring the police band and will pass on information as needed. We'll be in touch by headset and Misty will be on line. But no, they don't go in harm's way. They'll both bail at the first sign of trouble. We'll be on our own."

"Then we're set," Lamarcus said. "I'll meet you and Sal on site. I'll bring my boat in case we need it. Otherwise, we'll be at Wellington State Park next Monday night. That will give us two days head start before the meeting goes down."

The three men nodded their agreement. Jack and Sal loaded up in the white van as Lamarcus walked back to his car. He slammed the trunk closed as he watched his friends drive off. *Will I be a free man by this time next week?* Lamarcus thought. *Or will I be on my way to some hellhole prison in New Hampshire?* He decided that he hadn't done a good job shirking out of this one.

As he pulled out on the main highway he knew he would never have avoided this fight. He had taken an oath in the Marines. And though he was no longer with the Corps, one never really left it. He thought of Sal, clinging to life and still a jarhead to the end. *When they say Semper Fi, they really mean it,* he thought.

Chapter 23

Newfound Lake, New Hampshire

Darren pulled into the private drive leading to the house on the lake. A security guard manning the gate stepped out of his small building to check their identification. Darren buzzed the Subaru window down and the hot muggy air rolled into their air-conditioned compartment.

Elizabeth sat beside him still in her hiking shorts and boots. They had spent the last two days of their hike getting down off the Presidential Range. They knew they had some extra time built into their schedule and they took advantage of it by camping next to the Saco River.

At the lower elevation camped among the trees, they took advantage of the warm weather with a warm flowing river nearby. They had skipped clothes as they frolicked from the water to lay on the sandy beach lining the river bank.

Even the occasional boat floating by failed to deter them from their natural ways. If caught in a compromising position, they would stop and wait for the intruder to clear around the bend. Otherwise, it was two days of sex like nature intended. Long forgotten was the mystery couple high on the side of the mountain, although Darren and Elizabeth added the new position they had observed. At least they attempted several times to add it only to discover it was harder than it looked, and it had looked hard from afar.

Now they were arriving early for the scheduled meeting. Two days in a house on the lake to clean up, wash clothes and eat real food. All in the lap of luxury provided by ENOUGH's benefactor which included servants that came with the house.

The guard checked his sheet of invited guests and stopped. He looked up and lowered himself so he could see the woman in the passenger seat. Darren watched as he eyed the person who he knew wasn't on the list.

"Sir, I have no Elizabeth Jamison on my list. Is there an oversight that I wasn't informed about?" he asked.

"No oversight. I sent an updated request to Frederick. They obviously haven't gotten the new list to you," Daren answered. Frederick, Maryland was the home of the billionaire that financed ENOUGH along with his other various political organizations centered in Washington D. C.

"I'm sorry Mr. Honeyman. You know the rules. No one is admitted unless approved by Mr. Vlade himself."

"I know," Darren said as he switched off the car's engine. He retrieved his cell phone from its hiding spot in the car and dialed Frederick. Turning to Elizabeth he said, "This shouldn't take a minute. They'll send an email to our friend here and we'll be in. Wait till you see this place," he stopped as the party came on the phone. He spoke briefly and hung up.

In the guard shack an old dot-matrix printer announced itself as a new print-out zipped out line by line. The paper fed up at each line and the guard retreated into the shack to retrieve it. He soon returned and bent low.

"All set. Ms. Jamison is now official." The large gates swung open. "You know where to go. Have a nice day Mr. Honeyman."

Darren pulled the automatic shift into drive and nodded to the guard. As soon as the gate was open sufficiently for passage, he stomped on the gas. The Subaru sprung up the hill through a tree lined driveway. As the car climbed into the forest, all other signs of civilization disappeared, the few private homes near the entrance fading from sight.

By the time the car had traversed the one mile long driveway, the lake came into view. The driveway now descended through the forest to an open area holding a large house. Actually more a compound, the site held a large complex of buildings.

Located on the point jutting out into the lake, the main house was huge. Garages and servant quarters spread out from the house along with a tennis court and an indoor pool - everything that a billionaire and his guests could want.

Darren picked a spot for his Subaru. He knew he wouldn't need it until the end of the meeting and the two climbed out, Elizabeth in shock.

"This is something," Elizabeth said. "I've never been to a compound before. I could get used to this and I haven't even seen inside yet."

"Then don't linger. Let's go find our room, clean up and hit the lake. We can leave our dirty clothes by the door. They'll be taken care of," Darren said.

He was excited. He had never brought female companionship to any of the meetings and the women that did show up weren't his type. And there was always that Dr. Fisk who showed up early, too strident for any male.

But she wouldn't be here for this meeting, he thought. *She wasn't able to control her subject well enough and had paid the price with her own life. And then that idiot went out and muffed the whole job. Only a handful of people killed in New York*. They had hoped for the kind of job the copycat crazy had created in Newark. *Now that was bloody mayhem worthy of at least three or four states banning guns.*

* * *

244

Elizabeth climbed the steps up to the front door and felt her knee buckle slightly. She bent over and rubbed her joint and felt the twinge of pain shoot up her thigh causing her to wince.

Darren had seen her stumble and asked, "What is it? You look in pain."

"I jammed my knee coming down that steep trail from Mt. Madison. The long sit in the car tightened it up. I think I must have wrenched something."

"If you can make it to the room, I can get some ice for you," Darren said as he grabbed their small travel bags.

That would be great, Elizabeth thought. *I can ice in the room while Darren does whatever he was going to do.*

Carrying their gear upstairs to the bedroom wing of the sprawling house, Darren opened their door, revealing an immense suite overlooking Newfound Lake. Elizabeth hobbled over to a chair by the window and plopped down.

"Can you set out my bag right here beside me? I'll ice before I clean up."

Darren followed her instructions and then quickly disappeared into the bathroom. He took a shower and emerged in his nylon shorts.

"I'm heading to the lake for a swim. I'll have one of the servants bring the ice up."

As soon at the door closed behind him, Elizabeth dug into her bag and retrieved a concealed cell phone, immediately dialing a number.

"I'm in," she said when the call was answered. "The main guy will be here in two days." There was a pause in the conversation while she listened, then, "I'll be careful." She punched the button, ending the call. She sat back and waited for the ice to arrive.

Her plans were finally coming together for the answer she had sought so long ago. She pushed aside what she had had to do to get to this place. It was all worth it she told herself.

But she wasn't alone in her conversation. Unbeknownst to her was the fact that each of the bedrooms were monitored by Mr. Vlade's security. As a billionaire, he hadn't got to those riches by not using every means available to gain an advantage. Bugging his guest's rooms had offered plenty of information to persuade reluctant parties to comply with Vlade's desires.

A soft knock on the door announced her ice. "Yes, come in."

A male servant with a plastic bag of ice opened the bedroom door. A glass of ice water with lemon was on a tray in his other hand. He handed the water to Elizabeth while placing the ice on her injured knee. He adjusted the bag so it would balance itself while he asked politely if there was anything else she needed.

"No, I'm all set, thank you."

Alone again in the room, Elizabeth stared out the window as a flock of birds swooped by the window. Her knee grew numb from the cold while sun streaked in the south-facing windows. A door to a deck beckoned, so grabbing her drink and her ice pack, she hobbled out onto the deck. An umbrella over two seats made the perch a perfect spot to relax.

As she settled into her seat with her leg elevated, she placed the ice back on her knee. That's when she noticed it. What should have been going on below her on the lake was missing.

Where was Darren? she thought. *He said he was going swimming, but no one was in the water. Strange.*

* * *

"Night vision?"

"Check."

"Comm headsets?"

"Check."

"Sal, you got the headset?"

"You bet, boss. Misty, you with me?" Sal asked as he clicked his radio handset twice.

Misty's radio crackled as the signal came through. She looked up and smiled. Jack knew she was enjoying this adventure.

"OK, that checks out," Jack said. "I think we're set. Daniella, you know what you're assignment is, right?"

Daniella nodded. She knew her job was to monitor the police side ban radio for any sign that the team had been spotted. Misty would be ready to move in the white van to a spot closer to the compound if the radios didn't carry the distance to their cabin.

They had been lucky to find a waterfront cabin on Newfound Lake on short notice. When they discovered where the meeting was to take place, Misty had scrambled to locate a building they could work out of. A last-minute cancelation at the Hebron Bay RV Camp on the west side of Newfound Lake had fallen into their lap.

While not ideal due to the distance to the compound, at least it was located on the lakefront. Lamarcus had brought his fishing skiff so that they could enter the compound by water.

The team just had to await darkness. Lamarcus and Jack, the former Marine sniper team, would infiltrate and reconnoiter the compound. Sal would remain in the boat dressed as a fisherman to await their return. They would all remain in secure radio contact with each other for changes in the plan. They knew that the meeting was scheduled in two days, and they would be ready when the conspirators arrived.

Jack went to smearing camouflage grease on his face as Lamarcus rechecked his rifle. He pulled a sound suppressor out of his tactical bag and locked it onto his M-14.

"Lamarcus, where do you get that?" Jack asked of the suppressor. He knew that nothing could silence the sound made by the supersonic .308 caliber round that the M-14 fired, but with a suppressor, any enemy would have a difficult time seeing a muzzle flash or fixing on where the sound had originated from.

"Don't ask," was all Marcus offered.

An unlicensed machine gun and now an equally illegal sound suppressor. Jack stared at his friend in amazement. *For someone living in a state like Massachusetts, he sure had balls owning this stuff,* he thought. *Hell, even in Wyoming I'd be busted if they caught me.*

Lamarcus took the suppressor off and stowed it back in his tac bag. He shoved his rifle in beside it so that it would be less noticeable when they took to the boat.

The downside of the cabin they were in was that it had neighbors. Jack had noticed them perk up when three older men showed up the day before with two younger women. He had acted casual and had chitchatted about the fishing prospects found on Newfound Lake.

But he couldn't get over that they were being watched. *We'll see how they like our early morning fishing forays,* he thought.

Jack had walked by the compound the previous day with Tree. What had appeared to be a local out for exercise was the initial surveillance of their target.

Observing the obvious guard at the front gate, Jack had noticed video cameras strategically placed along the fence that surrounded the property. That information had tipped the decision for a water intrusion.

The water recon had not shown the level of security that the road had offered. Jack and Lamarcus had found a quiet cove just north of the main house that offered seclusion. *It might even be good for fishing,* he thought. *Sal will be anchored there so it might be good if he caught a fish or two.*

When the lights in the other cabins started going out, it was time for the crew to go to work. People in bed would offer fewer eyes to see what they were doing.

Lamarcus and Jack humped their gear down to the boat tied to the dock in front of the cabin. Stowing it under the seats, they untied the lines. Sal climbed in and hit the electric start. The outboard sprang to life as the lines were released and pulled into the boat.

The Boston Whaler slowly moved out from the dock and Jack pulled in the rubber bumpers. Sal hit the running lights as he increased speed across the lake.

The darkness kept the shoreline barely visible, more a change in texture rather than a clear definition of land. Sal maneuvered north on the lake as the large compound came into view. The lights from the house made the hillside bright and Jack could make out all the details.

Sal slowed so the two recon members could take in their target, keeping out of the range of the lights. While anyone inside the house would see their running lights, any details of the boat or anyone in it would be invisible.

Sal made a wide swing around the point that separated the main house from the cove they had chosen. He flipped the boat back around while killing the running lights and came back into the cove from the north. The outboard slowed to an idle as Sal nosed the boat into the cove.

Jack turned on his head-mounted night vision. As he scanned the shore line for human activity the night vision did its job. Seeing no one, Jack picked up the anchor and gently dropped it over the side. Sal killed the engine and let momentum carry the boat toward shore. While the anchor line played out, the boat drifted close to the land. Lamarcus lifted his leg over the side and lowered it into the water. He hit bottom and motioned to Jack who pulled the anchor rope tight. The Boston Whaler stopped.

Lamarcus grabbed the bow line and stepped onto the bottom. With water up to his knees, he slowly walked the line ashore, wrapping it around a tree and then walking it back to the boat. He tied it off on a cleat on the gunwale.

If there was trouble, Sal could easily untie and pull in the rope, all without getting out of the boat. Jack stepped out of the boat and followed Lamarcus to shore, each carrying their tactical bag of equipment.

Lamarcus had his night vision on his head as the two moved up the hill. They were headed toward the spot they had determined would offer the best spot for reconnoitering the house. They turned to see Sal donning his life jacket and placing his fishing hat on his head. A pole was brought out and a line went over the side as they continued their climb.

The main house lay in a leveled off spot in the center of the compound. A hill rose above the house to the north that was heavily wooded, making an ideal spot for observation. The two-member team chose a spot slightly to the northeast so that the front of the house was visible.

They spread out their gear and pulled out their camouflage net that would keep them concealed. Jack tried the radio headset to make sure they were in communication with the rest of the team.

"Red team in place," he said in a soft voice.

"Blue team set," was the response he received. *That would be Sal in the boat around the point,* Jack thought.

"Green team set," Jack heard, indicating that the two women in the cabin were within radio range.

Jack gave a tap to Lamarcus lying beside. He had just heard the same in his headset. Jack knew everyone was ready. It was time.

Chapter 24

Harvard, Massachusetts

Dr. Hillary Sumner rose at daybreak. She had to pack and run errands before heading to New Hampshire. She wasn't anxious to arrive early to the designated meeting.

Her work had been foiled by a lucky cop being present as her tormented patient had finally been motivated to act out. She had spent months finding the perfect candidate to manipulate. Then there were the months of turning the correct brain switches to get her demented person to respond at the right time.

Everything had worked perfectly to her design only to be foiled by a local cop waiting at the school for a gang member to arrive. At least that had been the story the police had presented at the news conference.

And Dr. Sumner had no other reason to believe any other motive had taken place. She had seen no sign of anyone snooping around her or her office. *But I'm glad for whatever happened that took those damn gravel trucks out of the town center,* she thought. *Those had been a nightmare, coming and going all day and idling as they got their coffee. But my patient had failed, miserably. They won't be happy with me even if I did everything I was supposed to. They don't accept failure well.*

After the New York shooting had only left five dead, the person on the phone had berated everyone on the job they were doing. She had been taken aback by the vitriol that their handler had thrown out.

I'd like to see him try to convince some troubled person to go into a school and shoot small children, she thought. *And then to live with the consequences afterward. Poor Dr. Fisk in Albany had found out how dangerous what we are doing was to the doctors.*

Dr. Sumner knew that this meeting would be entirely different than the previous meetings. Like Dr. Fisk, Hillary would typically arrive early to enjoy the compound before the others arrived. The two women had struck up a relationship that she looked forward to renewing at each gathering. While the others seemed to look on their time together as a distraction from the main goal, Hillary hadn't cared. She so enjoyed the time she spent with Dr. Fisk that she would have given up on their mission if Dr. Fisk had asked her too.

But Dr. Fisk had been one of the more strident ones and would never have abandoned the dream. An America without guns drew Dr. Fisk into the conspiracy and sustained her.

But without her partner to lean on for support, Hillary wasn't sure she would be able to withstand the scrutiny of the others as they second-guessed her failure. Dr. Sumner debated not showing but realized the type of people she had climbed in bed with. *They don't let you out, no matter what*, she thought.

To alleviate some of her loss, Hillary had contacted her counterpart in Rhode Island. That state had yet to join the list of school shooting sites and Hillary wondered if the doctor there would be ready in the fall. The Rhode Island doctor recognized the concern in Hillary's voice about the meeting due to the Massachusetts failure. She had offered to meet her in Harvard so they could ride together.

Hillary waited patiently at her home when she saw a car coming up her driveway with Rhode Island plates. She stepped out onto her front porch and waved. A woman parked her car and stepped out onto the gravel drive. She waved back at her colleague.

"Dr. Favreau, so good of you to offer to ride together," Hillary said.

"Fran, please. I could hear it in your voice, Hillary," Dr. Francis Favreau replied. "All that work for nothing. I had to be here for you."

"Thank you Fran," Hillary said as she gave her colleague a hug. She received a stronger one back, one that lingered longer than she anticipated. The two parted and looked at each other, neither one speaking.

After an awkward pause, Hillary said, "I guess we should load up. The Friday afternoon traffic will be its normal mess heading up Route 3."

"Yes, we should leave. We can talk in the car," Fran said. "There's so much I want to discuss with you. All that work and nothing to show for it. You must feel terrible."

Dr. Sumner bowed her head. She had wanted to avoid this when she had first contacted Dr. Favreau. Now it was already coming at her. The recriminations of failure on her part just wasn't fair. *How did I know that a cop would be waiting?* she thought.

Fran took her hand and squeezed it tight. She placed her other arm around Dr. Sumner's shoulder. "It's OK. You did your best. Look at Newark, it wasn't even part of our group. Some copycat did a better job than we have done. Don't worry, the momentum will carry us to our goal. Now, let's get going. We can take my car."

Hillary submitted to the offer and climbed into he passenger seat after loading her small bag. The meeting over the weekend didn't require much packing, different than when she had gone for a long weekend with Dr. Fisk.

* * *

"Hey you, old man. What do you think you're doing there?" a voice in the dark yelled.

Sal ignored the voice as he sat with his back to the shore, fishing pole in his hands.

"I'm talking to you stupid. You can't be here," the voice added.

Sal felt the line from the boat to the tree on shore go taut as the person on shore began to pull him. Sal turned to see a dark figure with a semi-automatic gun in one hand, his line in the other.

"Hey, leave my line alone. What are you trying to do?" Sal said.

"Get your attention you old coot. You can't be here. This is private property and they don't like strangers."

"Well, I'm fishing and these are the waters of the State of New Hampshire. They don't belong to any one person. I've fished here for years and you and whoever pays you can't make me leave. I know my rights," Sal threw back.

"Well, your rights stop at the waters edge. You can't have a line tied to shore, so untie right now," the security guard demanded.

"Boy, you're real neighborly, aren't you? One little rope on your damn tree is going to stop the world."

"Just untie now."

Sal untied the rope and pulled it in. The line snaked to the tree and then back to the boat as Sal coiled it neatly on the deck of the boat. "Satisfied, shithead?"

"What the hell you doing out here fishing anyway? Fish don't bite in the dark. It's three in the morning you old fool."

"Don't tell me how to fish and I won't tell you how to carry your machine gun, OK, dipshit." Sal retorted.

He saw the security guard pull a radio off his belt and talk into it. He knew that he was now on report to wherever the main security was located. Sal smiled as the guard slowly walked into the forest lining the shore. He double clicked his radio and received a double click in return. His team had heard the entire conversation and was acknowledging.

Sal listened to the whispered instructions. He stood up and reached for the anchor rope. As he began pulling in the anchor, he doubled over from the pain in his abdomen. He reached for his pain pills as he collapsed into the bottom of the Boston Whaler.

When the pain relievers finally knocked down the fire in his body, he retrieved the anchor and started the outboard. He was back at the cabin where Misty was waiting. When safely in the cabin, Misty acknowledged the message.

"Will Jack and Lamarcus be safe on site all day?" she asked.

"They know their work. If they don't want to be spotted, they won't be. Not by the minimum wage security guard I just dealt with," Sal replied.

"Then I suggest we take turns getting some sleep. We may have a wait before something happens. Sal, why don't you take first shift while Misty and I turn in," Daniella said.

"You girls get some sleep. Nothing is going to happen today. Mr. Big hasn't arrived," Sal said.

* * *

Lamarcus rolled to one side to urinate where he was lying. For a sniper concealment is everything. The daylight had forced the two-man team to remain in place to keep from being spotted. That meant normal bodily functions took place in spite of everything.

"Seems like old times, don't it?" Lamarcus said as he zipped up the plastic bag filled with urine and stowed it under a nearby log. He rolled back into position, his slight movement only noticeable to a fellow trained sniper, and an extremely lucky one at that. They were surrounded by trees and brush and with their camo covering, the two men were barely perceptible.

"Oh yeah. I really missed this. Laying on the ground with bugs crawling over you while I have to smell your piss all day. I don't know how I ever made it all these years," Jack said.

"What, and your piss doesn't stink? That what you going to tell me?"

"Not as bad as yours. Man, what have you been eating. You need to see a urologist or something. You never smelt that bad in the old days."

"Yeah, yeah. It's my prostrate. Here I am only 55 years old and my prostrate is acting up already. I can't believe it," Lamarcus said.

"It was all those places you put it over the years. I told you to be more discerning with your night time company. Now its coming back to bite you."

"Hey, when you're young you never think . . ." Lamarcus went silent at the sound of a branch cracking behind them. They had been whispering softly, but not that softly. The two waited and listened to see if the footsteps were coming their way.

Jack retrieved a small mirror from the upper pocket on his web gear and slid it carefully out from under their camouflage net. He turned it slowly to scan the scene behind them. *Nothing visible,* he thought. Then he caught a glimpse of movement. He touched his microphone switch twice to warn Lamarcus.

He stared as the security guard walked along the ridge about one hundred feet behind them. They had seen the well-worn trail along the ridge the night before and knew to avoid locating close by. Guards with little training tended to walk the same routes each time. It got the job done with as little energy expended as possible since the established trails would be free of obstacles.

A quality security detail would vary their patrol by time and location. Well-trained personnel would know to avoid any established trails and to randomly search the grounds. That would offer the best chance of catching any intruder.

But Jack and Lamarcus weren't ordinary intruders. Trained by some of the best combat veterans in the world, a Marine sniper team was among the elite. And Jack and Lamarcus had been experts in their craft for three years. The skills learned so long ago still came back to them as they waited for their searcher to pass.

Jack settled back down and put his mirror away. The two men knew that they needed to maintain good cover standards. They would remain silent and still the rest of the day so observations could be made to determine a plan of action.

As spotter, Lamarcus was on the spotting scope as cars began to arrive. Watching carefully, he would report to Jack on his findings. Jack had a small notebook out and recorded each arrival.

"Rhode Island plates. Two women. Oh lookie here, our friend Dr. Sumner has arrived. I'd like to be a fly on the wall at her reception," Lamarcus said.

Jack made a note of the two women. They had previously observed the couple that had arrived the day before. The woman was limping noticeably for some reason and the man had seemed distracted all day as the two lounged by the lake.

I think I'd be paying a lot more attention to a good-looker like her if I were you, Lamarcus thought. He and Jack quietly discussed what the couple's relationship was while they waited for more guests to arrive.

The two servants, a man and a woman, had been noted. *Obviously a couple that got to keep things ship shape at the compound in between visits. Nice work if you can get it,* Lamarcus thought. *Enjoy a nice big house on a lake and only put up with assholes a couple weeks of the year.*

Other cars arrived and Lamarcus noted their occupants. All were women as he surmised that the anti-gun cause was more powerful in female doctors than male doctors. *Ideology would run stronger in female psychiatrists,* he thought.

As nighttime settled over the lake, car lights could be seen approaching on the driveway. Jack and Lamarcus had their night vision monoculars strapped on, ready.

"Suburban, darkened windows. Can't see inside," Lamarcus reported.

263

The two waited for the vehicle to come to a stop. As the doors of the Suburban opened, three men stepped out. They scanned the area as one reached for a back door to open. He stepped aside as a man in a suit stepped down onto the driveway.

Two of the men escorted him into the entranceway of the house. The third man climbed back in the Suburban and drove it around the circular drive. He backed into a garage under one of the wings off the house and the garage door quickly shut behind it.

"Well, I think our Mr. Big has arrived. And those don't look like dime store security guards. I think the main event is about to start.

Chapter 25

Newfound Lake, New Hampshire

Darren Honeyman's blood pressure spiked when he heard the doors slam on the Suburban. Things were not going as planned and this new information wouldn't be well received. That he was responsible for risking it all was about to be discovered by someone who didn't accept failure well.

With his billions, he could command success, Darren thought. *My dream of a big payday for a job well done is slowly slipping away. Hell, it was quickly slipping away. What can I do to correct it?*

He waited on the outside deck overlooking the darkened lake for what fate would unload on him. He put down his drink and let the alcohol ease some of his torment. Knowing one drink would help him relax in spite of everything, Darren also knew more would only compound the problem.

He was alone with his thoughts when the first guard arrived. Right behind him came the man he was dreading. A second guard took up a position by the railing.

"Darren my boy, so good to see you again," Mr. Vlade said. He extended his arm and shook Darren's hand.

Maybe he doesn't know, Darren thought. *He knows, you stupid shit. He knows everything.* Darren collected himself and replied, "Mr. Vlade, so good to see you again. I'm sorry that Massachusetts didn't work out."

"To be expected my boy. Every event can't be guaranteed. That's why we have back-up plans," he said. "So, is everyone here?"

"I'm having them wait in their rooms. We have another issue to discuss first."

"Ms. Jamison. Yes, I've been informed." Vlade said. His demeanor took a recognizable turn. "Very sloppy of you, I'm afraid."

Darren watched as the third personal body guard arrived on the deck. He knew from past meetings that all three were former British-trained special forces now mercenaries working for the highest bidder. And Mr. Vlade paid extremely well for his safety. Darren knew that his boss received death threats routinely over his political stances and the money he threw at them. Darren also knew that the three guards were well-armed and highly trained.

Not like the four cheap guards Vlade kept around the compound when he wasn't here. One maintained the listening devices that had fortunately caught his assistant making brief but damaging statements. The other three were responsible for outside security. And now he was about to find out what resolution the boss would require for the intrusion.

"Have Ms. Jamison brought out here. It's such a pleasant evening I'd like to enjoy it," Mr. Vlade said.

Darren waited as one of the body guards disappeared into the house. The two men stared at the night as they awaited the man's return. *He's not talking. This isn't good,* Darren thought.

Soon a bound Elizabeth was brought out onto the deck and thrust into a chair. The guard stood over her with a knife handy.

Vlade looked at the knife and then back at Elizabeth. "I'm sure the knife isn't necessary. Do I have your guarantee that you won't scream or try to escape?"

"You have my nothing. What's the meaning of this?" Elizabeth strained at the plastic ties that held her wrists behind her back. "I thought I was a guest here. Is this the way you treat your guests?"

"If we have to. Especially, if they're here to do us harm," Vlade said. "Are you here to do us harm?"

"I don't know what you're talking about. Darren and I have been involved, you know physically, and he invited me to come with him to the lake," Elizabeth said.

Darren blanched as his name was mentioned. He looked at Mr. Vlade for a reaction.

"Yes, Darren was a bit sloppy in his invitation. But I'll deal with that later. First, I need to know who you called from your room yesterday?"

"I was just checking with some friends, is all. What's the big deal? Can't a person call from your house?" Elizabeth said.

"It depends who you call and what gets said. I'm afraid that we don't like spies coming to our little festivities."

"Well, if I'm not wanted, I'll just leave. Just undo my restraints and I'll get my things."

Vlade held up his hand at Elizabeth's' feigned attempt to stand and leave. "Not so fast my dear. You'd miss all the fun." Turning to his guard he said, "Take her back and lock her up. I've heard enough."

Elizabeth struggled as the guard grabbed her arm. She turned to plead, "Darren, are you going to let these thugs get away with this?"

The two men remained quiet until she was gone. Then Vlade focused in on his ENOUGH Director like a laser.

"OK, who is she and who is she working for? How much damage do we have here?" Vlade demanded.

"Mr. Vlade, I had no idea until they played the tape for me yesterday. If you knew what we had been doing you would never have guessed. No one could put out like that without having some feelings," Darren said.

"Yes, I'm sure your sex life was outstanding. I've gotten reports on your extracurricular activities on my money," Vlade said. "I've put them aside as the callings of an over-achieving male. But this one is different. We traced the call she made to a throw away phone somewhere in Maryland. Normal love interests don't use throw away cell phones."

Darren sat open-mouthed at the allegations. *How could Elizabeth have been such a passionate partner all this time and it was all to gain his confidence? It was all a lie to get in position to do what?* he thought. There was much to expose in their activities, but how much did she know? Not that what he thought mattered, it was appearing the issue was out of his hands.

"Darren, go get the others. We need to discuss next year's plans," Mr. Vlade said.

"Yes sir, Mr. Vlade. I want to apologize for any trouble I've caused. It won't happen again," Darren pleaded.

"I know it won't. Now, get the others."

Darren hustled off to get the seven psychiatrists. They had been asked to remain in their rooms until called and he moved fast to comply with Mr. Vlade's instruction.

* * *

"Are you getting all this?" Jack asked as he and Lamarcus looked intently at the receiver lying in front of them. Each had an earpiece in one ear, their secure handsetscommunications in the other.

Jack had crawled down in the early morning darkness and planted three bugs on the deck. Knowing that breaking into such a secure house would be difficult, he had hoped that with the warm evening air any meetings would take place on the deck.

And now that assumption was paying off as they had just listened to Vlade and Honeyman discussing this Jamison woman.

"Not sounding too good for this woman, does it?" Lamarcus asked.

"I'm not too sure I'd want to be in Darren's shoes either, from the sounds of it. Wait, they're talking."

Over the receiver they heard Vlade talk to one of the guards. By the night vision they could tell they had moved to the rail by the water. Luckily, that was right where Jack had placed one of the microphones.

"We need to close down this whole operation. We have too much exposure here," one voice said through the earpiece.

"Understood Sir," a second voice said. "Here or off site?"

"Here. I think a tragic accident is about to consume my vacation home. I'll collect the insurance and build something nicer," a voice spoke. Jack now knew the voice belonged to Vlade.

"And the caretakers, sir? I assume . . ."

"Expendable, I'm afraid, as well as the guards. I'll hire new ones," Vlade said. "I'll take Matt with me. You and James can handle it, I'm sure."

"Of course, sir. Now, you need to leave here while we get to work."

The quiet on the receiver indicated both men had left the deck area. Jack confirmed that the deck was now empty, as he scanned the house for activity but saw nothing. Soon, the garage door raised and a black Suburban drove straight out. It didn't stop as it headed up the hill toward the town road.

A few minutes later, Jack and Lamarcus saw the front guard trotting down the road toward the main house. Soon the two roving guards showed up at the front door as all three went inside.

"Jack, is what I'm thinking about to happen?"

"The rattlesnake den is about to be eliminated."

"What are we going to do? We can't let everyone in there die," Lamarcus said.

"Let's think for a minute. We're a little past ten now. They have about seven hours till dawn. I'm sure they'll want to be out of here by then. They'll want their boss a long way from here before they act."

"Shit, I don't know. Let's get Sal over here with the boat so he's ready. We may have to scoot fast ourselves."

"Good idea," Jack said as he switched his radio net to contact Sal. He got confirmation that he would be moving out within the minute.

The two snipers waited as the night progressed. They heard Sal in the Boston Whaler and imagined him tied up in the cove. No movement or sounds from the house stirred the quiet night air. By about four in the morning nothing had happened.

"Jack, we need to get down there. Things should be about to pop."

"Remember, there's five of them with guns that we know of, and two are very capable. You ready to storm into that?"

"Hell, I don't know. What else can. . ." Lamarcus was cut short by a terrific explosion. The house immediately went up in flames as parts of the building blew up into the air. As the two snatched their night vision monoculars off their heads from the bright flash, a succession of pops exploded behind them. They turned in the direction of the noises and witnessed a tree crashing down onto the driveway.

"What the hell is happening? What's behind us that's popping?" Lamarcus yelled over the commotion.

"They're blocking the driveway so the fire department can't get to the fire. Making sure all the evidence burns completely. But did those body guards disappear, I never saw them? They would have had to come right by us to set those charges on the driveway," Jack said.

"Prearranged. They covered their bases long ago in case this was needed, I'm afraid. We sat and let them cover it all up."

"We need to get out of here, now," Jack admonished his friend.

The two put their night vision back on and policed the area. They picked up any evidence of their being there and loaded up their bags. The two men quickly hiked across the point to a waiting Sal.

As they walked out to the boat, Lamarcus grabbed the shore line. He tossed his tactical bag in the boat and climbed in as Sal warmed up the engine. With Jack aboard, Sal put the boat in reverse and backed out into deeper water.

He hit forward and pushed the throttle forward. He left the running lights off as he swung wide around the roaring inferno that had once been the main compound. The light from the conflagration lit the night far out onto the lake.

Wiping the grease paint of their faces, the three saw the flashing lights of the fire department following the lake edge road as they responded to the fire. Jack knew with multiple trees to cut out of the way, they would arrive in time to water down the foundation.

Dejected at their lost opportunity at catching the conspirators, the three men unloaded the boat and disappeared into the cabin. The two women were waiting.

"What the hell happened? We heard the explosion from way over here," Misty asked.

Jack looked out the cabin window. He noticed all his neighbors were out in the early morning air watching the flames across the lake. He knew they had better make an appearance to ward off suspicion. Motioning everyone outside, he finally joined the others as the neighbors all gathered.

"Man, that's one big fire. Looks like the Malcolm Estate," someone said.

"What's the Malcolm Estate?" Jack asked. It was the first time he had heard the official name.

"The Malcolm's were an old family that had a house out on the point. They added on to it over the years. But when they died, all the kids fought over it and they had to end up selling it. Rumor has it some rich billionaire bought it. Never uses it though," one of the neighbors offered.

"Well, I'll be," Jack responded. "I hope no one was in there when it went up."

"There's the caretakers. Maybe they got out before it went up," the neighbor continued.

"Hope so. Nobody could survive that big a fire if they didn't," he offered in return.

Everyone watched as the flames slowly subsided. As Jack predicted, the flashing lights of the fire trucks finally announced their arrival to water down the foundation. By then the neighbors had returned to their cabins. Jack motioned everyone inside.

Daniella was the first to ask, "What do we do now?"

"Sit tight. We'll see what the day brings. But for now, we all need to get some sleep," Jack said.

Jack walked to his room with Misty right behind. Lamarcus and Sal stretched out on the two couches in the main room which left the second bedroom for Daniella. Jack started taking off his clothes when Misty came up behind him.

"I'm too tired to take a shower. I'm afraid I won't be good company tonight. If you want, I can sleep on the floor," he sagged at the nights events as his frustration overtook him. *We had been so close to capturing the whole lot of them,* he thought.

"That's OK Jack. Was there anyone in that house tonight?"

"Thirteen, I think. They were bad people, but they didn't deserve to die that way. And the poor caretakers. I'm sure they had no idea what those meetings were about. Just people thinking they had a great deal living in luxury at someone else's expenses," Jack said.

"My God, they were all killed?"

"We'll have to wait to and see," Jack said.

His estimate was off by one when the news hit the next day. The New Hampshire State Police were called in when one burnt body was discovered in the debris of the house. Soon, state forensic personnel were shifting through the ash and discovering all twelve bodies.

The three men continued to pretend to fish while the two women sat on the front porch pretending to read their books. To the neighbors, they were vacationing just like everyone else.

That evening they went out to the local diner. No decision had been made as to what they needed to do next and the meal was decidedly quiet, all five deep in thought.

Returning to their cabin after dinner, each knew that the morning would bring an end to their group. Daniella would return to New York and seek out new employment. Lamarcus would load up his boat and return to Cambridge and await his promotion to Captain.

Sal would return to his sister's house in Providence and await his death sentence. And Jack and Misty would return to their boat journey around the United States. They could be satisfied that they had stopped one known school attack and with the deaths of so many conspirators, who knew how many other tragedies had been averted?

Walking up to their cabin, a stranger stood from the Adirondack chair he had been occupying on the porch.

"Beautiful evening, isn't it folks?" the stranger said.

The five hesitated in returning the greeting until Jack offered, "Yes, it is a beautiful evening. Something we can help you with mister?"

The stranger stepped down off the porch and turned toward the lake. He stared a long time looking across the lake at the sight of the recent tragedy.

"Sure was a tragedy, all those people killed," he offered.

As the others acted sympathetic to the man's statement, Jack added, "It was a tragedy, that's for sure. Have you heard if they know what caused the fire yet?"

The stranger didn't answer. He just continued his gaze across the lake to the point. Lights were visible as the investigation continued to sift through the wreckage.

While the tension built at the non-response, Jack turned to get his party indoors. That's when the man finally answered.

"I think you know how it happened. Seeing as you and the black man were there and didn't do anything to stop it."

The group froze. The accusations hit home as all five looked at the stranger. *How did he know?* Jack thought. Jack looked at Lamarcus and by the size of his eyes knew the concern his partner suddenly had.

They all stared at the stranger in the dark before someone spoke.

The stranger looked around for any other people before speaking. Satisfied they were alone, he said, "I'm Bruce Jamison. It was my niece Elizabeth that you saw on the deck before the fire. Perhaps we might chat inside where we have some privacy."

Safely in the cabin and settled on the couches, Jack's group listened intently to Bruce as he explained. "I was watching from the hill opposite you. While you two were observing from north of the house, I was about 150 yards to the west. I had a clear view of the front of the house and the deck. I saw both of you infiltrate to your position and watched as one of you went down to the deck. I assume you were setting listening devices. Was I correct?"

Jack nodded his head without saying anything. Bruce continued, "I had night vision on the scene and saw everything. My niece came to me over a year ago with this wild idea of a conspiracy to take our Second Amendment rights away. I said she was crazy but the more she talked the more I became convinced. And as the school shootings continued, the pattern seemed to fit."

"But what got her on the trail in the first place?" Lamarcus asked.

"She never really said. But she asked for my help at being her outside protection. I'm retired military and since my brother died a few years back,

I've been stand-in for Elizabeth. I couldn't let her take on this whole thing by herself."

"So how far did she get in discovering the whole plot?" Jack asked.

"She was right at the point of putting it all together. I don't even want to know what she put herself through getting their confidence. She never asked me and I sure wouldn't have condoned any of it. But she is headstrong and couldn't be dissuaded."

"We're sorry for your loss, Mr. Jamison. I wish we could have done more to save her," Jack said.

The entire group hung their heads at the man's loss. Her quest for justice had ended in a fiery explosion. The room was quiet as each person reflected on the consequence of the fire.

Bruce broke the mood. "I don't think she's dead. I have a feeling she wasn't in the house when it went up."

Jack looked at Lamarcus. They had listened to Vlade and his security man discus the options and the woman's fate had never been mentioned. They had assumed that the fire consumed all the evidence. Now they were hearing a different theory.

Jack spoke first. "Bruce, we listened in on their talk on the deck. We heard them order Elizabeth locked in her room. What leads you to think she wasn't in the house?"

"I went out to the site and asked some questions. I volunteered to the authorities that I thought my niece had been staying at the house at the time. When I showed them my retired military ID, they offered some professional courtesy. Seems the State Medical Examiner was a veteran."

"But of all those bodies, unless they do DNA testing on you and each body, they couldn't know. And testing will take time. If she's still alive and with Vlade, we don't have much time to get her out," Jack offered.

"I know we're limited on time. But my niece wore a necklace with a locket on it. It was given to her by my brother and I know she would never take it off."

"And the forensic team hadn't found any locket?"

"None of the bodies found had any such thing. I believe they took her with them so they could work on getting information out of her. They needed more time that they didn't have here," Bruce said.

"But why come to us? We're just here at the lake fishing," Misty lied.

Jack and Lamarcus looked a little sheepish as she said it. Jack knew their cover had been blown and that Bruce had seen them staking out the house right before the fire.

"Hardly, ma'am. I think you were all chasing the same thing as my niece and I. Not sure who or what you are, but I'm guessing former military on you three." Bruce looked straight at Sal, Lamarcus and Jack.

Jack jumped in. "You talk of you and your niece. But we heard Vlade mention that she called a cell phone in Maryland. If you were here in New Hampshire, you couldn't be in Maryland taking the call at the same time. Who else is on your side?"

"I guess if we're going to come clean, we all come clean. I have an Army buddy down there. He's had the Vlade Estate under observation for some time. Keeps track of the big guy coming and going."

"So what did he report after the fire?" Jack asked.

"They must have traveled by jet as two hours after they left here a black windowed Suburban entered the estate. The windows were too dark to see anyone inside, I'm afraid."

"So, if your niece is alive, we could assume she's at the estate?" Jack offered.

"Vlade has many holdings in the D.C. area. She could be at any one of them. But his estate is the logical place for them to interrogate her. The place is very secure but we've never gotten close to plant anything so I can't tell you for sure."

"Well Bruce, if we are working on the same thing you are, what are you proposing?" Jack asked. He wasn't sure he was ready for the answer.

Chapter 26

Piedmont, Maryland

North and west of Washington D.C. holds the exclusive area for wealthy people tied to the Nation's Capital. While the suburbs of Virginia hold the communities of the upper middle class and their government-supported wealth, the truly rich settle in Maryland.

Whether it's the more liberal policies of the Maryland state government or the more refined inhabitants, the truly rich all gathered together outside the small community of Piedmont.

Once leaving the confines of the District of Columbia, each suburb grew richer the further out one went. While the close-in communities had the middle managers that kept the Federal government functioning, the next ring of towns held the upper crust.

Many had their stately homes in Georgetown for their use during the week. But they returned to their estates and their families on weekends. It was here among the grazing horses and long white fences that one's wealth stood out.

At least the Vlade estate would have stood out if one could have seen it from the road. From the air, the large mansion made its presence known. But the heavily wooded grounds and long circuitous driveway hid the entire estate from casual observation.

Inside, Mr. Vlade sat and admired his view across a small lake to the wooded grounds in the distance. His money had bought him the privacy he desired. His money also had bought him hired underlings to do his bidding.

As he sipped his coffee he contemplated the changes he was attempting to inflict on his adopted country. America had taken him in after his escape from Communist Bulgaria

Arriving with nothing, the next thirty years had seen his wealth grow as he used his considerable intellect to invest in winners. Soon he was manipulating the market to create his own winners. As his wealth attained massive stature, he learned that he could control entire events, often to his benefit.

But he felt that his adopted country was flawed. His sense of fair play shouted back at him that things needed to be changed. And he knew his life experiences offered a unique perspective on what needed to change.

While he supported many groups with his millions, his work on eliminating America's love of guns was the closest to his heart. He had seen the results of guns in the wrong hands as freedom-seeking Hungarians had battled Russian tanks. The results could have been predicted.

But where others saw the need for controls on government, Vlade came away with the opposite feeling. It wasn't the size of the government, it was who was in charge that mattered. And he knew just the person who needed to call the shots.

But first he needed to disarm the American public so there would be no proletariat revolt against the chosen one's rule. *Such nasty work these plebeians can be,* he thought. *Always yelling about individual rights. Didn't they know that they were lucky the government gave them any rights? The ingrates.*

Vlade was deep in thought about his next move when John, chief of security, entered his wood-paneled office.

"Mr. Vlade, I think the woman is ready to answer some questions."

"I do hope you didn't have to exact too much pain in the process?"

"Just the measured amount to get the job done," John said.

The two descended into the basement and opened the heavy steel door to one of the rooms. Sitting in a chair that was bolted to the floor was Elizabeth. Her wrists were handcuffed to the chair and hung down at her side. Her head drooped onto her chest while blood dripped down on her torn tank top.

James had been guarding her and walked over from the side as Mr. Vlade entered the room. At a nod from John, James pulled Elizabeth's head back by her red hair.

Vlade stopped at the sight. He had seen it before but he would never get used to it. The woman's face was bruised and bleeding. A cracked lip oozed red blood down her front onto her top. Her right eye was swollen shut and already the blue discoloration was setting in. But the other eye stared up at her tormentors, her mouth firmly clenched.

John asked first, "You said you were ready to tell us who you're working for. Well, we're all here now as you wanted, so tell us."

Vlade waited at a safe distance in case the woman spit or did whatever trapped people could do. He had no desire to get blood and spittle on his expensive tailored Italian suit. He left the dirty work to his underlings.

But there was no answer forthcoming. James pulled harder on the woman's hair, stretching her neck back as she arched her back to compensate for the force. Vlade noticed her hands pull tight against the handcuffs as she squirmed at the discomfort. She still didn't answer.

James offered, "I'm sorry, sir. She was ready to talk just a minute ago. Maybe a little more persuasion will get her to open up."

"Yes, maybe some more persuasion will do the trick. I'll be in my study when she's ready." Vlade turned and left the room. As the door swung shut, he heard the first blow land and the scream from its target. The door latched tight and the screams faded.

All this pain is so unnecessary, Vlade thought. *Just tell us who your working for and you can die quickly.*

* * *

Misty drove the white van while Sal and Jack slept on the mattress on the floor in the back. Daniella rode shotgun as the four headed into Baltimore. Their exit onto I-70 west came up and they turned onto the highway that would lead them to Frederick.

They had all left Newfound Lake early in the morning before first light had even broken the horizon. Lamarcus had loaded up his boat and would join up with them as soon as he had checked in with his job at the Cambridge Police Department.

He would cover himself with the continuing investigation on the attempted Lancaster school shooting. The department was giving him wide latitude in carrying out the investigation. With the good publicity they were receiving after one of their own had stopped the crazed killer, the higher-ups weren't real concerned when Lamarcus said he had more work to do. Lamarcus would soon join the others as they laid out their plans to rescue the Jamison woman. That was, if she was on the Vlade Estate.

Bruce was also driving to Maryland to join in the rescue attempt and had called his local contact before they had left. No news or additional information kept the group in the dark.

Jack awoke when Sal rolled over and kneed him in the back. He rubbed his eyes at the intrusion and sat up.

"Someone stirring back there?" Misty asked.

"Where are we?"

"Just to the west of Baltimore. We should be in Piedmont in about an hour."

"No, we need to set up away from Piedmont. If what Bruce said about the place is true, we'll stand out like the proverbial sore thumb there."

Jack pulled the porta-potty over and sat on the lid between the two women. He scanned the road side signs for an innocuous exit of commercial establishments. Someplace that wouldn't notice a white van with out-of-sate plates lurking around.

"Take this exit," Jack ordered.

Misty hit the turn signal and slowed for the off ramp, the Ford van slowing. Ahead was a large strip mall of mixed shops and restaurants. Across the street was a business park of commercial buildings. Further down the street was a slew of gas stations and motels. Jack pointed at one of the off-brand motels and Misty swung into the parking lot.

"I'll call Lamarcus. He needs to stay at a different motel close by. We don't need a Bay State convention here. People might notice something," Jack said.

He knew that Bruce would be staying with his Army buddy. One of the agreements they had reached with Bruce was that they didn't want their identities known to anyone else. Jack wasn't sure what was about to happen, but he was damn sure the fewer people that knew, the better. Bruce would be middle man as Jack's team went about their business.

Not having eaten since leaving New Hampshire, they decided food was the first priority, except for Sal. Jack realized the man was suffering and made sure Sal got to his room. He helped Sal take his pain meds and promised that he would check on him as soon as they were back from eating.

"I'm worried about Sal," Daniella said at dinner. They all had seen the pain on Sal's face as they had helped him to his room. Each knew that his cancer was progressing fast and that he would be limited in what he could do.

"Me too," Misty offered. She had tried to talk Jack out of taking Sal with them back in New Hampshire. Better to send him home to Providence and a quiet bed at his sisters. But his loyalty to his old comrade was too strong. Sal would be part of the team, even if it meant his lying in a motel bed through the whole thing. He couldn't leave Sal out on this final mission.

"Sal is tougher than you think. He just needs some rest and he'll be back," Jack lied. He knew his friend was dying and there wasn't anything anyone could do about it. Jack just hoped if the situation was reversed that someone would let him go out with 'his boots on'.

Lamarcus arrived in the early evening and he and Jack readied themselves for their first reconnoiter. Jack had driven the roads around the estate earlier and had determined the best point to interdict the property. After studying the aerial photos of the land that Bruce had provided, they were ready.

Misty drove the van with three interlopers ready in the back. Jack's dog Tree would be accompanying them. Misty's dog Jackie sat in the passenger seat as Misty swung around a corner and came to a stop. The rural Maryland road was deserted. Heavy forest lined both sides with no signs of humans anywhere. With the large estates in the area, all the roads had stretches of emptiness in between gated driveways.

Jack, Lamarcus and Tree climbed out the side sliding door and quietly closed it. Misty slowly drove off, leaving the three standing there. Jack looked at the wrought iron fence and walked over to it. He scanned through his night vision monocular for any signs of security.

He assumed that with such a large estate that the entire perimeter wouldn't be scanned - too many cameras required for such coverage. The cameras would be closer in to their target.

Jack started to climb the fence as Lamarcus boosted his friend up. Carefully straddling the top of the fence and its metal spikes, Lamarcus threw their tactical gear bag up to Jack. Jack dropped the bag on the opposite side. Then Lamarcus picked up Tree and lifted him up to Jack. Jack pulled on a rope clipped into a small harness Tree wore. He lowered the dog onto the other side and climbed down. Lamarcus climbed his side of the fence as Jack reached through the fence and grabbed his boots as he climbed higher. Dropping on the inside, they scanned the way ahead.

"OK boy, you lead the way," Jack told his dog. He patted him on the back and gave him a slight motion forward. Tree walked carefully forward as Jack pulled his backpack on. Lamarcus slung their gear bag over his shoulder and fell in behind.

The two humans wore their camouflaged dark clothing with Jack's face blacked out. They had their secure radio link set and Misty would be monitoring it from a spot in the center of Piedmont that wouldn't attract much attention.

Jack spoke into his microphone to tell his team they were inside the compound. He knew Misty would use the throw away cell phone to keep Daniella and Bruce informed to their progress.

Once deep inside the trees, Lamarcus stopped and pulled two outfits from his kit. Jack took one and stepped into it. His legs covered, he thrust his arms in the sleeves and zipped up the front of the jump suit. A hood with a face mask finished their camouflage. Lamarcus pulled his suit on and placed the hood over his head.

Now covered entirely in their anti-thermal registering turkey suit, they would essentially be invisible to any thermal sights the opposition might have. These suits had been developed for the military to solve the problem of human body heat signature in night time operations. Jack just hoped they worked as advertised.

Suddenly Tree froze in position. Jack saw his dog go into alert mode and slipped down onto one knee next to his dog's head. With Lamarcus crouching behind him, Jack surveyed the area, but saw nothing. No sounds or smells registered to human senses.

But he watched Tree's nose twitch as the dog's nostrils registered something ahead. Jack waited while his dog made a decision. Tree turned ninety degrees to his left and began walking. Jack and Lamarcus fell in behind. Over his earpiece he heard, "What was it?"

Jack whispered back, "I don't know what he smelled, but something spooked him."

Knowing Misty would be privy to their progress from the short discussion, Jack wanted to keep the entire team focused After about two hundred yards walking, Tree stopped again, the two humans waiting for the canine's response. This time Tree turned back to their original heading and resumed the walk.

"What's he picking up?" Lamarcus asked.

"Hell if I know, but if he misses something, we'll know soon enough."

They could feel it more than see it as the lake appeared suddenly. Even with their night vision monocles the heavy forested property had kept the open area hidden to the last minute.

All three slipped down to the ground, crawling forward until the large mansion across the lake came into clear view. Lamarcus opened the tactical bag and pulled out a spotting scope. Jack pulled out a camouflaged ground cover and carefully pulled it over them. Even with the thermal suits on they still had to be careful with their human shaped outline. They were still visible to any nightscope using an enhanced light-imaging device.

"I've got eyes on the house," Lamarcus said. "Looks like our friend is in one of the rooms. Hold on, I'll focus better."

Jack waited for more news through his earpiece even though his friend lay right beside him. Keeping their voices low to avoid any audio detection system the estate might have, Jack patted his dog as Tree lay with them under the sheet.

"Yea, that's him. Mr. Big. Just sitting there."

Checking his watch, Jack said, "It's late for him to be up. Suppose he's waiting on something important?"

Jack knew that rich people didn't typically stay up into the wee hours of the morning. Not that he knew any rich people. He just assumed that people with more money than they knew what to do with could get a good night's sleep every night.

"Oh, we got some activity. The security guy we saw in New Hampshire just walked in. They're talking. Oops, they leaving. Something seems to have gotten his attention."

The three waited. The humans contemplated on what they had seen. The dog just enjoyed sniffing the night air.

As they lay and watched for Mr. Big's return, Tree's ears shifted and the dog turned his head slightly. Jack noticed the change in his watchdog and nudged Lamarcus. Both humans lifted slightly and scanned around with their night vision. Nothing was showing. But Tree continued his slight head adjustment to something coming their way.

Lamarcus pulled out his silenced .22 caliber semiautomatic pistol and readied himself. Jack studied his dog and waited for the threat to emerge. They didn't have long to wait.

Chapter 27

Piedmont, Maryland

"So, are you more willing to talk now? Please say yes so the pain can stop," Vlade said.

Seated in front of him was a battered woman with both eyes swollen shut, her upper lip puffed out in a grotesque manner. She forced one eye open and Vlade still saw the defiance in her stare back.

James pulled her upright and blood flowed down from multiple cuts on her face. The bruising on her right eye was greener now as the broken blood vessels oozed into the damaged tissue.

"Tell the man what he wants to hear, bitch." James pulled harder and Elizabeth squirmed from the pain. But no answer was forthcoming. The woman continued her defiant stare through one partially opened eye back at her tormentors. James slapped her hard across the face and her head jerked to the side.

"Enough you two. Obviously we have a true believer on our hands. Let her sit for the night. I'm tired. We'll try something different in the morning. If brute force won't work on you, maybe modern medicine will get different results," Vlade said.

"We can waterboard her," John offered.

"In due time. We will resort to those tricks if my doctor friend can't extract what we need. Sleep well tonight, tomorrows a new day."

Vlade left the room and the heavy steel door shut. But not before he heard John's radio announce that they might have an intruder on the grounds.

* * *

Jack and Lamarcus waited as the threat grew closer. Jack patted his dog to keep the low growl from giving their position away. Not sure how they had been spotted, someone was definitely coming closer.

Jack heard the slight snap of a branch on the ground of someone close. He lay tight to the ground. Assuming his adversary had similar night vision on, Jack reached into his vest pocket and pulled something out. He tapped his partner slightly and held the device up so he could see it.

Forewarned, Jack tripped the device and threw it toward where the intruder should be. As he and Lamarcus closed their eyes, a blinding flash exploded through the forest. Opening his eyes, Jack stood and rushed the place where the man should be.

Standing while holding his hands in front of his face was a security guard. Stunned by the flash, the man reeled from the pain in his eyes. Jack tackled him and wrenched his arm behind him. Lamarcus was right behind with a tie strip and pulled the guards other arm tight behind him. Securely trussed up, Jack pulled out duct tape and sealed the man's mouth.

The guard struggled on the ground until Lamarcus stuck the silenced pistol into the man's right eye. The guard froze as he squinted through his left eye at the threat. He remained motionless.

Jack swung around to see if the guard was alone or was working with others. Before he saw the answer, a shot rang out and Jack heard a bullet clip the branch above them. He and Lamarcus threw themselves flat on the ground as they swung behind the prone guard for cover. The pistol was aimed in the direction they thought the shot had come from.

Immediately, the captured guard's radio squawked to life as his partner announced intruders by the west side of the lake. Jack grabbed the radio and handed it to Lamarcus. Pulling his knife from the sheath on his calf, Jack crawled forward toward the voice on the radio. Tree crawled low beside him.

Jack swung off the straight line to where he thought the man was and came in from the side. He figured that as long as he couldn't see his adversary in his night vision his adversary couldn't see him. Jack relied on his extra sensitive smell detector crawling beside him. Tree knew where the threat was and led Jack around to a spot Jack figured was close enough.

"Put a couple over his head," Jack whispered to his partner.

Two quick shots popped and the rounds cut the branches in front of Jack. He saw the image of a gunman raise slightly before a louder retort answered Lamarcus's challenge. Giving himself away, Jack rose and sprinted as the man lowered himself back out of view.

The second guard twisted to his attacker and a wild shot rang out. Jack landed on the man as he grabbed the man's gun hand. Jack stuck his knife against the man's throat ending any resistance.

Informing Lamarcus that he had subdued the second threat, the two soon had the second security guard zip tied. Realizing Tree wasn't nearby, Jack looked around for the dog but saw nothing. He crawled back in the direction that he had attacked from.

Tree lay on his side panting hard. Jack felt over his body and found the wet spot. Tree had caught the stray round the second guard had fired wildly. A wound in his right front leg was bleeding and Tree winced and let out a yelp as Jack touched it.

"We've got a gunshot victim. Meet us at the extraction point," Jack said. He knew Misty was listening and would respond immediately.

"Jack, we don't have time. We don't know how many security are headed this way right now," Lamarcus said.

"I need to take care of him first," Jack said as he picked up Tree and started walking toward the fence line.

"OK, I'll circle around to the south and try and draw them that way. Meet up with me there."

Jack walked quickly back to the fence. Reaching the fence, Jack climbed and while straddling the top, lifted his dog up. Just as he was lowering him down onto the other side, Misty pulled up.

She unclipped Tree and hustled him into the van. She waved slightly as she drove off. Jack lowered himself back down inside the fence. Sprinting about one hundred feet back into the forest, the flashlight beams hit. A knock on the back of his head sent him reeling to the ground. Three men jumped on top of him and cuffed him.

"They've got me . . ." was all Jack said into his microphone before it was pulled off his head. A fist slammed into the side of his face just to get the point across.

* * *

Lamarcus heard the warning and knew that Jack was taken. He didn't respond as he knew the secure radio link was no longer secure.

They were all in now. There would be no turning back no matter if the Jamison woman was still alive of not. With Jack captured, his life would be counted in hours now.

Lamarcus sprinted south through the forest keeping plenty of cover between himself and the lake. As he ran, he slipped his silenced pistol into its holster on his combat vest. He reached in his bag and retrieved his father's war relic.

Pulling the Stg 44 over his head, he placed the automatic assault rifle's sling across his chest and pulled the bungee that would hold tight to his body. The machine gun nestled onto his body as he ran through the trees.

Nearing the south side of the house, Lamarcus slouched down on the edge of the forest. Ahead lay a large expanse of lawn before the main house. *Time to find out if this turkey suit really works,* Lamarcus thought

* * *

Misty had her receiving earpiece in and heard Jack's warning. Warned by both men to never talk over the net, they made sure that if someone was tapped into the network that Misty's presence on the outside was unknown.

She drove toward their motel room anguished over what she should do. Tree was lying beside her on the floor. His leg had been bandaged and the blood flow slowed. Luckily he had one eye open as he lay quiet, otherwise, she was afraid he had died.

Reaching the motel, she ran up to Daniella's room, but she wasn't there. Misty ran down the hall to Sal's room and knocked. Daniella opened the door and immediately saw Misty's panic.

"What, what is it? What's happened?"

Misty pushed her aside as Daniella closed the door. Misty stood next to a prostrate Sal as he sat up, wincing in pain.

"Report, I want a report right now," he barked.

Misty told Sal and Daniella of Jack being captured. Then she told them that Tree needed a vet right away.

Sal responded immediately. He reached into his bag and pulled out a Model 1911 Colt .45 Model. He racked the slide to make sure it was loaded and grabbed the van keys from Misty. "Daniella take care of the dog. Misty, you're with me."

Daniella grabbed the keys to Lamarcus's car and the three all headed down to the van. Tree was carefully placed in the car and Daniella headed to the front desk to find an animal hospital open. Sal swung the white van out of the parking lot as Misty waved at Daniella as they left.

* * *

As all good military plans soon fall into back-up mode at some point, Sal floored the gas and headed up the road toward Piedmont. Misty directed him to the estate as he kept the van just over the legal limit.

Sal marveled at how alive he felt. The pain almost gone, he was wide awake, the drug-induced stupor he had been living in just a memory. He took a corner too fast and the van jerked back into the main traffic lane. The twitch of pain in his side announced that everything hadn't totally disappeared.

Knowing he had to help his two friends, Sal thought through the best way to accomplish it. The two things he did know was the bad guys had to be defeated and that he was ready to accomplish it.

Misty passed on the information of the one security guard at the front gate as Sal turned off the main state highway. The rural road leading to the main gate of the estate wound past other gated estates and Sal's mind swirled with alternatives that he could do to help his friends. As he approached the gate house, he made up his mind.

He could see the guard sitting in the little house. A dim light provided visibility the guard would need to inspect any vehicle entering the compound. Sal didn't slow down to offer him a chance to examine anything.

Driving past the guard house he finally stopped at the secluded spot where Misty had dropped off Jack and Lamarcus. Sal moved to the back of the van as he explained to Misty what was about to happen.

Misty pulled slowly up to Vlade's security hut and stopped in front of the closed metal gates. The guard opened the door on the side of the hut and stepped out. A certain wariness showed at the late night guest. The guard looked Misty over carefully before speaking.

"Yes ma'am. What can I do for you?" the guard asked.

"Is this the Forsythe estate?" Misty asked.

"No, I don't know where the Forsythe place is. It sure isn't here. And what the hell kind of delivery happens at three in the morning?" The guard leaned closer to try and peer into the back of the van.

"Well, you're around rich people," Misty said, "When they want something, they want it right now."

"Ain't that the truth," the guard said.

Misty added female charm to the situation and the guard seemed to relax slightly. She jumped as Sal finally took out the guard with a blow on the back of his head from behind. The man collapsed to the ground beside the van.

"Took you long enough," Misty said.

"Sorry, I'm not moving as fast as I used to. Took me longer to get from the back door around behind him," Sal said.

He opened the side door and bent to lift the guard into the van. His pancreas screamed in pain from the effort and tears welled up in his eyes. Misty jumped down and helped lift the comatose man into the back. He was quickly zip tied to the side of the van and gagged. Sal hit the button to open the entrance gates and Misty pulled through. Pulling out his Colt after shutting the gates, Sal motioned Misty to jump in the passenger seat after telling he would drop her once the mansion came into view.

Chapter 28

Piedmont, Maryland

Lamarcus realized it was now or never if he was going to rescue his friend. Lifting himself he sprinted across the lawn holding his pistol in one hand as he went. Lacking any subtle way on entering the house, he crashed through the French doors that lead to the formal dining room.

He heard the alarm go off throughout the house and sprinted toward the room where he had previously seen Vlade. *If I can get my hands on him, I can use him as a hostage to get the security to back off,* he thought.

As he turned a corner in the main hallway, a guard came out from the foyer. Lamarcus lifted his pistol and shot him twice. The man crumpled to the floor. Lamarcus's radio from the first guard was cackling with traffic as security scrambled to deal with the threat.

Lamarcus had no idea how many guards a rich guy like Vlade would have, but he assumed there would be plenty. Locating the room he had seen earlier from across the lake he found it empty.

Hearing security announcing a white van approaching the mansion, Lamarcus knew he had to respond. He sprinted up the formal staircase and swung toward the front of the house. He reached a second story window in time to see the white van speeding up the driveway. It was still about two hundred yards off but closing fast.

Lamarcus pulled the French doors open and stepped out on the small balcony overlooking the front yard. In the residual light of the house, he made out four guards crouched behind the low brick walls of the landscaping.

He shoved his pistol into its holster and gripped his German machine gun. He lined up the first guard and paced out his planned sweep. He pulled the trigger and the Stg 44 came to life.

Taking out the first guard, he swung to a suddenly startled second guard. He collapsed in a heap. The third raised his weapon toward Lamarcus but not before he was cut down. The fourth actually got a shot off which broke the window in the door behind Lamarcus. He died as he stood.

The white van slammed on its brakes as the driver jumped out the driver's door. Lamarcus watched as the person rolled a somersault and landed on his stomach behind a large lawn feature. *That could only be a Marine dong that,* he thought. *Sal has come to the rescue.*

Shots rang out as Sal's lawn feature was hit. As pieces flew into the air, Lamarcus could see through his night vision two armed men to his left behind one of the Suburbans. The shots continued as they focused on the white van.

Lamarcus aimed at the Suburban, and with a new full clip in place, opened up. On about the tenth round of the full auto barrage, the Suburban's gas tank blew. Two men flew out of the fire ball and collapsed on the driveway.

Sal stood up and charged the mansion. Lamarcus could see his old sergeant carrying his service piece. A shot rang out followed by two more. Sal hit the grass and low crawled quickly up to a retaining wall for cover.

Lamarcus swiveled his head in the direction of the shots. A figure on a similar balcony off a first floor room held a rifle. Lamarcus swung his rifle around and trained on this new antagonist. Two shots caught the man's attention and he ducked back inside for cover.

Sal was back up and sprinted for the front door as Lamarcus raced back into the building. Stopping to check the hallway before entering, Lamarcus flew down the stairs, crossed the foyer and let his friend in the front door.

"Where the hell have you been? I've been waiting half the night for you to get your sorry ass here," Lamarcus said, a half smile on his face giving him away.

Sal grinned back. "Don't think I'd let you young fellas have all the fun. You can only keep an old jarhead down for so long."

They slid along the wall of the foyer when an armed guard appeared from around a corner. Sal had his Colt ready and shot him twice.

"About time you got that beast into action. Didn't they take all those away and give you those wimp-ass 9 mm?"

Sal threw back, "Not me brother, nothing like a .45 to knock someone down and keep him down. So, what's the plan? Where's Jack?"

* * *

Almost directly beneath the two Marines, Jack lay on the cold floor handcuffed to a chair. As he slowly regained consciousness from the blow he had received, he realized he wasn't alone. He moved and the handcuffs announced that he was attached to something. The something was immovable as he attempted to pull.

As he opened his eyes and found himself staring at a woman's leg, he shifted and saw a second leg. He looked up and saw a slumped woman in a chair above him. He sat up on the floor and reached up with his free hand. The woman stirred in protest to his touch

"Elizabeth?" he asked.

"Mrrrrr," was all the woman offered.

"Elizabeth, I'm a friend of Bruce's and I've come to help you."

The woman stirred more from her semi-comatose state. Jack saw her left eye open slightly and glance down at him. Both eyes were swollen badly and her face was a mess. Somebody had hit her a lot with their fists to cause the damage he saw.

Finally she mumbled, "How can you help? You're stuck in here with me."

"Have faith, the Marines are coming to the rescue."

A slight smile came over her battered mouth, or what looked to be a smile to Jack. It disappeared in a flash when the sound of the steel door opening announced the return of her tormentors.

"Ahh, you're awake. I haven't had the pleasure of meeting you, Mister . . ." Vlade said. He left the sentence to linger hoping that his captor would offer him something.

"Mr. 'I gonna shove it up your ass'."

"Tsk, tsk, such an attitude, whoever you are. And your friends outside. They will be soon joining you as they realize the futility of dealing with me. I'd love to call the cops on you but under the circumstances, you understand."

One of the security guards walked over and kicked Jack in the ribs. Jack pulled himself into a ball to protect his vitals.

Vlade ignored him and ordered, "Take them both. We'll move to the secure room until security handles those upstairs."

John and James each took one of the prisoners but not before James trussed Jack up so he could barely move. Elizabeth stumbled on her feet as John held her tight. Jack shuffled along in tiny steps as the five made their way down the mansion's basement hall.

They reached what looked to be a vault door and Vlade spun the combination lock. John pulled the heavy steel door open and Jack looked at the protruding security bolts on the door. *Whatever the secure room Vlade had talked about, if this was it, it would take an army to break in,* he thought.

John handcuffed Jack to a metal wall fixture and shoved him to the floor. Elizabeth was dropped beside him and locked to the metal bar. Vlade and his two guards went further into the room and sat down.

Jack looked around and noticed that the room had all one could want in a siege. A toilet room was just off the main room as well as a small kitchen. A pantry of food lay beside the toilet room. It appeared that the room was stocked for a long wait.

Looking at his attachment, Jack lifted his handcuffed hands and gently rattled them against the heavy steel bar. Both ends of the bar were firmly attached to the concrete wall with large bolts. He studied Elizabeth's restraints and found them equally secure. From their being moved to this room, Jack figured Lamarcus had made progress on the outside. *And Vlade had said 'friends'*, Jack thought.

Jack lay on the floor and spent the time conjuring up who might be the friends Vlade had mentioned. *Could Bruce and his ex-military friend be out there helping?* he thought. *Or Sal. Could Sal be healthy enough to campaign one last time?*

No sound penetrated to the inside of the vault which held only a mechanical sound as the air supply was refreshed. The three others in the room were busy chatting about something but were too far away for Jack to make out any details.

Jack's mind raced as to how to retrieve the situation. If extra security showed up, whoever was on his side would be overwhelmed. As he thought he stared at the woman beside him. She had gone through too much to have it end like this. He knew their lives where done as soon as Vlade thought he had the attack contained.

And if Vlade missed anyone, his money would buy the required number of lawyers and media time to explain it all away as terrorists bent on destroying a successful man. There were all sorts of anti-capitalists, whack jobs Vlade could hide behind. And even if the authorities got serious about him, a billion dollars buys a lot of lawyer time to tie it all up.

Meanwhile, millions would be passed quietly on to the political class to make all Vlade's troubles go away. So even if the truth came out, it would get lost in the media campaign to smear the truth-tellers. Before it was over, the public would loathe the whistle-blower and continue to hold Vlade as a great American.

Jack had to think of something. Someway to end it right here, right now. *Don't let Vlade get away with it,* Jack thought.

That's when Jack's eye caught it. Or at least a small part of it. The necklace and pendant her uncle had described. Elizabeth still had her father's gift around her neck. The security guys had failed to strip her of it. Jack smiled. They were about to pay a price for their oversight.

He reached over and checked the pendant. The woman stirred at his touch. He quietly gave her a, "Shhhh." to keep her quiet. She moaned slightly in return.

Jack ran the necklace around her neck until he reached the clasp. He carefully released the clasp and the necklace and pendant fell into his hand. He grabbed the pendant with his opposite hand and held it tight between two fingers.

Grasping the opening part of the pendant, he yanked on the small door. It came off in his fingers. He noticed a picture inside the pendant of two people, a man and a woman. *Her parents,* he thought.

With the broken portion of the pendant, he reached back toward the handcuff. *If I can get this into he key hole, maybe.*

From his days as a police detective, Jack knew that handcuffs had a simple lock mechanism. The key had to be fairly simple so various police agencies could undo an arrested perpetrator. Jack had even practiced during his police training on opening a set of cuffs with a paper clip. The instructor had wanted to demonstrate the vulnerability of handcuffs to make the point an officer shouldn't totally rely on them.

He worked the broken pendant into the lock mechanism and twisted the metal. The soft gold pendant bent at the pressure and Jack got nervous that the pendant wouldn't hold up.

Being more careful as he turned the pendant, he kept his fingers close to the lock opening. The more he supported the soft gold, the more resistance he got to unlock the cuffs..

With one final twist, his right hand came loose. He grabbed the metal cuff to keep it from clanking against anything and removed the cuff. Checking to see if anyone had noticed, the three men continued chatting. As he began work on releasing the second handcuff that held his left hand he heard a shuffle. Jack looked up to see the one named John stand up, announcing he had to take a leak.

Jack continued his work while John was in the toilet. As he was about to get a final twist out of the pendant, it broke. Part was in the keyhole, and part was in Jack's hand, the soft gold succumbing to Jack's abuse. He sat back and waited, but not before he carefully placed the cuff by the steel bar and placed his free wrist next to it. At a quick glance, no one could tell.

John came out of the toilet and walked toward the two prisoners. He didn't notice the changed circumstances of his prisoners until it was too late. Jack swung his leg in a sweeping motion and caught John's feet. John landed in a heap as Jack immediately smashed his one free hand with its improvised brass knuckle into John's temple. The one free handcuff although still locked on Jack's wrist, now acted as a lethal weapon as Jack slipped his hand into the metal device. It fit his hand much like a set of brass knuckles with similar results to John's consciousness.

The noise brought the other two men out of their seats, James pulling his semi-automatic pistol out of his shoulder holster as he rose. But Jack already had John's weapon out. He raised it and shot James, with the second shot catching James in the chin as he fell from the first. Blood splattered over Vlade as he recoiled in terror.

Jack held the gun on Vlade as he searched John's pockets for the key. Finding it, he freed himself and then released Elizabeth. As Jack stood up, he watched Vlade carefully, helping Elizabeth to her feet.

"OK Vlade, open the door," Jack said.

Silence. Vlade's defiance told Jack everything.

"Once more and once more only, open the door."

No response as Vlade crossed his arms in front of him.

Jack lowered John's weapon and shot Vlade in the upper leg. Vlade screamed in agony and collapsed on the floor.

"That looks pretty bad," Jack said. "I'd say I might have hit an artery or something. You probably have about fifteen minutes to reach a hospital."

Vlade squirmed in pain as he gripped his upper thigh, blood oozing out as he thrashed about. Jack took aim at his other leg.

"No, stop, I'll tell you." Vlade quickly listed the combination to exit the vaulted room. Jack helped Elizabeth over to the door and twisted the dial. The big door clicked as Jack spun the wheel releasing the locking bolts and pushed the door open.

"Don't leave me here," Vlade cried.

Jack ignored the man's pleas as he carried Elizabeth into the hallway. Jack found the stairs to the main floor and slowly opened the door into the foyer. He was met by a .45 shoved in his nose. Jack smiled when he saw Sal on the other end of the weapon. Lamarcus was standing guard close by.

"Lamarcus, we may have reinforcements arriving," Jack said as he placed Elizabeth onto the floor. Sal handed him a rifle.

"I took this off one of the guards. You can have it. I know where there's another one."

Sal returned with his own rifle taken from one of the guards. Jack instructed him to maintain duty on the main floor for any stray guards they had missed.

A quick search of the mansion located the security room on the main floor. Concealed behind the kitchen storeroom, Jack rounded up the lone figure. He was escorted back to the study that Lamarcus had first seen.

Jack and Lamarcus quickly located the two guards they had captured still tied up in the forest. Their friends had never gone and looked for them after capturing Jack. They were moved to the study overlooking the lake. All the other guards were checked and two more were found still alive.

With the security hut guard from the van added to the collection, seven security guards sat with Vlade in the study. Seated in the middle was Vlade with a tourniquet around his leg. Sal stood guard over him and an now-awake John.

The surviving security guards were handcuffed to the oak table and pushed into more side chairs. Sal took an empty chair and sat down opposite his charges. The strained look on his face told Jack everything. The adrenaline of battle was wearing off and the pain of terminal cancer was kicking in. Lamarcus motioned Jack out into the hallway.

"What now? We could have visitors anytime now. Whatever call that may have gone out for reinforcements may catch our asses here," Lamarcus asked.

"I know, we don't have much time. And I think the answer is fairly obvious, don't you? With the body count we've created, there's no going back. And with Vlade's billions, we'll be squashed like a bug."

"So what are you suggesting?"

"Go take over for Sal and send him out here," Jack said.

Chapter 29

Piedmont, Maryland

Daniella got the cell call on the throw away phone just before day break. She needed to drive Lamarcus's car to the extraction point right away.

The drive was quiet as she imagined what had transpired at the mansion. When she reached the small turnout in the road that they all had seen the previous day, four people waited outside the fence. Daniella leaned over to look at the people getting in the back seat and exclaimed, "My God, what happened to her?"

Misty jumped into the front seat as Jack helped Elizabeth into the back seat. Lamarcus threw their bag into the trunk and climbed in on the other side of Elizabeth. He slammed the door shut.

"Where's Sal?" Daniela asked.

"Drive," Jack barked.

The two women in the front seat faced forward and the car sped away.

"That women needs a hospital," Misty said.

Jack was already on the cell phone to Bruce. Jack passed on some directions to Daniella as she drove. After several turns onto rural roads, Daniella was totally lost. But up ahead parked by the trees was a lone car.

A solitary individual stood next to it leaning on the door. He stood upright when they approached and Daniella stopped next to the car. Lamarcus opened the door and began to help Elizabeth out. Her uncle gasped when he saw her face in the overhead interior light.

"She's alive. I'm sorry we couldn't have gotten to her sooner. Get her to a hospital and when they ask, you never saw us here or anywhere," Jack said.

"I've never seen you guys. And thanks, I'll make sure she gets good care," Bruce said.

Jack reached into the back seat and pulled out an envelope from his backpack. "And take these. If things play out as they should, you won't need them. But if something happens, take these to the authorities. They're copies of Vlade's correspondence to his minions around the globe laying out his evil plans."

Bruce carefully loaded his niece into his back seat and turned to say something. Daniella was already driving off. Jack caught Bruce's wave out the back window in the taillights. He waved back but doubted Bruce could see him.

At the motel, they unloaded and gave Lamarcus back his car. Jack humped the gear bag up to their room and collapsed on the bed. Daniela and Misty both sat on the other bed and waited.

"Where's Tree? How's he doing?"

"Tree's fine. I left him at the animal hospital overnight. They wouldn't release him till I answered how he came to have a gunshot in the leg."

Jack panicked. They still had to extract everyone from a very messy deal. The two women knew something had transpired at the mansion, but Sal had carefully left Misty in the woods by the front gate before his charge into the mansion. Neither one had a clue how deep things had gotten.

"What did you tell them?" Jack asked.

"I said he's a cow chaser and that I try to keep him in the house. But he got out and some farmer shot him chasing one of his cows," Misty said.

"And he bought that?"

"We'll find out when we pick him up today. If the entire Maryland State Police force is waiting, we'll know otherwise," Daniella said.

"OK, tomorrow Daniella will take a rental car and go pick up Tree. Then we're out of here. We'll deliver Daniela to her car in New Jersey before Misty and I get back on our boat."

"What about Sal and Lamarcus?" Misty asked.

"I'm afraid they're on their own now," Jack offered.

* * *

The first signs of light in the eastern sky shown through the motel window as Lamarcus finished putting on his Cambridge police uniform. He wanted the authority it conveyed for what came next.

He closed his motel room door and headed to his car, his cell phone ringing as he descended the stairs toward the parking lot. He listened and hung up. As he walked by the motel's dumpster, he carefully dropped the expendable cell phone into the trash.

Now that he knew Jack, Misty and Daniella were safely out of the area in the rental car he could close out the final act on Vlade. He drove the short distance to the Maryland State Patrol building he had spotted upon his arrival yesterday.

Lamarcus swung his car into the parking lot and selected a spot to park. Locking up, he walked slowly in the front door to the seated desk sergeant. The man looked up and recognizing a fellow uniformed officer, perked up from his long night on duty.

Through the heavily glassed viewport the sergeant leaned toward the microphone. "Can I help you?"

Lamarcus introduced himself while holding up his identification to the sergeant and then asked, "Can I see your watch commander, please?"

The man picked up the desk phone and a side door buzzed open, a Maryland State Patrol Lieutenant stood in the opening. Lamarcus shook hands with his counterpart before saying, "I have good evidence that a crime has taken place at the Vlade Estate. I would suggest that we take back-up and investigate."

Lamarcus noticed the lieutenant's eyes widen at the mention of the local billionaire's compound. He seemed to hesitate slightly at the political implications of invading such a high powered individual's home.

"And Lieutenant, I believe there's some urgency to this," Lamarcus added.

"OK, I'll radio for one of my patrol officers to meet us there."

The two men headed out to the Maryland State patrol car and Lamarcus climbed in the passenger seat. The lieutenant grabbed the radio and made his request to dispatch as he slammed the car in reverse. Pulling the shift lever into drive, the two rear tires chirped as he floored it heading out of the parking lot.

"Care to enlighten me on what we might find when we get there?"

"Hopefully nothing, but I'm afraid things may have progressed too far," Lamarcus offered. He knew he had to maintain his act of having no knowledge of what they were about to drive into.

Suddenly the radio came to life with an urgent appeal to any unit in the vicinity of the Vlade Estate to respond. "We have a request from the local Frederick police for back-up on a 459 in progress."

The lieutenant looked at his passenger as he hit the lights and siren. He reported his location and that they were en route to the address, the radio dispatcher acknowledging the transmission. Soon, Lamarcus heard two other Maryland State patrol units reporting their destination as the Vlade Estate.

The cruiser flew over the rural roads past the ambling estates of the well-heeled. The traffic was light due to the early morning hour and they soon pulled up to the flashing lights of a Piedmont patrol car at the entrance.

The lieutenant stopped and buzzed his window down, "We need to check the estate."

The Maryland State lieutenant asked the local patrol woman to open the gate. As the metal gates swung open, he glanced over at Lamarcus who was doing his best to maintain a surprised expression on his face.

"Is this what you were expecting?"

"I wasn't sure what to expect. But this fits the MO, I'm afraid," Lamarcus offered.

"You have a suspect already?" The lieutenant drove quickly up the driveway as he talked. The cruiser rounded the last turn, stopping behind the white van. The Suburban continued to burn off to the side. Obviously dead bodies lying in front of the house had the lieutenant on the radio demanding more units.

Lamarcus sat and waited and soon saw more police cruiser's lights flashing as they squealed to a stop on the estates driveway.

They stepped out, the lieutenant placing his hand on his service weapon. Lamarcus copied his counterpart although he already knew it was unnecessary. Everything had been decided hours before. They waited as the Piedmont officers did their work

A patrolman came over to the two lieutenants. "My sergeant is just finishing up calling in for more support."

"Anyone still alive?" the State lieutenant asked.

"None so far. We have five dead out here in front. From the looks they were taken out by someone with a full auto rifle. They're chewed up pretty bad," the Piedmont patrolman said.

The Piedmont sergeant got off the radio and came over to the other three. Lamarcus was introduced as they waited for the mansion to be searched. Soon two more Maryland State patrol cars arrived followed by the Piedmont Chief of Police. The Chief made the call that they could enter the mansion.

Lamarcus stuck close to his Maryland State Patrol lieutenant who was sticking with the

Piedmont police chief. The three followed the other officers into the building as the search continued.

The radio crackled with a request for the chief to make his way to the study on the northwest side of the building. Lamarcus followed along as the three men headed down the main corridor. They stepped into the room overlooking the lake and stopped.

Sitting in chairs were seven handcuffed men slumped over. From the blood on the floor and the large holes in each one's head, they were all dead.

Across from them, in a leather overstuffed reading chair, sat a lone man. With no visible injuries, the lieutenant reached down to check for a pulse.

"He's dead."

Lamarcus held his composure at the sight of his old friend sitting there. *Sal looked peaceful at last in that soft leather chair,* he thought.

The police chief gave the others a quick look and announced, "This ones Vlade. He was in my office a couple of times. Looks like a large caliber to the head."

"Maybe this?" one of Piedmont's patrolmen said as he pointed to a Colt Model 1911 laying on the floor next to the man in the leather chair.

The Chief looked down at the weapon. "That would make a hole to match."

Lamarcus stood slightly to the side as his fellow officers went about their work. He suddenly felt the long stare before he actually saw it. He turned to the lieutenant who was finally focusing on the outsider in the room.

"You knew this was here, didn't you?"

The Piedmont Chief looked up at the suddenness of the question and added, "Yeah, what the hell is a local Massachusetts cop doing in my jurisdiction?"

The Maryland State lieutenant turned on Lamarcus, "Start talking now or I don't care what agency you're from, so help me, I'll ..."

Lamarcus held up his hand for both to stop. "I can explain. Yes, I knew this might be happening. I drove down here yesterday to try and head off this man." He pointed to Sal.

"You know this man?" the chief asked.

"He's an old friend, from the Marine Corps. He was my sergeant in the Corps and we recently got together after he saw me on TV."

The two other men studied Lamarcus for a minute. The Maryland State Lieutenant recognized him first. "You're that officer that stopped the school shooting in Massachusetts. Now I recognize you."

Lamarcus explained how Sal tracked him down after that. He told how Sal suffered from terminal cancer but had wanted to help in Lamarcus' investigation. Not wanting to hurt his dying friend's feelings. Lamarcus explained how he had involved Sal. When he began his explanation of the conspiracy to shoot up school children, the two other officers took on an incredulous look.

"I was afraid that Sal was going to take matters into his own hands. From the looks of that white van with Massachusetts plates, he came up here with all guns blazing. Seems he was determined to end Vlade's attack on the American people all by himself."

"One man did all this? I can't believe that," the chief said.

"Sal was a lifer in the Marines. Most of that time was on long range patrol duty. The Marine Corps doesn't have any special forces per se, but LRP personnel are as good as any of the others. He was quite capable of this."

"And with these, I could see how," the Maryland State Patrol Lieutenant said. He had located the StG 44 and the H&K 91 rifles standing in the far corner of the room. We'll check them at the lab, but my bets they will match up with the bodies lying around here."

Lamarcus knew some would match up. They had been the weapons he and Jack had used to clear Vlade's rats nest out. They had made sure they were expertly wiped down before Sal handled them and fired off a few shots. Along with Lamarcus' silenced handgun, Sal would be matched up with the weapons found on site.

"So this Sal knew about the conspiracy from his help on your investigation. You contend that he drove down here to take matters into his own hands," the Piedmont Chief said.

Lamarcus walked over to his old friend's body and searched through his pockets. The two others started to protest that he was disturbing a crime scene. But Lamarcus carefully extracted a prescription bottle from Sal's pocket and held it up by the outside edge of the lid. He was careful not to touch the smooth bottle itself.

"I know for a fact that this was full two days ago. I drove him to the pharmacy to pick them up." Lamarcus placed the pill container back in Sal's pocket. "He drove down here on his final mission. Took out his enemies' position and then took all his pain meds at once to end his life. If either of you two were veterans, you should understand."

"But it's not how we meter out justice in our country," the police chief offered.

"Maybe this helps explain?"

Lamarcus and the Piedmont chief turned to where a Maryland State patrolman stood over a pile of paper on the desk. They walked over as the lieutenant flicked on the desk light.

A pile of files were strewn over the desk top and the desk drawers hung out empty. Someone had intently searched the desk and had left the evidence for authorities to find.

But on top of the whole mess was a large sheet of blank white paper. On it, someone had written something. A felt-tipped pen lying beside it matched the lettering size and texture. The three men moved around to the opposite side so they could read the note without disturbing it.

"All enemies, foreign and domestic," the note read, part of the oath all inductees swear upon entering service in the military. *Sal had fulfilled his oath to America*, Lamarcus thought.

*

Chapter 30

Beaufort, South Carolina

Misty Duran checked the anchor lines to the Tiki 38 as it swung in the gentle breeze. Anchored 100 yards off shore in a protected anchorage, the catamaran rocked easily on the small chop coming in off St. Helena Sound. They had been sitting in their little piece of heaven for a week now, just enjoying the warm Southern hospitality that matched the fair December weather.

Jack Wesley was below decks cooking dinner. Even though Misty was a superior cook, Jack did his domestic duties as they each shared work on the sailboat. Tonight was spaghetti with meat balls, his specialty.

Lying beside him was a recovered Tree. Misty's dog Jackie lay beside her buddy. Tree's leg had healed but he now had a permanent limp. With Tree's advanced age, the two combined to slow the dog down considerable. While Jack still took his friend for a walk each day on shore, the frisky canine he remembered was gone.

A small television broke the silence as Jack switched on the news. The set was mounted over the dinette table where it was attached to the bulkhead. Jack typically didn't follow the news but since the

Vlade escapade, he and Misty had taken up watching.

It had been three months since the shootout in Piedmont. The subsequent release of information on Vlade's attempt at coercing America into passing strict gun control measures had come out. So far, their names and identities had been absent in any of the news reports. Along with Daniella, the three had resumed as close to a normal life as they could find.

Jack had received an email message a short while back that Daniella had decided to return to school. She would be studying criminal justice with the goal of becoming a police detective. Jack approved of her career choice.

After that night in Piedmont, Daniella was driven back to her car in New Jersey while Jack and Misty had continued on to Greenbush, New York where they picked up Jack's brother's sailboat. They soon returned it to Annapolis, Maryland and his brother's marina slip.

Misty's new catamaran was waiting for them and they celebrated both events. Jack on his becoming a 'looper' and Misty on receiving the boat she really wanted.

Jack wasn't sure whether he would receive a certificate from somewhere on his accomplishment of circumnavigating the eastern United States. He still chuckled over the whole 'looper' thing.

As the national news came on, Jack stopped chuckling. He never cared for the talking heads they put on the news and when the topic for the night's session were premiered, his attitude took on an even fouler mood.

"Misty, they're talking about the hearings tonight. Come on down, dinners ready. We can watch as we eat."

He heard Misty cross over from the opposite hull and could tell that she stopped at the cockpit pod, probably to grab a wind breaker for the cool evening breeze developing. Her feet announced themselves as she dropped down into the hull. He leaned forward as she squeezed by on her way to a seat at the dinette.

Wharram cats weren't noted for spacious accommodations. Narrow hulls and no cabin between hulls meant close living. Jack certainly didn't mind the close personal contact he had with his boat mate on a constant basis. And the inviting main deck was an open expanse any time one wanted some personal space. He could see the appeal the boat had for Misty. Fast and safe, she could cross any ocean with a measure of confidence most boats lacked.

The ad ended as the two settled in to eating dinner. The first two stories came and went as the spaghetti disappeared. After another block of ads, what they had been waiting for came on.

"As the Merrill Hearings, as they have become known, continue, we take you to our correspondent on Capitol Hill," the television news anchor said. "Chuck, where have we gotten to?"

"Good evening Peter. Senator George Merrill of Wisconsin broke these hearings wide open yesterday with his announcement that he had a witness to this whole Vlade affair. That broke with his fellow Democrats who had been stonewalling any attempt to give life to the theory that one man was attempting to twist the mentally ill into heinous acts all for the benefit of the anti-gun crowd."

Jack stopped eating as he and Misty watched intently. They had purposely kept their distance as the Merrill Hearings got under way. Jack received news from Lamarcus regularly by an anonymous computer link.

Jack knew that Elizabeth Jamison had recovered from her beatings and had come forward to substantiate the conspiracy. The anti-gun crowd had been working overtime with their friends in the media in an attempt to put a lid on the whole mess. Now that the committee chairman seemed to have turned against his own Democrat Party, it appeared things were about to get interesting.

"I can't believe this guy is deep-sixing his buddies in the Democrat Party," Misty said. "It's not like them to break ranks."

"Remember, he's up for reelection next year and he comes from a state with a lot of hunters. I'm sure his office has been lit up constantly with concerned gun owners pressing for the truth," Jack offered.

"Maybe, but he's not endearing himself with the party leaders, taking this stand."

"Political survival is a strange thing. Most of these guys would sell their mother to stay in Washington. So he pisses off a few Senators from New York or California. From the news on the web, all the Democrat Senators from rural states are feeling the pressure. That guy from Montana is really catching hell."

Misty jumped right in, "I can't believe Montana would even have a Democrat U.S. Senator."

The news report switched to the Senate hearing room as a red-headed women sat beside an older man at the witness table. Sitting beside the two of them was Lamarcus. The liner at the bottom of the screen identified the two as Elizabeth and Bruce Jamison. The name Captain Lamarcus Lewis came trailing along afterward.

"She looks good considering her condition when we pulled her out of Vlade's tender mercies. And I see Lamarcus finally made Captain," Misty said.

"Yeah, she looks a hellava lot better than that night. Lamarcus told me she's had four surgeries and has worked hard in physical therapy to get her full mobility back. She's one strong woman to go through all that," Jack said. Then he almost put his fist through the television screen.

The news report showed the Senior Senator from New York cut into the young woman witness. "I have proof that you were having an illicit affair with the Director of ENOUGH before his untimely violent death in a house fire in New Hampshire. Do you now deny such an affair, Ms. Jamison?"

Misty and Jack watched as the young woman held her composure through the blistering attack that the New Yorker laid out for the television cameras. Jack's blood pressure sky rocketed at the attack.

"Typical Democrat response," Jack said. "If the facts don't agree with your position, than substitute character assassination. Smear everyone involved and let the media carry that message. Meanwhile, ignore the real facts."

"I understand now why Sal went for his final solution. I thought him wrong to end it like he did, but I understand now. Vlade would have used his money to buy himself out of the whole thing."

Chuck, the news reporter turned the news back over to Peter at the main news desk. Once again, left unsaid were the details of the whole Vlade conspiracy. The American people were being fed the Democratic Party line that the anti-gun crowd wanted.

"Do you think it will ever change?' Misty asked.

Jack hit the remote and the television went dead. He pushed the remaining spaghetti away. His increased stomach acid was mixing with the marinara sauce and he could already feel the effects. He turned his head and stared at the woman beside him.

"I hope so, but I'm not holding my breath."

Acknowledgements

First I would thank Timothy Johns, my tireless editor. Though he works hard that my writing is presentable, place no blame on him for the final product. That all rests with me.

My proof readers offer valuable feedback at different phases as my draft is put together. Dick Martin, Jeanne Crownover, Larry Stoddard, Tiffany Martin, Barbara Foster, and John Briggs have all kept me from straying too far off on tangents.

Charlie Cremeans was an early supporter who encouraged my storytelling.

Finding Morwenna Rakestraw to do the cover layout was a relief.

Mitch Press of World Book has offered his wisdom from his family's years in the book business. While not all encouraging, his guidance as publishing transforms in the digital age has been invaluable.

Lastly, my wife, Agnes, deserves recognition for tolerating my swerve into being an author.

Dear Reader,

Thank you for your selection of reading material. I hope this book measured up to your expectations. The most critical part for a new author is getting the word out to other readers.

I would appreciate your help in spreading the word. There are three important things you can do. You need to understand the importance of the first one to my becoming a successful writer. If you do anything, go to Amazon.com and write a review.

1.   Go to Amazon.com and leave a review
2.   Tell a friend about this book
3.   Tell your social network about this book.

The more positive reviews that are made in various places allow readers to find me.

Again, thanks for your support.

W.B. Martin

Check out my website at wbmartinauthor.com

Read an excerpt of the new exciting Jack Wesley
adventure from W.B. Martin.

Chasing the Blackbird

Available April 2018

Chapter 1

Sete, France

Jack Wesley stood on the open platform of the Sete train station, his older brother Ed beside him. Although still not happy about the turn of events, Jack knew his brother well enough to understand his situation.

"Well, we lasted longer than our last boat trip together," Ed said trying add some levity to the situation.

Jack knew he was referring to their short time together on Ed's sailboat. A sailing trip that circumnavigated the East Coast of the United States had been their last time together. And Ed had only managed to get away for a two week section during his Christmas break. Jack had completed the trip with no additional time with his brother.

Holding a powerful position in Washington D.C., Jack knew Ed lived for his job. Years as chief of staff for Wyoming's lone congressman had fixated Ed on the levers of power. It was only his congressman's sudden retirement after his wife's death that had freed Ed for another chance at brotherly adventure.

The phone call yesterday had changed everything. The retirement announcement of Wyoming's senior U.S. Senator had quickly ended the former congressman's bereavement period. Ed had a campaign to run and Jack found himself a solo boater once more.

"Hey, we had a good time in Italy at least," Ed continued to soften the hard feelings between the two. "And the Midi Canal was fun. We did get a month in this time."

Jack remained sullen and silent. *Yes, driving a Ferrari with the crazy Italians had been fun*, Jack thought. It had taken him a little time to get used to the aggressive driving shown in Italy, but it was his brother's dime that had sprung for a flash car. And Jack knew Ed could certainly afford it. More so than Jack who lived well on his police retirement check, but not well enough to afford a Ferrari rental.

"Look Jack, I'm sorry our trip got cut short," Ed said. "As we've discussed, my friend won't be needing his canal boat any time soon. You have the boat two more months. Just make sure its in Belgium for the next people that are going to be using it."

The train heading toward Toulouse and a direct flight to Washington D.C. screeched into the station. Ed bent down to grab his two bags and readied himself. Jack finally relented.

"I understand brother," Jack said. "I just don't know why you like that political crap. I can't imagine we're even from the same gene pool. You sure Mom didn't sneak out on Dad and find some politician in Salem on the side."

Ed broke out in a big grin at the mention of their growing up in Eugene, Oregon. Jack had stayed in Eugene, retiring after thirty years as a police detective. Ed had been incredibly lucky on his investments and hitched himself to a young Wyoming politician headed to the nation's capital.

"And knowing her, it was probably a damn Democrat," Ed said. The statement got a smile out of Jack finally.

"Just make sure your guy wins," Jack said. "I may need his help someday." Ed rolled his eyes at the reference to Federal help. There had been more then once that Ed had used his office to intervene on his brother's behalf.

Ed climbed the steps of the train and turned to Jack. "Hey, it's Europe. No guns allowed. How much trouble can you get into?"

* * *

Jack took a couple of days off from canal boat touring to enjoy the nearby beach. The Midi Canal ended near Sete and so had the Wesley family vacation. Now alone in France, Jack wanted to regroup before setting off on his now solo journey across France.

A couple days on the beaches helped revive him. The French were famous for their topless beaches. And the scanty bottoms the woman wore left little to the imagination. Jack gladly took in the scenery while catching some sun.

He had noticed that life on the canal lacked certain opportunities for female companionship. Most of the women on canal boats were with a male partner and most were decidedly middle aged at best. *Not a lot of young single women seem to enjoy the sedate life of motoring along at three knots looking at trees and fields,* he thought. *And that was when you could see some fields. Many times the canal was ensconced in a tree lined depression.*

Tomorrow Jack would return to his journey. His trip would cross the bottom of France on the Canal du Rhone a Sete until he gained the Rhone River. He would pass through Avignon on his way to the Saone River which would take him to the Canal de 'Est and Belgium.

As he walked back from the beach, Jack stopped at the local market to stock up on groceries. There were plenty of small communities along the route but he had learned to have plenty of spare food on hand for any uninhabited stretches.

Reaching his boat as the sun set, he stowed his provisions in the galley. He had purchased a croque-monsieur at a local shop and sat down in the boat's salon to enjoy it. *Just a good ham and cheese sandwich squashed in a toaster,* he thought.

Opening a bottle of French red wine, he poured himself a glass. Maybe the sandwich tasted better because of the wine. The croque-monsieur definitely tasted better than any American ham and cheese he'd ever eaten. The sandwich disappeared quickly and Jack took his glass and the bottle of wine out on deck to enjoy the evening.

As he sipped his wine, the warm breeze gently rocked his boat. The lights along the harbor illuminated the nearby boaters enjoying the fine weather as they came in from a full day out on the Mediterranean Sea.

As the bottle's contents slowly disappeared, the commotion settled down. Soon the bottle was empty and the harbor quiet. A lone ferry slid by ending its journey from Africa. On his walks to the beach Jack had noticed the sign directing traffic to the nearby ferry landing where a boat connected Sete to Tangiers in Morocco.

The lights along the large ferry lit the water as it passed and Jack saw people on deck heading below to their waiting cars. The long sea crossing from Africa was about to end as they scrambled to disembark.

Jack guessed the time to be close to midnight. *No hurry heading to bed on such a pleasant evening*, he thought. But as the breeze grew cooler, Jack moved into the doghouse situated in the middle of the boat.

Being a Dutch built canal cruiser, the steel hulled craft had its helm in the middle of the boat while other countries placed the steering control on the ends. With the doghouse on his boat in the center, it left room for two separate cabins, one aft, one forward. A main salon sat forward separate from the V-berth in the bow.

The large doors on both sides of the doghouse allowed sufficient air flow in to be pleasant but the roof over his head kept the cool night air out. He placed the empty wine bottle by the helm as he sat down in the large captain's chair.

As he sat looking out the windshield at the night scene, he grew tired, a day on the beach in the sun and the wine doing its work. *I guess I need to hit the sack,* he thought.

Just as he was about to get up, he heard a muffled splash. Jack scanned the harbor for a late night swimmer but saw no one. He surveyed in all directions looking for water movement but the onshore breeze stirred up small waves, hiding any other. As he sat, he tried to decide what held him. Sleep called and he forced himself to stand up.

That's when he felt it. The boat rocked slightly from it's resting position. As a steel hulled boat, unlike a lighter fiberglas boat, the heavy Dutch cruiser took a lot to make it move. Jack turned away from the dockside door to find a woman standing in the opposite doorway.

He stared at her as she dripped water onto the deck, some spilling into the doghouse. In the low light, Jack could tell that this woman hadn't been swimming for pleasure. She had panties on and a torn tank top, both soaking wet and revealing everything underneath.

"Can you help me? I need a place to hide," the woman said.

Jack froze for a second at the request. Out of the corner of his eye he saw movement on the dock. Turning for a closer look, he saw three men methodically moving toward him, searching each moored boat as they went. He turned and took her arm as she stepped into the cabin. Standing beside him, Jack realized that the woman was as tall as he was. And in the added light, Jack saw that she had a dark complexion with short curly hair.

From her looks, Jack surmised that she was late twenties, but he didn't stop to ask. He escorted her down the ladder into the main salon. Pulling a hatch open, Jack pointed to the engine compartment. She bent down and lowered herself into the confined space. Reaching for a blanket lying on the settee, he handed her a coverup. The hatch placed back, he climbed back into the doghouse.

As he tried to think what he had just gotten himself into, he saw the three men growing closer. Searching each moored boat, they were obviously looking for something or someone, they steadily approached his slip.

He looked around and noticed the refection of water on the deck. *They might see the wet deck,* he thought. With no time to mop the trail of water the woman had left leading down to her hiding spot, Jack stuck his fingers down his throat and gagged twice. A liter of wine along with the remains of his ham and cheese sandwich spewed out into the doghouse, splattering across the deck. The smell quickly overwhelmed the cabin.

He reached over and opened a cabinet, inside sat a mop and a bucket. He was out on the boat's waterside deck lifting a bucket of water out of the harbor when he turned to discover a man standing in the doghouse doorway.

"What are you doing?" Jack demanded, flashing as much menace as he could at the man. His two compatriots stood on the dock watching.

The man said nothing as he stood, checking Jack's boat.

Jack placed the bucket down and reached for the mop. He flipped the handle around so it could act as a weapon and asked again, "What are you doing on my boat?" He moved the mop handle to imply he was ready to use it if no answer came. The man in the cabin said nothing, but one of the men on the dock climbed on board and stuck his head in the door.

"Oh shit. What a mess."

The first man that had been standing mute babbled in a foreign language.

"My friend wants to know if you have seen a young woman?" Before Jack could answer there was another exchange between the two men in a foreign language. "He also wants to know why your deck is wet?"

"Well, as you can see, I'm cleaning up an accident. Too much to drink, I'm afraid."

The man in the doghouse doorway leaned forward to smell Jack's breath, being careful to avoid the mess on the floor. He said something to the other man.

"American? To much French wine, no?"

"Yes, to much French wine. Now. please leave so I can clean up."

After some additional foreign language discussion, the two men climbed down off the boat. They resumed their determined search of the moored boats. Jack bent to the task of cleaning up his mess and dumping the results into the harbor. He rinsed his bucket and sat down.

He ignored the rumble in his stomach. *I can grab a slice of baguette in a minute,* he thought. *But first I need to know who just landed in my lap and who those characters were.*

Waiting an appropriate amount of time for the three strangers to have cleared the marina, he closed the doors to the doghouse and climbed down into the salon. He lowered the blinds and turned the interior lights down to a minimum. Opening the hatch, Jack motioned his guest out of the engine compartment.

The woman crawled out on all fours and stood up. The low light provided enough light in the salon to make out details. She wore the wool blanket wrapped around her. Reaching under the blanket, she slipped her panties off. Then she struggled out of her wet tank top, hanging both on an overhead line running along the cabin roof. She snugged the blanket around her sarong style and sat down on the edge of the dinette.

"Thank you for your help," the woman said. Jack noticed a strong accent in the woman's words.

"Don't mention it. Those three men didn't seem to be the hospitality committee."

The quiet of the early morning took over the boat's salon. The initial greetings had been made and now the two sat in silence. He didn't want to pry into this woman's problems, even if she had gotten him involved.

Jack broke the silence. "I'm Jack, Jack Wesley."

"Nice to meet you Jack. I'm Valentina. And again, thanks for the help."

A short quiet spell ensued until Jack offered, "I sort of lost my supper out there. Figured it would distract the welcoming committee as well as cover up the wet deck. I have some bread and cheese if you'd like some."

Valentina sat quiet without any response.

"It's French bread and cheese, but it's still good. I think I have a bottle of Italian wine handy though."

Jack noticed a slight smile break out on his guest's face at the mention of the Italian wine. *So, as I suspect, there's an Italian connection to her accent,* he thought.

"Yes, thank you. A little food and drink would help."

Jack moved to the galley. As he worked away in the subdued light he noticed Valentina looking furtively around the salon. He stopped and watched, waiting for a response as to what seemed to be bothering her.

She met his gaze and smiled again. "Scuzi, where is the toilet?"

Jack smiled back and the tension eased some. "Ah, the head, as its refereed to on a boat, is down the passageway and to the left."

Valentina nodded her understanding and moved across the small room. As she reached the start of the passageway Jack stopped her.

"Almost forgot. The toilet, or head, on boats don't do well with toilet paper. There's a little plastic bag in the can to the side for the that."

"Thanks for the heads up." They both smiled at Valentina's bad pun before she disappeared.

Jack had the snacks ready by the time she returned and they both sat down at the dinette. Jack took a healthy swig of wine to clear the vomit taste out of his mouth. With a sweeter breath, he ate, looking across at the woman that had landed on his boat.

Though the blinds were drawn, enough light filtered into the dinette to make out details. He assumed Valentina's height to be six feet since he was looking straight across the table at her eye level. When she looked down for more food, Jack took the opportunity to study her face.

Her dark complexion spoke of African heritage mixed with European. *She could easily pass for Halle Berry's tall younger sister,* Jack thought. Her hair looked to have dried and now hung in medium length perfect curls. When she moved her head her hair literally bounced on her head.

Jack admired her beauty while trying not to be too obvious about it. She looked up as she took another slice of bread with cheese and took a bite. Jack glanced down so as to not appear to intrusive.

"So, are you alone on the boat?"

"My brother was with me up until a few days ago. He got an unexpected call and had to return to work."

"I'm sorry, family time is special."

"Yes, we were looking forward to three months together on the canals through France and Holland."

"So do you intend to carry on by yourself?"

"I don't see an alternative. But I've boated solo before, so its not new to me."

Valentina looked at Jack as if her brain was busy processing something. He let the moment linger.

"So, do you often take midnight swims escaping from three thugs?" Jack asked. He figured it was a little forward but he wasn't getting anywhere with the polite routine. He watched for her reaction.

Cooly, she hesitated to answer as she took another bite of baguette. She looked Jack straight into his eyes as she slowly chewed.

"Not to often. But sometimes I even do it without three thugs chasing me," she said with a certain challenge in her voice. Then she smiled to ease the tension. "And you, do you ever take midnight swims?"

"Every chance I can. But I try to leave the thugs out of the experience."

The two smiled at each other again. Each took their glass of wine for a sip. Jack held his up for a toast. "To midnight swims." Valentina clinked her glass against his and they drank.

"So, I expect you'll be heading out tomorrow?" she asked, "To continue your trip across France."

"I had planned to. Do you have a better idea?" Again he watched for her reaction. *I know I'm pressing a little but why not. Tomorrow she'll probably be gone anyway,* he thought.

"No, but if I can catch a ride to get away from here, that would be helpful."

"Be glad for the company as long or as short as you choose. I sleep in the forward berth. You can have the aft cabin. Just go up through the doghouse."

Valentina looked at the ladder to the doghouse and craned her neck to see the hatch that led to the aft cabin. She switched her gaze and settled on the pilot berth across the salon from the dinette.

"If it's all right with you, can I sleep there tonight?"

Jack followed Valentina's gaze to the pilot berth. "No problem, but I might disturb you in the morning getting coffee ready."

"Expresso or cappuccino?" she asked.

Definitely Italian, Jack thought. *Only Italians thought of cappuccino when coffee was mentioned.*

"Sorry to disappoint, but American I'm afraid."

Her frown told it all. *If I want to entice my guest to stay longer, I need to invest in a expresso machine for the boat,* he thought.